COLD BLOOD

JANE HEAFIELD

Print ISBN 978-1-913942-58-8

ALSO BY JANE HEAFIELD

Dead Cold

Don't Believe Her

PART I

1

———

Elvis Presley's ghost aside, the very last person Bennet expected a call from was the mother of his child.

'Liam, hi, how are you? How are things? How's work? Are you still a sergeant?'

A blizzard of questions that made his head spin. Ten *years*. It had been ten years since their last contact, not an ounce of animosity lost on his part, yet she talked as if they were old friends on an annual gossip catch-up. 'Anyway, I know it's been a long time, but I need to talk to you. I'll call you tomorrow night about eight. Bye.'

And that was it. The event flashed into existence and winked out again so fast he almost wondered if he'd imagined it. The call had come just before midnight last night, but he'd been fast asleep and the landline answering machine had taken it. Bennet deleted the voicemail and planted his ear against the living-room door. No sound of feet thumping down the stairs: Joe hadn't heard the message from the mother he couldn't remember.

Still in his coat and shoes, ready for another working Friday, Bennet stood at the window, looking out at the dark garden, and tried to calm his nerves. Ten *years*. Ten years since Lorraine had walked out, abandoning her baby son and his father like a crappy motel room.

But Bennet hadn't been able to so easily scrub Lorraine from his mind. Joe had been a baby and unable to compute what just happened, but that wouldn't last. One day he'd understand what a mother was, and that his wasn't around, and he'd want answers. One day, he'd have the urge and the muscles to go out and find her. Until that day, Bennet had to make sure she was alive and well and able to answer her grown boy's knock at the door.

This had been a simple case of keeping secret tabs on her, made easier in a world with social media and the internet. True to prediction, as Joe had grown, he'd come to understand that the old lady neighbour who often looked after him wasn't his mother. Then the questions had started. That had been a tricky first conversation, and it had lost no sting by repetition over the years. Bennet had had all the answers Joe could have wanted, and the kid could have watched her life progress almost real time. Joe could have learned what his mother looked like, her hobbies, everything. But there were some things Liam didn't want him to discover just yet.

But Bennet hadn't provided those answers. Instead, he'd claimed no knowledge except that she was alive, somewhere. His father-of-the-year award was probably in the post.

He'd always wondered if Lorraine had mirrored his interest, but now he knew she had paid scant attention to her son and his father. Still a detective sergeant? Minimal research would have informed her that Bennet was now a chief inspector working with Barnsley's Major Investigation Team 2, one of four covering the four boroughs of South Yorkshire. Worse, that brief one-sided conversation hadn't contained a single mention of her son.

But she'd called, and it had to be about Joe, didn't it? No

other theory made sense, leading him to assume that Lorraine had finally reached that point, be it the product of curiosity or guilt, where she desired to get to know the son she had abandoned when he was small enough to hold in one hand. He'd always suspected the day would come. And planned for it.

But, here it was, and he wasn't sure how he felt, or what he should do. He hit 1471, the last-call return number, but Lorraine had withheld hers.

Now came the footsteps bounding down the stairs. Joe bounced into the room, full of energy. Full of oblivion.

'Dad, yo. What's new?'

The question was nothing but their form of hello, but Bennet felt spotlighted, under pressure to make a snap, possibly life-changing decision.

'Nothing, son. Nothing at all.'

2

In the chilly incident room at Barnsley's Churchfield police station, Bennet's murder squad was working a stabbing at Buttery Park. At this morning's briefing, one of his team was outlining the results of a phone call trace, but Bennet was having trouble concentrating. His mind was a loose kite, sailing away.

Fifteen days ago, on the second day of the new year, a group of six teenagers had come across another group of six who were kicking a ball in Buttery Park in the early evening. A witness walking her dog said a game blossomed, then wilted when one kid slide-tackled another. The two fought like alley cats, which she found somewhat amusing until a blade appeared. Twenty seconds later, all but one of the tearaways scattered to the winds. Eighteen minutes after that, the remaining boy, Mick Turton, was in an ambulance, bleeding from two holes in his chest. He bellowed for revenge as the ambulance zipped out of the park, cried for his mother as it blasted down the road, and gave up inhaling as it turned into the hospital grounds. Major Investigation Team 3's hotline buzzed soon after.

But for four days, they had nothing, until a lucky break.

Twelve teenagers, one clear witness, a wide, open park, but the team hit a brick wall, and stayed there with their noses pressed against it for ten days, until a blind piece of luck dropped in their laps. A mile from Buttery Park, an old man hit triple nine because a neighbour's kid had busted his window with a football. When the old guy refused to hand back the ball, the kid's dad took a corn-on-the-cob fork to his car tyres. While mediating between the two men, one of the police officers saw blood on the football and remembered the Buttery Park incident.

Off went the blood for testing. Back it came as Mick Turton's. The ball went next and gave up a fingerprint. It belonged to a sixteen-year-old petty drug dealer known as Don The Man. Don The Man had been arrested many times, so high respect for the police's investigative powers must have been the reason why he reported his ball stolen on the same day a kid got knifed. In his garden one moment, gone the next. But Don was all for helping the police and the stabbed boy's family get justice: 'Killer must have lobbed the ball into someone's garden when he legged it. You can keep it for more tests and shit.'

Because they weren't born yesterday, Bennet's team had obtained records of Don's contract phone's whereabouts on the night of the stabbing. At the important time, the device was in the vicinity of Buttery Park. Don The Man's explanation: 'Shit, man, I was so pissed about my ball, I forgot to report my phone got nicked as well.' His alibi for the time of the attack? At his girl's house, watching news about the ongoing Australian bushfires. He even quoted lines from the newscasters, as if that was proof ('Shows I didn't just watch some earlier news programme, eh?'). The girlfriend, sixteen-year-old Erica Smith, had backed him up ('So, what, you peelers saying I'm lying as well?'). The Man's abrasive mother moaned that her son had asked his girlfriend to marry him a couple of weeks ago, and why would someone who's planning a wedding go out and kill someone? ('He'd have to be mad, wouldn't he? You saying my son is mad?')

But in terms of real evidence, they had nothing. Don's mother and Erica and all his cronies remembered the ball and the phone getting stolen, and would swear it in court. The only decent piece of CCTV showed a figure in what appeared to be bloodstained clothing and carrying a football running past a shop near the park, but a Crown Prosecution Service lawyer who'd viewed it said the ball might not be a ball, the bloodstains might not be blood, and the figure looked too fat to be Don The Man. Many had witnessed teenagers fleeing along streets and down alleys, but no one had managed to identify anyone, so none had been traced. No DNA or other fingerprints had been found at vital spots at the scene or on Mick Turton's clothing or body.

Bennet's team talked to Don The Man's crew, but they knew nothing about a football game: they'd all been hanging out in a friend's house, miles away from Buttery Park. By weird coincidence, on that very evening they'd given all their phones to a pal to carry in a bag, and hadn't the idiot gone and left it on top of his car. All missing and now dead. And none of them could supply phone numbers, so tracing these unregistered devices was looking like a bust. Likewise, Erica, the girlfriend, had an unregistered phone and apparently broke and tossed it on the same night, and, lo and behold, not a single one of her friends or family knew that number or had it stored in their own devices. A highly unlikely set of circumstances, but CPS lawyers only gambled on dead certs.

Yesterday had almost provided a breakthrough. A female with a voice disguised by helium, believe it or not, had called to say she had proof of who killed the boy in the park, and would call back. She hadn't yet. The call had been traced to a phone box in Darnall, but it was on a busy main road, which meant anyone could have used it. No CCTV covered the phone box. Witnesses were being traced.

Don The Man's custody clock had expired and he'd been released, and for almost two weeks the case had vented heat like a joint of cooked beef left out in December wind. The team was disheartened. Losing a suspect was worse than never finding one in the first place.

The detective up front of the incident room finished his outline of the Darnall phone call trace and took his seat. Someone else stood to give her updates. Bennet found himself restless, but not because of the stale smell of the investigation.

He was still thinking about Joe's mother, Lorraine.

3

———

Later that night, asleep on the sofa, Bennet woke to find his son rooting through his coat, which was hanging on the back of the nearby armchair. In the light from the TV's screen saver, he watched the ten-year-old slip out his wallet with a scary skill. The detective in him assumed something more sinister than a kid needing money for sweets, so he said nothing and pretended to sleep. Wallet in hand, Joe crept out and back upstairs. Bennet checked his phone and saw it was just past midnight.

He gave it a minute, then did his own creeping. Liam's bedroom door was ajar, so he put an eye to the crack. The room was dark except for the light from a laptop screen on Joe's lap. He was sitting in bed with his back to the door, and his dad's debit card was in his hand. Bennet pushed the door open slowly and stepped inside so he could get a better look at the screen. Again, his detective suspicion told him this wasn't a kid sneakily trying to buy the new UFC game on Xbox that he'd been begging his dad to buy for a week now. And he was right.

The website was called XODeepRichessOX.net, but it wasn't an online store. According to the tag line, it was a forum for people eager to make money on the dark web. The dark web? That was a portion of the World Wide Web hidden from the normal internet-surfacing community, using encrypted data accessible only through certain browsers. You didn't get there riding Google. Some of it was legitimate, hosting intranet systems such as those of the military and big businesses, but it was also a territory of criminals. He didn't know much about the dark web, but he was damned certain a ten-year-old boy shouldn't be crawling about down there.

There was a chat screen open. Joe – username GuestLBoe – was conversing with someone called KingHack555. He saw a mention of the Department for Work and Pensions.

A hacker on the screen and a bank card in Joe's hand? Bennet snatched the laptop away.

Horrified, Joe almost jumped out of his skin. But he said nothing as his dad scrolled through the conversation. Joe and KingHack555 had been talking for three days, with all entries taking place at night. At night for Joe, that was. Who knew what time it was in whatever country this bastard was plying his scam from. Bennet typed MY DAD IS A COPPER AND YOU'RE IN TROUBLE NOW, closed the chat box, exited the forum, and shut the laptop.

'Joe, what are you doing?'

'You won't find her, that's why I did it,' Joe snapped, his face now one of anger instead of fear and embarrassment.

Liam had hoped he was wrong, but now couldn't shut his eyes on the truth. 'You wanted to pay a hacker to find your mother? Joe, you can't trust people like this.'

'So who do I trust? The police, like you? Oh, sure, you can find her, but you won't, will you? So I had to do it this way.'

Bennet's heart went out to the boy. Ten years old, and smart enough to sink into the dark web and find someone who could sneak into government computers for information. It also showed his level of desire and reminded Liam that Joe wouldn't have had to employ such drastic measures to find his mother if his father hadn't been such a barrier.

'Joe, I think–'

'Why won't you, Dad? Why won't you use your police people to contact her?'

He wasn't even sure, not fully. But he gave Joe a reason that was easy to admit: 'It's against the law, Joe. Police resources aren't for personal use.'

Crying, Joe flung himself back onto his pillow in outrage, and nearly cracked his skull against the headboard. The smart, mature kid was once again just that – a kid. 'But it's my mum. I don't remember her.'

'Joe, I–'

Joe told him to go away, then turned over and buried his face in the pillow, even pressing its edges over his ears. Liam didn't want to leave him upset, but this wasn't a conversation for past midnight. He left, but halfway down the stairs felt guilt become a heavy ball in his gut. Back he went.

'I know where she is, Joe.'

Joe sat up. 'How? When? Where is she?'

The 'when' wasn't going to be part of this: *I've known since the year she left* was an answer that might put an eternal wedge between father and son. 'She's living in Birmingham. It's about a hundred miles away. I found her using the electoral register and Facebook. Her surname's Cross now. Lorraine Cross. That's why you couldn't find her. But I did.'

'Not Taylor? She changed her name? Was that so I couldn't find her?'

'No, no, it's not because of you. I... I don't know why she changed it.'

Joe knew Mum and Dad had never married, hence why she'd never been a Bennet. Thankfully, he failed to consider marriage as a reason for the surname Cross. The lie had felt like chewing broken glass, but Liam wasn't yet ready to broach this subject. Once he did, he would have to go all the way. And he might just tear his little boy's heart in two. A marriage wasn't the end of it.

'Have you talked to her?' Joe asked. He seemed almost high on fabulous news.

'Sort of. She left me a message. She says she wants to talk to me.'

'Just to you?'

He gave his next claim careful thought. 'Well, it might be about you. I think she might be ready to meet you again.'

'Can I have her number? Can I hear the message?'

Joe had never heard his mother's voice. For the second time, he opted to lie to his flesh and blood rather than risk scorn: 'It got automatically deleted. And it was a withheld number. But you'll talk to her soon. When I talk to her tomorrow, we might be ready to arrange a meeting. So you can meet your mum.'

'And go out with her?'

He had to be careful not to go too far with this, before he knew the whole story. He still wasn't certain what Lorraine wanted to talk to him about. 'Maybe. We'll work it out.'

'Has she got a new family now?'

The question hit him like a fist, but Joe didn't look upset. It seemed to be genuine curiosity, and it swayed Liam's hand.

'Yes. She has a husband. And a child.'

'A new boy?'

'Well, it's a daughter. Five years old.'

'Is this because she didn't want me? She didn't want a son?'

Bennet sat on the bed and stroked Joe's shoulder. 'No, not at all. Me and your mother... we didn't work out. She moved away and made new friends and a new life. She met a man and they married. Married people have children sometimes. That's all it is.'

'So she won't move back home?'

'I don't want you to expect that we'd be a family again. But she wants to see you and that's good. It means you can get to hang out with her at weekends, or once a month. She'll be in your life again. Will that be okay? Do you understand what I said?'

He nodded. 'She won't be my proper mother.'

'She will, but she won't live with us. Is that okay?'

'Yes. I can play with her. And I have a new sister.'

Bennet wasn't sure Joe did fully understand. 'Half-sister. But, Joe, you have to understand something. You might not see your mother as often as you'd like. It might not be often at all. You might not meet the rest of her family, at least not at first.'

'So I won't ever meet my sister?'

Bennet felt he was tying himself in knots. God, he'd interrogated and broken down vicious killers, but he didn't know how to proceed with a ten-year-old boy.

4
___

On Saturday afternoon, while out bowling with Joe, Bennet got a call from one of his team. Six months ago, Detective Constable Henderson had thrown up at her first murder scene and announced she was quitting; now she had her sights on promotion and often did weekends off the clock.

'Liam, we got another call from Helium Girl. Same silly disguised voice trick. It was about twenty minutes ago. I have a copy of the recording on my phone. It's the same phone box in Wombwell.'

Bennet watched Joe send a bright-green bowling ball into the gutter. 'Okay, send me it. Thank you.'

On Thursday the 16th an anonymous female caller, with a voice disguised by sucking on helium, had claimed to have information and was willing to talk to a senior detective, face to face. She had promised to call back with details of a meeting place, but so far hadn't. The call had been traced to a payphone on a busy commercial street in Wombwell.

It was one of myriad calls the incident room had received, but this one had gotten interest because the caller sounded like a teenager. Everyone involved in the lethal football game at

15

Buttery Park had been a teenager: maybe she knew one or more of them. But with no clues found at the payphone, all the team could do was wait for the tipster to call again.

DC Henderson sent the recording by email. Once more Bennet listened to a voice made comical by helium: '*I don't have anything for you peelers. I was wrong.*' A pause here, probably while the caller loaded her lungs with gas again. '*So I won't be coming in. But I know it was a black man from Bradford what did it.*'

Helium Girl's first call had mentioned a black man. No witnesses had reported a black man amongst the teenagers though. He called Henderson back. 'Helium Girl mentioned a black man again. Go through the files again and see what we have on any other mentions of a black man in the park.'

'I did that. No joy.'

In the neighbouring lane, a family of three was having the time of their lives. The kid was a boy about Joe's age. Bennet tried to picture himself there with Joe and Lorraine, but it felt wrong. Maybe there was a chance Joe and his mother could make such a social trip, but not with Bennet. Too awkward. And it threw him a new worry: what if Joe enjoyed his time with her so much that he wanted a lot more? A lot more than she was willing to provide? How would he feel when their time was up and she basically dumped him in order to return to her daughter and husband?

'Dad? Your go.'

'Sir? What should I do?'

Bennet snapped back to the moment. 'Try the files again,' he said to Henderson, then hung up the phone. 'Okay, Joe, watch the master.'

For the remainder of the game, Bennet couldn't take his eyes off the family in the next lane.

5

As eight o'clock approached, Bennet popped round to his neighbour's. Patricia was in her seventies, widowed, no children, and loved to babysit Joe, even at a moment's notice. When he rapped the window and she appeared, a thumbs up from him was all it took. She mirrored it and Bennet went to fetch Joe. Minutes later, his boy was next door, probably destroying Patricia's chocolate collection, and Bennet was sitting in the living room, staring at the landline. The minutes dragged. He was torn between a couple of tactics. Should he insist that Joe was eager to see his mother? Or pretend he was willing to let Lorraine see the boy because a mother shouldn't be denied access to her son? He didn't know why it would matter either way, but the worry was there.

At two minutes to eight, he started to pace. God, it felt like he was waiting for news of a blood test. He'd waited to give evidence in court with less tension in his muscles.

The phone rang. The display said UNKNOWN. Bennet was known amongst his team as unflappable, like a cyborg, but if this horrendous timing was a colleague's doing, they'd soon alter that opinion of him.

'Oh, Liam, you're in, good. How are you?'

It was Lorraine. The wait had been the worst part, because now he relaxed. 'Good. You?'

'Always good. How's Joe?'

Last time she hadn't mentioned their son, but now had at least acknowledged his existence. 'Always good also. So, you wanted to talk to me?'

'Yes. It's about my old place, Lampton. You remember it?'

Of course. It was a Peak District village, Lorraine's former home. But he didn't want to give the impression that their time together, a decade ago now, was still vivid in his mind. So he gave a pause. 'Lampton? Oh yeah, that place. I remember a little. What about it?'

'Not long after I left, there was that missing girl, you remember?'

Vaguely. He recalled hearing something on the news, back when Lorraine had been pregnant with Joe and just a few weeks after she'd left Lampton and moved in with him. But he'd been a detective sergeant with South Yorkshire Police, not Derbyshire Constabulary, and the investigation had nothing to do with him. He hadn't known much back then and hadn't learned anything new since.

'I remember hearing about it. Did they find her?'

'No, that's the point. It's been ten years in March. Not a single clue, no suspects. But the anniversary is the perfect time to bring the story into people's minds again.'

'I'm getting lost, Lorraine. Why are you telling me this?'

'I saw an article on a Facebook post. A friend sent it to me because it was about Lampton. It was asking for help with a documentary about the missing girl. They wanted people who knew Lampton. So I called them, and they hired me. They've got a lot of their background sections filmed and now they want a walkaround. Round Lampton, filming certain places, and they want me to talk to them about the village and what it was like back then. Back when the girl was taken. And then we're going to Chesterfield. We're doing it over the next few days, starting tomorrow. I can't wait. It'll be such fun.'

She was starting to ramble, and he was lost. 'Sounds great, Lorraine, but what has this got to do with me and Joe?'

'Well, the film-makers are hoping to examine old clues and see if they can find something new. Wouldn't it be great if they could solve it after all these years? So I told them about you. I told them you're a police officer. I said you could get into the files. You can get all the police information from back then, including stuff the public didn't see.'

The tension came back with a vengeance, almost locking every muscle. 'Wait a minute, Lorraine. That's why you called me? That's all you want?'

'I know I haven't been in touch for years, but if we can solve–'

'And Joe?'

Her pause said everything.

'Don't call me again, Lorraine. I thought you wanted to meet up with Joe. I thought you gave a shit about your own son. Some detective I am, right?'

She stammered. 'I... Liam... I have a... I can't just...'

He felt anger pushing to the surface, but long practice had made him adept at subduing it. Calmly, he said, 'You have a what, Lorraine? A new family now? That's cold. There's something wrong with your mind. You're not wired right. But it doesn't matter. Joe doesn't need you. In fact, he's better off without you. Has been for the last ten years. So don't call me again and stay away. Stay away from me and stay away from Joe.'

He hung up. Now he felt the anger bubbling up again, and

this time he let it. It wasn't directed at Lorraine, but at himself, and he deserved to let it gnaw and pound at his insides. He had earned this abuse because he, not Lorraine, was the fool who'd made a promise that was now fated to crack his son's heart.

6

____

Bennet woke in the dead hours of Sunday with the urge to do something. He felt antsy and needed to work his muscles. He considered washing his car, a five-year-old Nissan Pathfinder he'd recently bought because Joe loved the idea of a big four-by-four. He thought about doing Joe's unfinished homework. He debated cleaning out the garage. All would burn energy, but none would satisfy a need to... progress. That was the best word for it. Something that furthered his life, or meant something in the great scheme of things. He even got dressed and got the front door open, his plan to hit the station and work some more on the Buttery Park case. But even that had an air of the futile about it. He knew what the problem was. Same as all of last night: Joe and his mother.

He settled for jabbing a phone number. Detective Liz Miller answered quickly, even though Spain was only an hour ahead of the UK.

'Stake-out?' he said.

'Can't sleep. Our man's doing just fine in that department. And you? Raid?'

She'd understood his question: why was she awake so late?

The inspector, part of MIT 3 in Sheffield, was in Barcelona as part of an investigation into the armed robbery of a jeweller's in broad daylight just a hundred yards from her station. The suspect was Spanish and had fled home, and they were staking him out. And Bennet understood her question: was he awake because of an upcoming dawn raid?

'Can't sleep either,' he said. 'My son's mother just got in contact.'

A moment of silence from Liz. She knew his history. Lorraine had fallen pregnant with Joe and they'd decided to live together. Bennet was newly promoted to detective sergeant and hadn't wanted to leave Barnsley, so Lorraine had cut her roots. A year later, unable to deal with having a child she'd wanted to abort, she'd abandoned her new family and lived alone in a bedsit until she'd met her current husband and relocated to Birmingham.

Bennet had met Liz in December last year, when she'd inveigled her way into a double murder investigation his team was heading. There seemed to be a hint of something beyond the professional to their relationship, but nothing had coalesced so far. Bennet hadn't realised how much he liked Liz until he heard about her Spanish trip with a male colleague. He hadn't liked it. Now, Liz's silence suggested she wasn't impressed by the resurfacing of Bennet's old flame. Unless he was reading it wrong.

'Does she want to see Joe?' Liz asked.

'So I thought. But it turns out she just wanted my police clout to help her with something.'

Liz didn't ask what exactly. 'Does Joe know she got in contact?'

'Yes. I told him there could be a chance they could meet. I was impatient and it was stupid. And now I've got to tell him he means less to his mother than some dusty old crime file in a basement.'

'Did she say she won't see him?'

Ah. No. He had to admit he didn't really give her a chance. 'I might have told her to get lost and never call again.'

She tutted at him. 'Mr Unflappable, eh? Call her back and find out for sure.'

'I can't. I don't have her number.'

He wasn't sure he would have called anyway. He was still annoyed at her. He and Liz spoke for a few more minutes, on subjects not involving family or work, and after the call he didn't feel as tense. Getting his feelings off his chest, onto that of someone impartial, had eased him a little. But not enough to sleep. He sat on the sofa, surrounded himself with Buttery Park files, and sank himself into the world of a young man whose mother loved him but would never see him again.

He was still there come daylight and a call from his boss. Superintendent David Hunter got straight to the point. 'A little gift was left for you at the station late last night. It's a herbal stress remedy. With a little bow on it and a note telling you to take it easy. I sent it for prints.'

Bennet didn't need to ask who'd sent it. Since the Buttery Park stabbing, Don The Man hadn't exactly laid low and kept silent: he'd been calling himself Teflon Don, after mafia boss John Gotti, who got the nickname because multiple charges by the law authorities never stuck to him. Don The Man clearly rejoiced in the fact that he'd been arrested and released, thus outwitting the police. His sending of a herbal stress remedy to the man leading the murder hunt was a taunt. It managed to get Bennet's mind off Lorraine for half a day.

That changed when Joe went for a bath just after a roast lamb dinner. Joe hadn't mentioned his mother thus far today –

surprising because he knew she had planned to call the previous evening – and the question came out of the blue.

'Mum didn't call, did she?'

'No. But she's busy, and she didn't say it would definitely be Saturday night. She might call later this evening, or tomorrow.'

Joe nodded, but there was no conviction behind it. If the boy hadn't last seen her when he was a baby, Bennet might have thought Joe knew what a waste of space his mother was.

7

———

On Monday Joe's school class departed on a two-day trip to the cathedral city of York, an hour or so north, where the kids would learn about Vikings, Romans, and the Industrial Revolution, and spend the night camped under the stars. Bennet parked outside the school and checked Joe's knapsack to make sure everything was there. Joe gawped at the coach outside the school gates as if it was a rocket going to take him to faraway worlds.

Joe opened the door, but didn't get out. 'What are you doing today?'

'Just work, son. Files to read.'

'But you've got another two days off.'

'A policeman is always on duty, twenty-four-seven.'

'But they only pay you for forty hours,' Joe said with a grin. Bennet laughed. But he stopped when Joe quickly changed track. 'Will Mum call today?'

'I don't know, Joe. We'll see. She's probably very busy. Perhaps we shouldn't look forward to it too much. It could even be weeks.'

That put a frown on his boy's face. 'Okay. I've waited years. Can wait some more.'

Bennet ruffled the boy's hair, then pressed a twenty-pound note into his hand. 'Buy me something cheap and tacky from a gift shop and keep the change. Hey, isn't that your pal Shaun?'

Bennet pointed at a kid by the school gates.

'Yeah. Did I tell you his granddad's a policeman as well?'

Bennet's father was a former detective and Joe was very impressed that the two main male adults in his life had such 'cool' jobs, although he had no desire to follow in their footsteps. 'You might have mentioned it. Why?'

'Shaun says his granddad says it was harder back then. He says there were hundreds of serial killers because no one knew.'

Bennet laughed. 'If he's saying it was harder back then to connect crimes, well, today's technology makes it easier for sure. It's possible murders could have been committed by the same person and the police never discovered it. We're better at catching people who might have gone on to be serial killers. But I'm not sure serial killers is a subject kids your age should be talking about.'

'Shaun keeps winding me up. He says his granddad was better than you because he didn't have the fingerprints and phone tapping and DNA and stuff.'

'True, they didn't have those things. But the criminals are just as smart as us with the new technology. Shaun's granddad didn't have to deal with cybercrime. What rank was his granddad?'

'Don't know. I'll ask him.'

'Don't worry about it. Anyway, you don't want the coach to go without you.'

Joe fist-pumped his dad, and was gone a moment later. Sitting alone, watching teachers try to subdue frantic kids and herd them on the coach, Bennet found his mind wandering to

Lorraine. Where was she right now? With her new daughter? Did her new family even know about Joe? Had she told them he was living a drive away, or in another country and out of reach, or dead? He felt the itching muscle tautness again. That urge to... do something. He pulled his phone, determined this time to contact Lorraine.

Last night he had gotten as far as loading her Facebook profile before backing out. This time he managed to start a message to her before wilting. He couldn't go through with it because it felt too much like begging. Lorraine had to *want* to see Joe, not be convinced or cajoled into it. He drove home.

Usually a quiet house was enjoyable, but not this morning. Usually he kicked off his shoes a second in the door. Not today. He stood in the living room, coat and shoes on, and cracked his fingers. The itchy call to action felt worse now that Joe wasn't around. A few members of his team had sent updates about Buttery Park tasks they'd completed, but none of the information progressed the investigation or gave him something to do. But he needed some kind of action. Mr Unflappable was getting worked up by simple inactivity. No, impotency. A feeling of uselessness. He hated it. He felt like a hyper kid being forced to sit still.

So he drove to a crime scene.

8

____

Buttery Park was a place he'd never visited before a teenager got stabbed there. Almost three weeks ago, he'd arrived with his team, and ambulances, and there had been a host of onlookers, and a centimetre of snow, the darkness, and an ambience as chilly as the January air. Now, the place was tranquil, warmer, brighter, and devoid of any indication that a terrible crime had been committed here.

Except for the flowers on a bench on the hill by the lake. The car park offered a view of the water and café and tennis court and children's play area, but the vital area hid in a blind spot. Bennet had to stroll halfway down the hill before the crime scene revealed itself, a patch of land between two small woods that provided the sides of a makeshift football pitch. Anyone sitting on the bench had a perfect view of the spot where a bad sportsman had pulled a blade. On that fateful evening two weeks ago, nobody had been sitting here.

The backrest had a bronze plaque dedicated to the memory of a ninety-year-old woman who'd died eighteen months ago, but a second had been added. The stabbed boy's parents had been unable to afford the £1500 it cost to make and apply a plaque, and had written to Barnsley's District Commander to provide the funds. Bennet could see that their plea had either failed or was ongoing: the current dedication was a computer-printed piece of A5 paper, laminated and stapled to the wood, probably without permission.

He had visited today in order to shift his thoughts from Lorraine and Joe, on to solving a crime. But seeing that plaque only fed his guilt. Hundreds of hours put in by people trained to catch killers, myriad doors knocked and statements taken and CCTV tapes collected, and what did he, as overall leader, have to show for it? Two parents resigned to hearing bad news every day, and one lethal thug taunting his hunters. If Bennet couldn't help his own son have a chat with his mother, what chance did he have of providing justice for any other family?

9
____

At seven that evening, their prearranged time, Bennet called Joe. After giddily talking non-stop about his great first day in York, son asked father for a favour. None of his friends believed he still had his first birthday card, and could his dad take and send a photo of it? The card was in his middle desk drawer, under a small blue notepad. But there was a warning:

'Don't touch the blue notebook, Dad. You can't.'

Bennet found the birthday card, which he'd laminated wide open to keep it in prime condition. He hadn't seen this card for a few years and it brought a smile to his face. At first. A bunch of his then police colleagues had signed the card, some of them long gone from the team and some from the service itself. But Lorraine's name was absent, like a buzzing neon reminder that she had walked out on him months before the card existed.

He sent the photo. Joe said, 'Cheers, Dad. I asked Shaun and his granddad was a sergeant. But not a detective like you. Now he's saying all policemen today are fat because they don't do anything.'

Bennet would have laughed, but he was still emotional about Joe's birthday card. 'Your dad's not fat, is he?'

'His granddad says in the old days it was all about good old-fashioned coppering. They had to go out and work hard to catch serial killers. Knocking on doors and talking to people and searching dirty places. He says these days computers and internet do all the work and all the police do is sit on their bums and wait for the villains to come to them, and that's why they're all fat. Are detectives better than normal police?'

'It's basically all the same, but I'm trained in detection. There's aspects they do I have no clue about and vice versa. In terms of rank, though, DCI trumps sergeant.'

'I'll tell him that. Cheers. Gotta go. Remember, don't look in the blue notebook.'

After sending the photo and finishing the call, Bennet's eyes went where he'd promised they wouldn't. But what father wouldn't nosey into a notebook he'd been warned away from? It had a padlock, but it was a cheap thing easily popped open by the tip of a pencil.

The pages contained written details of special or memorable events in Joe's life. But these weren't diary-like notations for reminiscing. They were letters written to his mum. Together they created a mini-biography, informing her of everything important that had happened in his life. The later letters showed advancement in his English skills, suggesting he'd been keeping this record for a long time. Perhaps a few years.

Bennet was shocked. Joe had mentioned his mother periodically, but this book proved she'd been in his thoughts far more often than Bennet had realised. In one letter Joe mentioned that a friend had suggested his mother had left the family home in order to pursue a career of greatness, something Joe was keen to believe. He wrote of how 'amazed' he was by her commitment to 'saving the world' and his eagerness to welcome her back once her 'mission' was completed. It tugged at Bennet's heart to be reminded of how innocent and naïve and fanciful a ten-year-old could be. A major source of his constant tension the last two days had been his inability to come down on one side of the fence, but no more. All anxiety dumped out of him as if a trapdoor had opened. He'd chosen a side, finally.

Sitting at Joe's sticker-covered desk, he called a detective constable named Hooper. The young man had stalled his career with a number of errors during a double murder investigation a month ago, but since then had redeemed himself with long hours and dedication. The kid had promised Bennet he would be available for anything, anytime, and had since never failed to accept an out-of-hours task.

'Hooper, I need a favour. There was a missing person's case in March 2010, at a village called Lampton, up in the Peak District. A young girl. Get onto Derbyshire Constabulary and see what they can give us from the files. All of it, if you can. See if there's anyone connected to the investigation who will agree to be interviewed. For a TV documentary.'

'TV? Is this about the Buttery case?'

'No. Don't ask. But make sure you stress that this is a personal query. I'll explain later. Email me whatever you get. Don't tell any of our team about this until I say it's time. Thanks.'

Hooper didn't need to know any more. After the call, Bennet opened Messenger, ticked Lorraine's name, and this time there were no nerves when he wrote his message.

YOU WIN. I'LL DO IT. I CAN GET YOU THE POLICE FILES YOU NEED, AND THERE'S A CHANCE I CAN GET YOU AN INTERVIEW WITH ONE OF THE DETECTIVES WHO RAN THE INVESTIGATION. I'LL HELP YOUR DOCUMENTARY. BUT YOU HAVE TO DO SOMETHING FOR ME. NO, NOT FOR ME. FOR JOE. HE'S YOUR SON AND I WANT YOU TO MEET WITH HIM, EVEN IF YOU DON'T CARE FOR IT. HE MISSES YOU AND HE DESERVES BETTER THAN THIS.

10

If he'd been relegated to house clothes and a day indoors, Bennet might not have made the decision. But his boss decided things with a strange phone call that Tuesday morning, although Bennet didn't know it at first.

Superintendent Hunter launched with, 'The Buttery Park victim's parents just called the station. They've heard that we had a suspect and released him, and they're not happy. They've threatened to turn up at the station this morning, with a reporter. I know it's your day off, but any chance you could come in? Andrea's at the hospital.'

Andrea, the family liaison officer assigned to the Turtons, had blood tests scheduled for today, Bennet remembered. 'To talk to them? Did they give a time?'

'Well, no, it's just a threat. But it would be great to have you here just in case. Just hang around the station. That pool table is still in the rec room, right?'

'No. That got bust months ago.' Actually, Hunter had donated it to a charity shop after banging footsteps and laughter – the rec room was above his office – had interrupted a meeting between him and a caseworker from the commissioner's office.

'You want me to hang around the station all day on the off-chance that the parents will come in?'

'It's just to appease them. I don't think they'd like being fobbed off with someone who doesn't have all the answers. Free food at the canteen. Watch TV. I'd take that deal. And we'll call it overtime. I need this, Liam. Help out a friend.'

Bennet was the Buttery Park stabbing's senior investigating officer, but he didn't have all the answers, either. But, Andrea aside, his was the face the parents knew best, even though on the three occasions he'd met them, it had been as the bearer of inert news.

So, there he was, dressed, in his car, with the world available to him, and that was when he made the decision. That morning he'd woken to find that the message he'd sent Lorraine still didn't display the telltale tick indicating it had been read. Sometimes Facebook hid messages from a user if their algorithms figured the recipient didn't know the sender, so Lorraine might not even know Bennet had contacted her. Or she'd blocked him. Or she simply hadn't opened Messenger. Whatever the reason, her lack of reply gave him that itchy craving to act, to work, to... do *something*.

With the bitter taste of Joe's letters to his mother still forefront in his mind, he didn't make a right turn out of his driveway, for the station. Instead, he spun the wheel left, for the motorway, and hoped he wasn't about to make a big mistake.

11

———

10 MUST-VISIT PEAK DISTRICT VILLAGES.

4: LAMPTON IN THE PEAK DISTRICT IS A POSTCARD-WORTHY TINY COMMUNITY, ONCE A MILLING EPICENTRE, WITH MAZE-LIKE STREETS OF STONE-WALL COTTAGES AND AN ENCLOSED VILLAGE CENTRE. IN 1924, SOME FORTY YEARS AFTER THE FIRST FREEDOM TO ROAM BILL WAS PRESENTED TO PARLIAMENT AND VETOED, MOORLAND AROUND LAMPTON WAS THE SCENE OF A MASS PROTEST BY RAMBLERS DETERMINED NOT TO BE DENIED BY LANDOWNERS. YOU CAN FIND LAMPTON, WHERE A NOMAD PLANTED A LAMP AND BUILT A TOWN, BY TURNING NORTH ONTO BENDERS ROAD OFF THE A6 JUST WEST OF BAKEWELL AND FOLLOWING THE SIGNS (PAGE 84).

The closest major road to Lampton was the A6 near its south border, but there was no entry from the south for vehicles, so Benders Road hooked around the village on the east side and speared it from the north. Unmentioned in official guidebooks was a much shorter route: a private farm track beginning a few hundred metres along Benders Road that ran towards Lampton's eastern flank, where there was a secret parking area for residents only. The farm track was barred by a gate secured by a heavy-duty combination padlock. To dissuade those on foot who could scale the gate, the landowner – a hulking bear of a man called Crabtree, if Liam remembered correctly – had posted a WARNING sign with a picture of a snarling dog.

Because the secret car park and the track had been created for those living in Lampton, they all knew there was no guard dog, and they all had the combination for the padlock. Bennet hadn't been a resident but had visited Lorraine a number of times. After a decade, Liam didn't expect the code number in his head to be correct or that Crabtree wouldn't have changed it. He got a pleasant surprise.

A few minutes down this hedge-lined track, another led off it on the right, with a sign saying PRIVATE. OUT. YOU. KEEP. This would be the track to the Crabtrees' farm. He drove past.

The secret car park was behind the Red Lion public house. It was enclosed by buildings on three sides, with a small alleyway between the close sides of the pub and the Yorkshire Bank – too thin for vehicles, thus making it off-limits to tourists. A concrete ramp up to the raised tarmac had been painted with STOP CLEAN WHEELS, which he disobeyed. The car park was only a third full, so he cut a few turns and circles to dislodge most of the mud from his wheels before parking far from the majority of his mess. Stepping in the car to stepping back out: fifty-one minutes.

The eternally gloomy alleyway between the pub and the bank delivered him into the south-western end of the rugby-ball-shaped village centre. The area was known as the Well and it struck him, again, how apt that was. Dead centre was a pond enclosed by a green area for picnicking, itself encircled by the road and then a ring of old buildings with modern frontages. An aerial view might give the impression of a shallow well perhaps two hundred metres wide that had mostly emptied to expose items cast to the bottom.

Ahead of him, past the green, the main road left the Well between the old grey library, with its nice rear garden that Liam still remembered fondly, and the Anderson's supermarket, with its classy glass front and bright letters set against aged grey stone, like a young woman's face transplanted onto an old lady's head. Beyond these two buildings, Bennet remembered, the road curved out of sight, to run past an array of cheesy trinket shops, and reappeared above the edge of the Well as it climbed upwards towards the Porsche showroom, a Tesco, a church and a tiny school and the hotel. The place had hardly changed in the decade or so since he'd last seen it.

He crossed the road and dumped himself on one of the benches circling the pond to watch the village breathing. There was a black siren-style speaker atop the lamp post next to him, and he saw others dotted around the area. A civil defence system, given that the Well was effectively a sunken bowl and perhaps liable to flooding? It was a little strange that this area was covered by five or six small sirens instead of one large device. The system hadn't been in place a decade ago.

It was a cold January, so the tourists were spread thin. Duos and threesomes and a scattering of families moved here and there, mixed with Lampton's human furniture. He could instantly tell the two species apart, because the locals walked with a purpose, knowing where they were going and doing so on a timetable. The tourists ambled along with a constant look of awe on their faces, like lost children, as if city folk regarded quaint old England as another world. And they drew suspicious glances, like trespassers.

Amongst the locals, Bennet recognised a face here and there. He saw folks he'd been on low-level speaking terms with, and some he'd heard gossip about, but nobody he would have called a friend. Would anyone remember him from the – what, ten? – times he'd visited? Would he get the backslaps and handshakes of a returned kindred spirit, or the same sceptical glare accorded every other stranger? It was a long time ago.

So far, the latter appeared to be the order of the day. Eyes had run across him, then quickly moved on. Not even a double-take. It was a tourist spot, after all.

There was a fat man in a donkey jacket on a nearby bench. With shock, Bennet realised he recognised the guy. Crabtree, owner of a large portion of land to the east and one of the village chiefs, who became so by virtue of wealth, influence, or length of residence. The Crabtree in his memory had been a big ball of solid muscle from fifteen-hour days hauling weight on his farm; a lively, brash soul of the party who was rumoured to kill defective cattle with his bare hands. But the years had transformed the guy into a wreck. The former Hercules was vastly overweight, greatly aged, and stared at the pond with dead, zombie eyes. He didn't look much like a *Champion* or *Credit*, or whatever term they'd used to denote the important clique amongst the clan. He also looked like a man who'd suffered a great loss.

Bennet stood up. Reminiscing about Lampton not only wasted time, it also felt awkward. He'd sometimes wondered if things might have progressed differently had he moved here instead of dragging Lorraine to Barnsley. But he hadn't and his only connection to the village, Lorraine, was out of his life. He wasn't here to catch-up or to remember the good times or imagine what might have been, but to find Lorraine and convince her to agree to see her son. So he'd go do the find and convince, and get out of here.

12

The sandwich shop was a new version of itself, with a new name – Jenny's – and a new proprietor. The fresh look was just an update of the original, still designed to appeal to a city slicker's sense of rural England. Tied-back flowery curtains and a red carpet and wooden tables draped with gingham cloths and paintings on the walls showing craggy peaks and valleys. Soft music oozed from a speaker in a high corner. The menus were in chalk. Every table had a brochure displaying things to do in the local area and a little saucer bearing slices of Lampton rock. Meat and pasties and cheeses were arranged behind the glass counter, with their names in archaic script on little flags. One cheese was so grey Liam thought it should have a little toy astronaut on it. Signs everywhere promoted a local jam that was apparently 'world-renowned', probably meaning that a tourist from overseas once bought a jar and said it didn't taste like shit. He'd eaten here one time only, if memory served.

As he entered, he waited for someone to recognise him. Or all of them, turning their heads as if he was a cowboy entering a rowdy bar. No one batted an eyelid. Of the ten or so patrons, he was sure he recognised all but two of them. He clocked a lady at a table near the back, certain that she had lived on Lorraine's street: a retired school headmistress from Wales, if he remembered correctly. Near her was a beekeeper who'd been stung half to death but still loved his 'little babies'. There was a middle-aged man he was sure had cracked a water pipe digging up his garden and caused strife because the water board had had to shut the whole street's supply off for a while. And the young kid helping behind the counter – one of his old neighbours' nephews, fresh out of school and with aspirations of being a racing driver. So much for that. Bennet was surprised he'd learned so much about this place and its people and had to convince himself it was less about the 'what might have been' and more about his detective's brain.

The new proprietor – Jenny of Jenny's by her badge – was fat, in her late twenties, and very tanned. Her bark-like skin would have turned heads even on a beach, never mind a community of grey and green. Way back, this sandwich shop had been run by an old couple who'd been here as long as anyone. Maybe they'd made enough money to buy a place somewhere with decent wifi. Maybe the Reaper had called their ticket numbers.

The only spare table was next to a pair of unknown faces whose demeanour pegged them as tourists. Or was it aliens? The locals had a derogatory nickname for visitors, but he couldn't recall it. The pair were a little giddy, a demeanour more suited to Disneyland than a little Peak District village. The sour looks were reserved for them. He booked the empty table by leaving his coat on the chair and went to the counter. And told himself to chill out. The failed phone call to Lorraine, the whole reason he was here, had flared up the itchy tension again, and he was venting frustration with sour thoughts about the locals.

In front of him was a guy in oily coveralls who was waiting for Sandwich Jenny to wrap four baguettes in foil. Liam cocked an ear to some of the conversation around him, seeking a titbit about the film crew Lorraine had allied with. Nothing doing, although it was hard to net anything other than the giddy newbies discussing walking trails. But his interest piqued when he heard the guy in coveralls speak.

'Didn't my dad tell you to use cake domes on the cakes?'

The cakes on a shelf were uncovered. Sandwich Jenny looked quite horrified as she blurted an explanation about a delayed delivery. Coveralls Man shook his head. Jenny tried to lighten the mood, or change the subject, by asking if the young man's father was okay this morning.

In a mirror at the back, Bennet saw the young man's face. Under the left eye was a large mole, which had puckered the skin around it and caused the lower lid to droop. Otherwise, a pretty handsome chap. Bennet said, 'Did you find your cat?'

The young man turned. 'You what? Me?'

'You lost your cat. And you thought he was in someone's car.'

Puzzlement creased the young man's face. Bennet smiled. 'You were looking in cars for a cat. Or so you said.'

That did it: instant realisation. 'You're the detective man. You had a wife here.'

'That's me, although she wasn't my wife. You're Lucas Turner. You were about ten, right?' Joe's age. And, like Joe, motherless at that stage, albeit to cancer a couple of years before.

'Yeah. You thought I was trying to steal a car.'

Indeed he had been. Lucas Turner had been a known local tearaway back then, but he was also the son of a local councillor hotshot, so no one dared do anything about it. Given the cake-dome lark Bennet had just witnessed, that hadn't changed. Bennet had spotted him trying car-door handles and warned him. As the kid had been walking away, he'd called Bennet a tosspot. It would have been nice to have a little chat about that old event, but... *chill, Liam, chill.*

'So, given the outfit, you're still into cars. Where do you work?'

'Showroom up the road. I run the workshop. So what you doing back here? Business?'

'Pleasure. That old girlfriend of mine and some friends came up to film a documentary about a crime way back. I was hoping to find them.'

'Yeah, the missing person? I was ten when she went. She was my friend. You're reopening the case?'

'I'm not here about the missing girl. That's a Derbyshire police thing. I'm South Yorkshire. Any clues where the film crew are?'

'What they done?'

'You mean a crime? Nothing. Like I said, I know them. Got a message to pass on. So, any clue?'

'I heard they were hanging around. That's about it. Never saw them. I think they left.'

Jenny gave him his food and started to ring it in the till, but Lucas slapped Bennet's arm, said, 'Good to see you again,' and left. Quick. No payment for the sandwiches.

'Help ya, love?'

Bennet turned back to Sandwich Jenny. 'Yeah, four sandwiches if they're free, I guess.'

'Oh that, no, that's... they're prepaid.' She cancelled the unpaid items off the till and gave him a smile. This close, he could see that her deep tan and heavy make-up were camouflage. She was closer to forty than twenty. He ordered a cheese cob and she set to work on it.

He glanced out of the window and was surprised to see Lucas staring at him. The kid turned and left the moment he was spotted.

'You want ketchup on this, love?'

Ketchup on cheese? 'No.'

Bennet watched Lucas scuttle across the green, fast. The young man had become uncomfortable the moment he knew he was in the presence of a police officer. Might be worth tossing his name into the Police National Computer to see if he had a record. Or paying the car showroom a visit, just in case it was a mammoth chop shop.

'Visiting someone, love?'

She obviously hadn't overheard his conversation with Lucas. 'I'm here looking for a film crew. Four of them, I think. At least one was a woman, a former resident here called Lorraine Cross. Used to be Lorraine Taylor. Before your time though.'

Jenny didn't look up from the cheese she was cutting. 'I don't recall. I just mind my shop and don't catch much news.'

Interesting. She didn't seem the least bit interested in why a film crew would visit this little backwater. So he told her: missing girl, ten years ago.

'Oh, I know, terrible thing,' she said, buttering his cob. Still no eye contact. 'Before my time, like you say.'

'You didn't see the crew? They didn't come in to get an interview or anything?'

'No, they didn't come in here. And they wouldn't get much luck. What that poor woman went through. She deserves peace and quiet, not to have that terrible day dragged up again.'

'The mother? Is that who you mean?'

'Yes. We look after her. It's only right. You should stay away from her. She won't want to do any interviews.'

'Do you think the film crew might have contacted her? Where does she live?'

Behind him, a voice said, 'I wouldn't worry about where she lives, pal. Your people have been and gone. That's tourists for ya.'

Liam saw a skinny man in a thick woollen jumper and old jeans, sitting at a corner table with a tea and a newspaper and a dog curled under his chair. His was the only seat at that table, as if he owned it. He looked like he belonged right there, like a piece of the décor. He even had his own cup, given the tatty state of it, and was probably there come early morning or late evening, Christmas or Easter, rain or shine.

Liam took his wrapped cheese sandwich to the man's table. There were no free chairs within reach and he wasn't going to carry one across the room, so he squatted opposite the old guy.

'You remember them? The film crew? They were here.'

'Yep. Know all the Lopers in town, if you get my meaning. Upped and offed. You should do the same.'

Hallelujah. Lopers, that was the nickname for strangers that had eluded him. Short for interlopers, probably. 'By upped and offed, you mean they left?'

'Been and gone. Like the woman there said, that lass lost her kid and she needs to be left alone. We don't like reporters here and we don't want your sort hassling her.'

'Well, I'm not here to hassle her. And I'm not part of a film crew or a reporter. I'm a police officer.'

The old man looked surprised. 'I don't know anything about your film crew. Except they were Lopers sticking their noses into business they have no mind to. I mind my business. Sure you're not here about that missing person all those years ago? I was home with the wife when it happened. That girl will be married to some rich bloke in Spain or something by now. But you coppers never did believe she ran off. It's not respectful to come asking questions about that out of the blue.'

A strange claim. 'I'm not here about the missing girl. I'm South Yorkshire Police, not Derbyshire. My interest is just the film crew, about an entirely different matter. They came here on Sunday, right?'

Dog Man picked up a slice of Lampton rock from the saucer and popped it into his mouth. He sipped his tea, which had been sitting so long it had a membrane on the surface. He had to wipe the thin skin off his lips. 'So I heard. Been and gone. Left Monday. Probably because they got no help. Like I said, tricky business, that missing person, and that poor lass's mother deserves her peace and quiet. We look after our own here.'

A quick glance round told Bennet many eyes had gone back to their business. But not all. At one table, a set of eyes looked quickly away when he met them; at another, someone caught staring made no such cheap move and gave Liam a nod instead.

'Why are the police after them? Criminals?' Dog Man said. Liam turned his attention back to the man and lowered his voice.

'It's not actually police business. More a personal thing. I knew one of them. How did you know they were a film crew? Did you meet them? Did they say?'

'They came into the Lion Sunday night. Mouthy sorts, them out-of-towners. They must have said they were filmers, or someone else blabbed it. Can't remember how I know. But that can happen. Can't remember how I know JFK got shot. So, what have they done? They on the run? Bank robbery or something?'

'Personal issue, remember? Do you mean The Red Lion pub? Run by the Argyles?'

'Only pub we got. And the Argyles are gone.'

'They left?'

'Can't say. We don't talk about it. Listen, friend, we're in a time-lapse or something with these questions and answers. You going to tell me what the police want with these Lopers?'

Again the old man had ignored Bennet's claim that his interest in the film crew wasn't professional. He had no mind to repeat it. 'They might have information about a code 99. I can't tell you more than that. It would be very helpful if you could tell me anything else. Did they go to visit the mother? Is there somewhere they might be filming, like an old crime scene? Did they go home? Maybe you overhead someone, as you say, blab.'

Dog Man shook his head, and then he focused on his newspaper. End of chat, apparently. Liam stood to leave. He put his cheese sandwich in his coat pocket, grabbed a piece of Lampton rock, and headed for the door. Eyes watched, of course. In the open doorway, he turned to the room.

'You can all chat with that fellow with the dog now. He'll tell you everything I said.'

13

———

He had to pass the Red Lion pub to get to the car park, but he stopped outside. If the pub had been elsewhere in the village, he would have gotten his car and left this place for good. But it wasn't. It was right there, just feet away. The film crew had visited the Lion on Sunday night, so the staff might have a clue where they were, if still in the village. That information could be his within minutes, and it would be sheer laziness not to pop in and satisfy his curiosity. The publicans, the Argyles, were an old couple he'd always gotten on with, and they wouldn't be so reluctant to talk to him.

Curiosity? Who was he lying to? Joe expected to meet his mother, and damn if Bennet was going to let her just cast the boy aside without explanation. He wanted to have it out with her. She might be able to ignore words on a screen, but not his face in front of hers. It was why he'd made the journey and he wasn't about to give up so easily.

Although a timetable on the wall said the Lion was closed, the thick wooden double doors were wide open. Liam walked into the lounge. A man was sitting at a table, cleaning pool balls. He didn't know the face. The Argyles had a son Liam had never seen, but that guy had lost an arm, and this guy had both. On one wall was a large frame with four headshots, including the man himself: Tom Jonesy. The others on the picture were Erica Jonesy, probably his wife, and a couple of young females. One had a giant reddish-yellow birthmark across her lower cheek and mouth that looked like someone had lobbed a slice of pizza at her. Liam didn't recognise any of them. The young females had probably been schoolkids when Lorraine lived here.

Jonesy caught sight of his visitor in the doorway. 'Hey, pal. Too early. Pool league tonight, if you want to come back then. Pints a pound, 7 till 9.'

Liam walked closer. 'I saw. Sorry to intrude, sir. Are you the new publican? What happened to the Argyles?'

Jonesy spat on the black ball and started towelling it dry. 'Been here five months. Not from round here, then, you? Not if you don't know about the Argyles. Not my place to tell tales. Too late if you're here for them.'

'Did they move or get another pub somewhere, or something?'

'Or something,' the guy said, a little defiantly. 'That's a lot of questions. We're not open, I said. Come back tonight.'

'I'm really sorry to interrupt, but I'm looking for some people. I hear they were in here two nights ago. A small film crew. Mouthy sorts, apparently.'

'Oh, them Lopers. Yeah, Sunday, they were here. I heard about their big mouths.'

The guy seemed more willing to talk now, so Liam approached and sat at the same table. 'You *heard* they were here? You weren't here that night?'

Jonesy took his box of clean balls to the pool table, where he tipped them loudly onto the baize. 'Not at weekends. We go to the grandparents. Wife's, not mine. Vicky over there was on duty.' He nodded at the picture of four headshots. Vicky:

birthmark girl. Jonesy started sweeping the balls into the pockets.

Liam cast his eyes around. His detective habit had already looked for and found a CCTV camera aimed down from above the entrance. But reviewing the footage from Sunday night, if it still existed, seemed like too much trouble for little extra information. 'They probably asked some questions in here. They were making a documentary about an old crime.'

'The missing person thing from years ago? They were here for that? A documentary? I wouldn't have thought anyone cared anymore. Hardly a world-famous thing. They didn't ask me anything. Wasn't here. Wasn't living here when she went missing, either. Mind you, don't go asking questions all over about that thing, and stay away from that girl's mum. Protective people here, and they won't like reporters sticking their noses in.'

Jonesy was the second man to effectively give him a warning. 'I'm not a reporter. I'm a police officer, but I'm not here about the missing girl. So have you got any idea where the film crew are? Are they still in the village?'

'No. Look, they were just customers, and I wasn't here. If they'd lugged in video cameras and stuff, I'd have probably heard about it. I guess they just wanted to sample my great ale. That's all I know.'

Jonesy headed behind the bar and started cleaning a mirror. Like Dog Man's raising of a newspaper, it said this nice little chat was over. Liam considered hauling his warrant card, which always had the ability to loosen tongues, but figured Jonesy was the sort who'd definitely make a complaint. Informing this guy he was a policeman wasn't morally incorrect, but giving the impression he was on official business was another matter. There was a code of ethics to think about. He hated that he'd even considered such action. He left the wallet in his pocket and aimed for the door.

'Hey,' Jonesy called. In the doorway, Liam turned to him. 'Your turn. So why do the police want them? Rob a bank or something?'

'Or something,' Liam said as he stepped out.

14

As Bennet approached the alleyway between the pub and the bank, a man exited it right into his path.

'My apologies,' the man said as he moved past. Liam turned to watch him go. He was tall, lithe, grey-haired and handsome in a Paul Newman sort of way, and Bennet recognised him. Richard Turner, father of the mechanic in the sandwich shop. Parish councillor and veterinary surgeon, with a thriving practice on the outskirts of the village. And cake-dome fan. Way back, it had been widely known that the eligible bachelor slept with married women from the village and, like his son's troublemaking, it was something nobody complained about, not even slighted husbands. Ten years ago, the councillor had had a deity-like standing in the village and he reeked of it today.

Lorraine hadn't much liked Turner because of his sexual conquests, but Bennet hadn't cared about that. In fact, he'd respected the man because he was a single father, little knowing he'd become one himself soon afterwards. Now, the feeling was much the same. Lucas Turner had grown into a worthwhile adult, it seemed; Bennet only had hope his own son would prosper.

As he walked away, Turner cast his eyes back at Liam, but quickly averted his gaze upon realising he was being watched. Liam shook his head – what, did Lopers have a certain smell or something? He couldn't wait to get out of this place.

Back in the secret car park, Bennet sat in his car and wondered what to do. He checked Messenger, but Lorraine still hadn't viewed his message. If the film crew had been and gone, she'd clearly not needed his input for their documentary. Maybe they'd wrangled someone else's help in getting police files on the missing girl.

He'd entertained the possibility that Lorraine's access to Facebook and Messenger was via desktop rather than mobile: she hadn't posted a thing on the social media site since Saturday, so maybe she was unable to while away from home. Now, he found a more worrying idea take the helm. Perhaps there was a way to view Messenger messages without the software acknowledging it, and she'd read his cruel words and something had changed. He'd threatened that his help came at a price: see her son. Had she decided that was a price not worth paying and now wouldn't ever contact him again?

Having to bribe Joe's own mother to see him. What a damn joke. And if she had gotten the files, she no longer needed him and he had nothing to bargain with. All he could do was wait for her to call, if she ever would. Meantime, he was far from home for no reason and facing an awkward chat with his son.

He started driving, hoping to be home, feet up, within the hour. But at the end of the track through the Crabtrees' field, he didn't make a right turn on Benders Road, for the A6 and home. Instead, he spun the wheel left, for the main road into Lampton's northern end, and hoped he wasn't about to make a big mistake.

15

At the junction of Benders Road and Main Street, which ran all the way into Lampton's Well, there was what looked like a Guy Fawkes effigy by the village noticeboard. A sign on the effigy told Liam he'd missed the Lampton Scarecrow Festival by five days. He'd live. He turned left, towards the village.

Although Main Street led nowhere but the Well and dead-ended there, a sign pointed the way ahead. Just before a run of four modern, red-brick homes with a side street splitting them was a medium-sized Tesco on the right with a Shell garage next door and the Porsche showroom facing both across a wide road of smooth, bright tarmac, all of it indicative of an urban town instead of a remote village. Only beyond the final two houses did the effect change.

Here, the road thinned and its condition worsened, the houses aged and grew further apart, interspersed with small shops, and became a mix of taller and shorter, cheaper and affluent. A hundred metres later was the main residential area and here the land sank on both sides as the road coursed along the spine of a hill, with side streets slipping down like ribs.

Once past the final two side streets, the main road veered downwards at a slight curve towards the Well. The view from this spine road, through breaks in the buildings, was breathtaking, and probably the cause of many a vehicular accident.

The Pandora was ahead on his left. It was a timber-framed, three-storey, converted clergy house set back from the road behind its car park. At one time, back before the church had sold it, the house had sat in lush gardens, but in the sixties the new owner had widened the track into what was now Main Street, and built many of the houses along it. Out front, the only remnant of those gardens was a small walled lawn with a fountain dead centre of the cark park. That was as much as Liam knew about the place, despite having lived in Lampton for a year. A lady called Gemma had managed the hotel way back, but if the sandwich shop was anything to go by, she was long gone.

So was the name, or he'd remembered it wrong. The sign at the mouth of the car park said Panorama, not Pandora. As he waited for a tractor to pass so he could turn into the car park, he again had to remind himself why this was a good idea.

If he went home, he'd worry about that upcoming talk with Joe, wouldn't he? He still had a few hours until he had to pick his son up from school, so it wouldn't hurt to hang around a little longer, ask another question or two. And this was the best place. Given that the crew had visited the local pub at night, they'd probably overnighted in the village. There were various homes that owners had converted into bed and breakfasts, but the Panorama was the only bona fide hotel in the area. Maybe he'd find the crew still there, or one of them had left a phone number when booking.

His phone buzzed with a text message. Once his car was laid up close to the fountain, he read it. Not Lorraine. It was from DC

Hooper, who he'd tasked with acquiring information about the missing girl case in 2010. He'd forgotten about that.

Gave your number to a former tec Sarg Ford on case you mentioned, he said he will call you. Looked him up. Fired for misconduct, now works supermarket security. I think he thinks he can make a buck or two for his info, so be wary. Anything else?

Bennet's reply said thanks and, no, there was nothing else. Of course there wasn't, since the whole plan to bribe Lorraine with help had gone to pot. Hopefully the detective-cum-Asda-guard wouldn't call.

The Panorama's foyer retained timber framing bare brick, but paint had been applied to gloss it all up. The walls were hung with art depicting scenes from the ancient era of the house's construction, but were encased in modern frames. The furniture was clearly pseudo-medieval, given how it was all within bumping and fingering distance. The patterned carpet was dull pink along the traffic line and bright red at the untrampled edges.

The reception desk was on the right in a large arched alcove, but empty of life. He rang a bell and picked up a leaflet flaunting some local attraction.

'Hello?' a voice said behind him. A middle-aged black woman with curly hair appeared in the corridor. So Gemma Bowler had managed to hang on to her job, but the years had been cruel. Way back, Gemma had been on crutches because of debilitating arthritis in both feet. Now she was in a wheelchair. She'd also picked up a thick forehead scar somewhere.

She wheeled around his legs and into the alcove, and spun to face him across the counter. She wore jeans and a white T-shirt with a picture of her hotel on it. 'Visiting? Need a room?'

He'd met Gemma a couple of times in the Yorkshire Bank

queue. She was a chatty lady who made friends easily. 'How's the detective fiction going?'

At first suspicion, then realisation. 'Lee! How are you? That is you, isn't it?'

'Liam. Here I am. You still write detective fiction?'

She reached out to shake his hand. His was sweaty and he wiped it on his trousers first. 'Oh, I gave that up for fantasy because the research is easier and I've always loved it. Although I did consider having my detective chase a mythical serial killer. I imagine there isn't a police book out there that mentions a Bakhtak. That wouldn't sell.'

'Might get away with saying it once. Twice, no. Anyway, I don't need a room. Not staying. I'm just in the area looking for some people. Lopers. Three of them, anyway. One is Lorraine Taylor, my girlfriend way back. Lived here. Did you know her?'

Gemma thought and shook her head. 'I remember you saying you had a girlfriend, but I don't think we ever met properly. It happens, even in a place of just a few hundred people. She left to live with you, is that right? Bradford?'

'Barnsley. Over ten years ago, so it's easy to forget. She was part of a four-person film crew that came to Lampton on Sunday. Did they stay here?'

Gemma looked a little unsure, until he added a teeny white lie: 'I *heard* they stayed here.'

She remembered now. 'Yes. Well, one of them. A man who said he was a director. I remember that, because we don't get many directors. He was middle-aged, like fifty or so, if that helps. Oh, and he was black. A black man. I don't know what they were filming.'

'A documentary about a young girl who went missing here about ten years ago. He didn't talk to you about that?'

She needed to think again, which puzzled him. Did hordes

of kids go missing round here? 'Oh. Yes, I know the story. I was on holiday that week she vanished. But no, he didn't mention it.'

'You were here back then. You could have given some insight into the way of life here in those days. Good filler for the documentary. Are you sure this director didn't mention it?'

'Terrible thing, that girl running away. The family was devastated. We kind of don't much talk about it to people when they come asking. Reporters and tourists who know about it. Out of respect to the mother.'

He'd run face-first into a wall of protection around the tale of the missing girl, even though he'd stressed that he wasn't here about that long-ago event. 'And you didn't ask this director what he was filming? You're always one for chatting with strangers.'

'No. But the way he was casually dressed when he went out that night, I thought maybe he was videoing birds or something. Night animals, maybe. A nature documentary. You can film that sort of thing alone, I thought. He had a camera bag, so that was what I figured. I didn't really ask. We get all sorts in here and a lot don't like to talk about themselves. I tend not to chat to my guests unless they look like they want to, and he didn't.'

'He went out filming Sunday night? What time was that? I heard the crew went to the Red Lion on Sunday.'

She nodded. 'Oh, yes, I heard that too. But this was after. He came back, collected his camera bag and folder. Oh, I'd say about a quarter to ten. I thought he'd maybe had an important call or something, because he was a little rushed.'

Bennet put the leaflet back on its pile. 'Folder?'

'Yes. Like a file folder, yellow. And his bag.'

'A camera bag, you said. So no suitcase of clothes?'

'Nothing like that. And that was it, he left. I had to give him the code for the door, which made me think he was coming back, but he didn't. I get that sometimes when people have to rush off. They leave the key in the lock, and he did that. I know, strange that he didn't bring any luggage, but I didn't ask.'

Actually, the lack of belongings didn't puzzle Bennet – he'd sometimes been away overnight to survey or arrest a suspect in another city and hadn't taken much more than his phone and some cash. More intriguing was why the director had stayed at the hotel alone. A falling out with his crew? He needed space and peace to write a script, which might also explain the yellow file folder? Was he a diva-type, unwilling to bed down in a car or a cheesy bed and breakfast?

'He stayed here alone, but didn't anyone accompany him here? To drop him off, maybe?'

Gemma shook her head. 'At least not that I saw. I was inside. But other people could have been outside, in a car. He only stayed fifteen minutes or so after he checked in, so he might have had people waiting outside. I just don't know.'

'Fifteen minutes? And how long was he gone for?'

'Oh, until that night. He checked in in the afternoon and left and I didn't see him again until nearly ten, after, like you say, they'd been to the Lion. But a lot of tourists do that, because they're off sightseeing.'

Liam glanced at the guest register, where he saw only one person had checked in on Sunday. Room: seven. Duration: one night. Name: Donald Ducke. The contact number column was empty. But he hadn't signed out.

'You don't mind people using silly fake names?'

Gemma leaned in to look closely at the register. It took a few seconds for her puzzled expression to become one of mirth. 'Oh my, I didn't even notice. It was the E that threw me, I reckon. He pronounced it like duke. Oh, what an idiot.'

Did she mean the director, or herself? 'Any idea where they were heading next?'

'No,' Gemma said. 'I never ask such a thing. I can't help you there, I'm afraid. I only know they upped and offed. You could try the Lion.'

'What about CCTV? I don't see any cameras.'

Gemma rubbed at her legs, as if they hurt. 'No. Busted for a few months now. I keep meaning to get around to it.'

'You really should. You deal with strangers who don't live local and often use fake names.'

She shrugged. He thanked Gemma and turned to leave, but one final question begged to be asked. No name to trace or phone number to call, but perhaps there was a clue in the room Donald Ducke had taken. A forgotten driver's licence would do nicely. Could he see the room?

She gave him a key and he took the stairs. The room was the simple affair he'd expected. Bed, shower, TV with probably only a handful of channels, wifi with porn doubtless blocked, and a table against a wall with a pair of chairs and the paraphernalia for making hot caffeine. It was a blizzard of white, from the walls to the TV to the kettle to the towels, like an apartment in a sci-fi movie. Apart from odd snippets like the TV remote and coffee sachets, the only colour came from the window in the opposite wall to the door. He could see a corner of the housing estate, beyond which it was all green fields and snaking, thread-thin roads and walking trails set against a backdrop of faraway towns and villages.

Liam stood in the centre of the room, hands in his pockets, and ran his eyes around. The hotelier, Gemma, had joked about his seeking fingerprints, but she hadn't been wildly off. He was after some kind of clue as to where the film crew might have gone, but of course, the room had been cleaned since the director checked out. It felt a little odd to be searching a room without other detectives and crime-scene techs around.

Even if the room hadn't been cleaned, what had he expected to find? A handy little Post-it note with an address? There was nothing here that would move him forward, so he needed a new track. Lorraine had mentioned Chesterfield, so perhaps that should be his next location. But that was a big city and he had no idea what the crew was doing there, and it seemed like too much trouble. Even being here felt like a waste of time. He should just keep sending her messages on social media until she replied.

Back downstairs, he returned the key and thanked Gemma for her time. 'The room. Anything out of order when you went to clean it? Find anything?'

She shook her head. 'The tea table had been moved into the middle of the room, but that was it. Anything else you need me for?' she asked.

There wasn't, but simple curiosity prompted: 'Yeah. What happened to the Argyles?'

Her answer surprised him: 'Oh, that would be telling. Maybe over a candlelit dinner. Seriously, though, we're not supposed to say.'

'Small village, shock horror, eh?'

She just shrugged. 'Not supposed to say. At the last town meeting the Keys decided we shouldn't talk about it. Not to anyone.'

Hallelujah. Keys, that was the name for the handful of important residents who controlled the village. In Bennet's time here, he'd never attended a town meeting, but they were held once a month or when necessary. After dealing with community news, all nice and normal, most of the village folk had to leave the room so the Keys could vote on important matters not for mortal ears.

'Surely the rule is you just don't discuss the Argyles with Lopers? Seriously, what happened to them? Did they get eaten by Bakhtak?'

'No, I can't tell you. I really can't.'

Lorraine had given him the low-down on the Keys. Everyone had to follow their rules and disobedience was punished. A teenaged tearaway had been banned from the Red Lion and given a 9pm curfew. A shopkeeper had been forced to shut his shop for a week because he'd sold alcohol to underaged Lopers. And an event back in the 1980s was still shrouded in mystery – a man had been evicted from the village, with just the clothes he wore, for getting a facial tattoo.

Liam had cracked a joke about getting put in the stocks and pelted with tomatoes, but he hadn't really taken it seriously. He'd been consumed by police work and uninterested in village matters or gossip. Now that he thought about it, the whole shebang with the Keys seemed a bit scary.

'You know, there's no legal basis for what the Keys do, Gemma. They can't punish you for disobeying their unofficial rules.'

'I know, but we all agreed, didn't we? I mean, the Keys aren't councillors or anything, except Mr Turner. He's been one for about four terms now. He covers a few parishes and he's mostly involved with car parks and recreation grounds. But the Keys are something he put together off-the-books, if you like. They're not official but we've all accepted it and it's been that way for fifteen years or so. I guess it's like playing Monopoly, and the Keys are the banker. If you want to play the game, you obey the rules of the banker, but you can quit the game at any time.'

By leaving your home? Sweet. The Monopoly analogy sounded like a gem written by the Keys to justify their actions, perhaps the brainchild of their top dog, Richard Turner, bachelor, vet, councillor. Whatever. Not his concern. He had his own life to worry about and it was time to get back to it.

16

His detective paranoia buzzed as he left the hotel. The car park had space for thirty vehicles and the five that had been here when he arrived were scattered. Now a new car had arrived, and it was parked right next to his own, facing the opposite way so that both driver's doors were close. He approached casually, aware of all the times a police colleague had been attacked by a disgruntled criminal or angry family member of one.

He could see the outline of someone in the driver's seat. He approached his passenger side, for caution, and watched the driver wind their window down. It was a large woman, about sixty. She wore a blue-and-white uniform shirt and had a name badge, although he couldn't read it at this angle. She spoke rapidly.

'You're the detective who's come here. I need to speak with you. Quick. Please.'

Word had travelled fast. 'About what?'

'Not here. We can't be seen.' She tossed a ball of paper onto his bonnet and drove away, fast. He noted the registration number just in case a coming day required a trace and picked up the balled paper.

There was a sketch of what looked like a pair of lollipops with their heads facing each other. Between them was a circle with GRASS written inside. One of the lollipops was labelled ARTON PLACE and had an arrow running across to the other, GRODES PLACE, at whose end was a little square house with an X. The arrow said FOLLOW THIS. A rough map, it seemed. Apparently he was supposed to go down Arton Place, cross some grass, and meet the woman at one of the houses on Grodes Place.

It tingled his detective senses. This woman wanted to tell him something and was worried about eavesdroppers. But it was almost one o'clock and he had to pick Joe up at three. He considered his options and made a decision. He called one of his team, a sergeant called Sienna Todd, and asked her to go pick up Joe because he was stuck in a place called Lampton in the Peak District. She agreed and he called the school to inform them.

Google Maps told him Arton Place and Grodes Place, his destination, were cul-de-sacs with a small green area between them. But he also noticed something curious. Although the entry to Arton Place was just across the road, between the four red-brick houses, there was no through route for a vehicle. For a crow, the simplest way was to follow the arrow on the sketch map, as advertised, but a driver would have to take a more winding journey to reach Grodes Place. And the woman who drew the map knew he was in a car.

He exited the car park, turned right and just seconds later spun the wheel left, onto Arton Place. The street was lined with semi-detached homes with small gardens. Beyond the turning circle at the end was an alley splitting a pair of detached homes, with trees beyond. He parked.

At the end of the alley the trees parted for a cycle barrier.

This was where he stopped, staring out into a green area about a hundred metres long and ringed by trees. In the centre was a basic children's playpark. At the far side he saw the end houses of Grodes Place poking above the trees. Nobody was about.

Why had the woman wanted him to come this way, knowing he'd have to leave his car? Perhaps she figured he wouldn't mind a stroll, or maybe there were roadworks blocking the other route. The reason could be completely innocent, but he'd been a policeman too long to ignore a gut feeling. And his gut told him this wasn't about ease or practicality. He didn't like the fact that the only windows giving a view of the green area were those in the two houses behind him and the pair across the way.

He'd already googled the nearest police station and tapped its phone number into his mobile. There it was, on the screen, and with his finger hovering over the call button, he started walking. If he saw anyone who wasn't the large woman coming his way, he'd call the station, report his location, and keep the officer on the line until he got safely across the green.

Nobody appeared. While passing the playpark, he saw a metal post at its edge with another siren attached. The park's apparatus was clean, in shape, but its emptiness made him think about his son. Joe and his friends often chatted online and visited each other's houses to play Xbox games, and good old-fashioned days larking at places like this were minimal. It was a shame that technology had forced more kids indoors.

At Grodes Place he encountered another alleyway created by the high side-fences of two back gardens. He got partway down when a voice called out.

'In here, quick.'

A gate in the high fence opened and the same large woman poked her head out. An arm waved frantically. She locked the gate behind him and scuttled into the house. He followed her into a kitchen, and only when the back door was shut did she seem to relax. Clearly, she didn't want to be seen with a Loper. Or a police officer. Now he saw her name badge said Anika, Team Helper.

'Upstairs.' He followed her up, into a room with a large oak dining table loaded with boxes. They were also stacked beneath it and around the walls. At the window, she stared out. He watched, waiting, and she said, 'It's tough to see it every day. But this is my home. I can't leave.'

He didn't understand. 'The green?'

Anika turned to him, puzzled. Now he saw she'd picked up a large, padded envelope at some point. 'The playpark. It hurts to look out the window and see where Sally had her most fun. Where she had her worst experience. Where she might have died.'

Now it fell into place. Sally. The missing girl from ten years ago. Anika was her mother.

'This was her bedroom. I use it for storage now, because it hurts too much to stand in here and look out at the park. Do you think I should have kept this place as a shrine? I know some grieving parents do that. I couldn't. I needed to move on. That was the advice.'

Now he knew why she'd wanted to talk. She had heard a policeman was in the village, and she'd assumed he was here because...

'I'm sorry. I'm not here about your missing daughter.'

'Not here for Sally?' The thought dismayed her. 'But why not?'

'I'm sorry, I'm here on separate business. I'm not part of Derbyshire Constabulary, and they're the ones who would be investigating her case.'

'Oh, they are. It's still an open case. But unless they get new evidence, there's not much they can do.'

Sounded about right. He looked past her, at the playpark

beyond the window. He felt it wouldn't help to continue this conversation, but he couldn't fight his intrigue. 'She was taken from the park?'

'I know you police have theories it might have happened somewhere else, but I'm certain. I just know. So why are you in Lampton if not for Sally?'

'I'm here to find four people. A film crew. They came here...' He left it there, unwilling to state why the crew had come to Lampton.

'Oh. I know who you mean. They were here on Sunday. They wanted to tell the story of my Sally. So are you connected to this after all?'

She seemed buoyed again, and he needed to shut it down. 'No. Sorry. I need to find them about a separate matter. It's not connected to your daughter's disappearance, I'm afraid. I heard Chesterfield mentioned. You know why that might be?'

She gave a slow nod. 'Chesterfield. That makes sense. The party. Sally was at a party in Chesterfield the night she disappeared. I think the film people might have mentioned going to Chesterfield.'

'So they contacted you?'

'They did. I got a phone call. It was on Saturday afternoon. But I couldn't talk to them.'

'Why?'

'It wouldn't do any good, would it? They were just telling the story. They weren't investigating. They couldn't help me, so I didn't speak to them. I mean, I know the exposure might have helped. But... it was the correct thing to do not to talk to them.'

He didn't understand. But whatever she meant, she didn't sound that certain she'd made the right choice.

'It's old news now,' she continued. 'My Sally's disappearance was a dark time for this village, and it brings back bad memories. And I wasn't supposed to have something like this open old wounds. It's not good remembering Sally in this way. I shouldn't celebrate her birthday. I stopped honouring her death, you know. The anniversary of when she went missing. I wanted to plant small trees, one for each passing year. Ten years next March 6th, did you know? But it wasn't the correct thing to do. Just like not keeping her bedroom as a dedication to her. A shrine. I should move on. Move on and wait to see if she comes back, I mean. And I have.'

It didn't sound like she had. Something was off about her choice of words: the way she talked about things she *should* do or was *not supposed* to do. And a slip of the tongue she'd tried to slyly correct.

'You grieve in the way you want to,' Bennet said. 'If you want to plant trees, or keep her bedroom the way she had it, you can. You are allowed to.'

That seemed to strike a nerve, but she said nothing. He knew she had led him here via the playpark not to make sure no one saw, but to let him see the crime scene in order to stoke emotion about her daughter's disappearance. So that he would want to help her. And she still clutched that envelope in her hands. She needed a prompt and he gave it by asking what she held.

As if she'd long yearned for the opportunity, she opened the envelope and stepped close to him, and pulled out photographs and newspaper clippings. She held up a picture of a cute girl in black leggings under a short tartan skirt and a T-shirt with a sequined butterfly on the front. She was holding back tears.

'This wasn't taken the night she went missing, but this is what she wore. Her favourite outfit. She loved butterflies. She had a butterfly claw clip in her hair.'

She tried to smile at the photo, perhaps reminded of good times, but Bennet knew something else, beyond her daughter's disappearance. 'You talk as if you believe your daughter will be back. But you also mentioned her death.'

The tears started. 'Nobody talks about her, you know. I only have a handful of friends, and *we* talk about my girl, but it has to be in secret. I wanted to officially declare her dead, but I'm not supposed to. Sally might return. That's the theory. A lot of people think she's alive, living a nice life somewhere. So we have to go with that. So, to the world, she's alive. So there's no grave. But I know she's dead. And no one will help me.'

'You say you have no one, but what about family? Sally's father?'

'Family are scattered. I meet them now and then, but not here, not where it happened. They wouldn't be welcomed by the village if people knew they were here because of Sally. I go to them, instead. It's a much-needed break for me. I don't know why I don't just leave this place forever. And Sally's father... my husband and me drifted apart because of this. Perhaps Sally was the glue that kept us together, and without her... he left not long after she went missing. I don't hear from him. I don't want to burden him, because he's in enough pain.'

She thrust another photo into his face. He could tell from the computer-generated image that it was an age-progression depiction. He was staring at somebody's guestimation of how Sally would look today, aged twenty instead of ten. The creator had crafted Sally's head, shoulders and upper torso, and he'd put her in the same butterfly T-shirt. The existence of this picture meant the police were still investigating, still cared. This photo could help someone recognise her as she'd look today.

But before he could say this, he saw other computer-generated images in her hands and he took them. Sally aged about fifteen. And twenty-five. And thirty. And forty.

It made no sense. But he was certain of one thing. 'The police didn't create these.'

'No, Councillor Turner paid for them. Not long after she went missing. After Sally's father ran away. He wanted me to know how she would look. To ease my pain. He's very sweet. He looked after me in the first few days. The morning after Sally disappeared, he bought me a dress. A black dress for the TV, you know? So I would have the right look for appealing on TV and in papers to talk about Sally. And Sally liked him too.'

She thrust another photo at him. In this, Sally wore riding gear and was knelt by the front leg of a large brown horse with white markings. She seemed to be brushing the horse's white feathering, which was so thick it seemed to wear pompoms.

'Sally loved to ride one of Richard's horses and one of his friends was teaching her. Not this horse, although she actually renamed it. This one was too big. There was another. She would go at weekends mostly. She and Richard's son, one of her best friends, they were learning together. She had an ill cat and Richard helped it. He's a vet. Will you help me?'

The sudden swerve from history into a plea for help threw him. There wasn't much he could do, but the best detectives were people who cared for others and were desperate to help them find justice. It wasn't his case, and he wasn't a Derby sleuth, but he'd seen that possible crime scene, he'd seen photographs of the girl, and his mother had begged to his face. Now he was obliged by his own moral code to do at least something for this woman.

'I can't do much. I can talk to my boss and see if he'll find out anything new from Derby police. Maybe I can prompt an officer to come talk to you, or to do another round of publicity. But I can't investigate. I'm not allowed. But for now, I really have to go.' He didn't tell her he needed to pick up his own child, the same age the one she'd lost.

His agreeing to help seemed to satisfy her. She led him to the back door, but as he was about to step out, her fingers snapped around his wrist. 'Do you have children?'

'Yes, a ten-year-old boy. His mother left just a few months after he was born. She has a new life.'

'Such a contrast. A mother who knows exactly where her child is, but doesn't want to see him. And a mother who would do anything to know where her baby is. So you have some idea of what I'm going through. Will you promise to do all you can to help me? You know my pain. You have your boy, the same age as my girl when she was abducted. So will you promise to find my Sally?'

Agreeing to offer aid was one thing. But what she was asking was a step too far. 'I can't help you. I'm sorry.'

____

17

When he got back to his car, parked in the turning circle on Arton Place, Lucas Turner was leaning against it. He still wore his coveralls, but a biker jacket had been added. The bike it accompanied was nearby with a helmet on the seat. This wasn't going to be a scalding for laying his vehicle up in someone else's spot.

'Councillor Turner wants to talk to you,' the young man said. 'Follow me, please.'

Councillor Turner? A strange way for the kid to refer to his father. Intrigued, Bennet knew he would go and see what the top-dog Key wanted. But he wouldn't make it too easy for this kid. Given what Bennet had recently learned, all respect for Richard Turner and his kin had departed. He opened his door. 'I have a prior engagement, I'm afraid.'

A look of surprise came over Lucas's face. Then annoyance, suggesting a threat was imminent. But then he seemed to realise he was dealing with a policeman, or a Loper who didn't have to follow the rules, or maybe just a bigger, stronger guy. 'It won't take long. Please. My father is a parish councillor.'

It sounded like he wanted Bennet to be impressed, but his

narrowed eyes gave his words a sinister sheen, as if 'parish councillor' was slang for mafia hitman. Eager to go, but not eager to please, Bennet checked his watch and *hummed* and *hawed*. 'I guess I have a few minutes spare. Lead on.'

Bennet followed the bike out of Arton Place and down another side street closer to the centre. Two turns later, Lucas pulled up at the end of another cul-de-sac. It was much like the others Bennet had seen, except instead of two houses at the end, there was just a single large one. It was fifty feet behind an eight-feet-high brick wall that curved around half the entire turning circle. The high walls ran down each side, suggesting an enclosed plot, and he could see a fair splash of land behind the home. A sign by the large iron gates advertised TURNER'S – VETERINARY SURGEON. Bennet had expected Turner to have a lavish domain, but not this large, and not slap bang in the middle of a typical residential street.

Lucas Turner rode onto the pavement and stopped at an intercom by the gates. Bennet didn't catch what he said, but it was a handful of words at best and he didn't await a reply. He turned to Bennet, said, 'Don't lie to him, okay? He'll know,' and off he blew, far too fast down the road. Bennet watched the gates automatically swing open.

A driveway bearing a flashy Mercedes G-class four-by-four, led to the large porch, and the front door was ajar: another invitation. But Bennet stood his ground out on the road. Two minutes later the door fully opened and Councillor Turner stood on the threshold, dressed in the same suit as before but now without his jacket and with his sleeves rolled up.

Bennet waited. He'd gotten the impression that Turner had barked orders from behind a large, imposing desk and had waited there to receive his guest like a king. It wasn't going to go down that easy.

After at least thirty seconds standing on the threshold,

Turner realised he was going to have to give a little more. He made the long walk to the gates, braving the cold. 'You could have come in, you know, detective. That's why I opened the gate.'

'Oh, I'm sorry, sir. I felt it was rude to just enter your home. I waited to be invited in.'

'Well, that was my invitation to – oh, it doesn't matter. So, I hope my son was polite to you. He's not a fan of strangers.'

'He barely said a word. Maybe still smarting because I told him off years ago for trying to steal cars.'

'I believe he told me about that misunderstanding. He was making sure they were locked.'

Bennet kept a straight face. 'My mistake. So, you want a word with me?'

'Yes. Let's walk.'

Turner snapped his fingers, as if calling a dog. It made Bennet eager for a fight.

18

They strolled down the driveway, then Bennet veered onto the grass and alongside the house. Turner didn't look comfortable in the cold, but made no objection.

They went around the back, where Bennet saw a long extension to the house in white plastic and glass. The daylight made it hard to see much beyond the giant windows, more so because a security light above the back door of the main house had flicked on at their presence. But he made out a reception area and there was another sign for Turner's vet surgery on the door. The backyard was oval and large and pretty bare apart from a wooden building at the far end. Stables, by the look of it, although it looked unused as such; there was no equestrian gear and the area out front was spotless, no straw or horse poo or churned mud in sight. The retaining wall lay before a ring of high trees that gave additional privacy.

'This is a nice set-up,' Bennet said. 'Vet work must pay well.'

'Well, I do it part-time now, just weekends. My time is mostly taken up with my civic duties.'

The councillor had basically just admitted he made less money than Bennet had assumed, but elaborated no further.

Turner was probably financing himself by milking various well-off widows and divorcees in this commune and others.

Turner stopped. He looked cold but trying to hide it. Maybe he'd sussed that Bennet had angled away from the house specifically to keep him uncomfortable.

'I understand you're here about some visitors we had to the village. So this isn't about what I believe Sally's mother spoke to you about?'

'What would that be?'

'Sally Jenkins, the ten-year-old girl who went missing. Terrible thing. So you're not investigating that?'

At least this guy had the decency to refer to her by name. And he was the first person not to shove an alibi for that long-ago night in Bennet's face. 'No, although there is a connection of sorts. A four-person film crew came to shoot a documentary about that crime–'

'Crime?' Turner cut in. 'There's no proof that a crime was committed. She could be out there somewhere.'

Bennet didn't know the case, but he knew the odds and he wouldn't have bet on them. Even Sally's mother – and parents were usually the ones who lived in unfounded hope – thought she was dead. But he said none of this to Turner.

The vet approached the entrance to the reception and held the door open. An invite. Bennet entered what was indeed a reception, with a waiting room. The expected set-up: reception desk, chairs, table of pamphlets and magazines, posters all over the walls, including a framed photograph of Mount Rushmore National Memorial. A door in the wall that the surgery shared with the house was marked STAFF ONLY. Another said SURGERY and a third RESTROOM.

Turner leaned back against the reception desk, which had items for sale and a small hot drinks vending machine. A common interview tactic was to remain at eye level and close, but he figured Turner would open up his personality more if he didn't feel so scrutinised. So Bennet took a sofa ten feet away.

'So, the film crew? Don't ask me for their names, because I don't know,' Turner said.

'I know one of them. A helper they had, for local knowledge. She used to live here some years ago. Lorraine Cross, although she was a Taylor back then.'

'I recall. She was your girlfriend.'

Bennet nodded. He'd hoped to keep that piece of information in the dark.

'And now you want her back?'

'No, that's not why I'm here. I need information from the film crew, on another matter. Apparently they stayed one day and then left.'

'Yes. They were here Sunday. You spoke to someone at the café, so I gather you know they went in the Red Lion pub that night and caused trouble.'

'I heard. What trouble?'

'I don't know. Sunday is usually my night for a little drink at the Lion, but I was helping my son with his car and didn't go. But I heard they were quite arrogant. That's beside the point, though. I can't imagine Ms Jenkins had much to offer about these people, since she hardly goes out. But she would have had plenty to say about her daughter, I suspect.'

Word had travelled fast.

'She mentioned Sally liked to ride your horses. You taught her.'

'Well, an acquaintance of mine did. A woman. And my son, he loved to help her too. I had two horses. A gift from a customer. I had land, so went for it. Yes, Sally used to ride Reeve, a three-year-old filly, but her mission was to brave B'fly, a mature Clydesdale.'

Turner headed behind the reception desk and grabbed a

glass and a bottle of Hennessy VS 44. He raised the bottle in Bennet's direction, but received a shake of the head.

'However, B'fly was a hundred and eighty centimetres. He dwarfed Sally. Far too big for her at her age, but he was her mission. No astronaut or hairdresser dreams for that girl. Her destiny was to ride B'fly one lap around the field before she hit sixteen. I'll always remember how she used to stand right next to him, arms folded, looking up at him, as if contemplating the challenge. Like a mountaineer staring at Everest and thinking, you will not defeat me.' Turner gave a smile at the memory, then quickly lost it. 'It's a shame she'll never realise that dream.'

Curious. 'Never? But you think she's got a new life out there.'

'Don't be so quick with judgements, detective. Reeve and B'fly died about two years ago, just months apart. That's all I meant. I turned the stables into a workspace for my computer.'

Turner came out from behind the reception and sat on the same sofa as Bennet. Eye level, three feet apart. 'So, Mr Bennet, Anika had nothing helpful for you?'

'She seemed unhappy about the lack of progression in the case. Amongst other things.'

The councillor missed or ignored the accusation in Bennet's final sentence. 'No, unfortunately there wasn't much progression. I didn't feel the police did a very good job. My people were trying their best though. We tried to give them all the help we could, but the police didn't seem to care. They did a shoddy job. No offence.'

He smiled. Bennet smiled back. 'None taken. Different police service. I'm not part of Derbyshire. So why a shoddy job? Because they didn't buy your theory that she ran away?'

'I didn't say she ran away, detective.'

Bennet sipped his tea. 'You kind of did, councillor. You said there was no proof a crime had been committed. If she'd been taken away, even by a trusted uncle, or if she'd willingly gone off with a friend, she was not of legal age to make that choice and there was no permission from her mother, the legal guardian. That's a crime.'

'But I didn't say it was a fact. Just a possibility. Just like her being out there somewhere. I know the police believed she was dead, although they didn't dare say as much. Can you tell me Sally being alive and well this very day is not a possibility?'

'A ten-year-old just one day gave up her parents, friends, everything? Never changed her mind come adulthood? Didn't once get recognised from media appeals that would have gone out? Survived without a job or a home?'

Turner had finished his cognac and poured another. He again waved the bottle at Bennet, who again passed. But he noticed the bottle's label said it was a limited edition released in honour of Barack Obama. The bottle, and the Mount Rushmore photo, said something about this man. Did he think of himself as presidential, of his standing in Lampton as akin to that of the men honoured by the cognac and the national monument? More like a despot.

'So, Mr Bennet, you can promise me such a thing is impossible? *Impossible?*'

Bennet could have argued all day, but knew it would all be a waste. Ironically, the very circumstances he was denouncing – a street child able to fend for themself – had applied in his last big case less than a month ago. 'Do you seriously think Sally Jenkins just left her life and she's still out there? This is why the police did a shoddy job? Because they were open to other scenarios?'

Turner gave a sly grin. 'No, Bennet. I don't know that for sure. And that's entirely my point. Yes, some of my people theorised that Sally had run away, and the police steadfastly refused to believe it. But they also refused to believe that a stranger must have taken that little girl.'

'Ah, so the police did a shoddy job because they considered

the possibility that a local had snatched her? The police explore all avenues, Mr Turner.'

'Everybody knows everybody here and she would have been spotted if she'd been with one of our own. Or someone would have gossiped. I asked my people, and they said they knew nothing.'

'Well, a child abductor is hardly going to admit it.'

Turner gave a wry smile, as if his guest had made a childish mistake. He continued without a response to Bennet's claim. 'But, just like with the runaway angle, the police ignored this advice. I can assure you, as someone right here at the time, that the police refused to use extra resources to search in other towns and cities, instead focusing on my people. And even Sally's father, at one point. And when they hit a dead end, they lost interest.'

'Lost interest. I can assure you that the police don't just–'

'Her disappearance didn't get the nationwide exposure that some of the famous cases do, and doesn't even today,' Turner cut in, angry. 'The police make a half-hearted show of still trying to solve it by sending a low-level detective to ask useless questions once a year or so, but irreparable damage was already done. Time was wasted, evidence lost. Sally has been missing ten years in March. You're defensive and blind because you're a police officer.'

Defensive, yes. Blind, no: he knew police investigations were often flawed. But Turner was missing a point and Bennet saw a route back to the reason he was here.

'Let's say you're right, Mr Turner. Bad police, missed opportunities, and now it's been ten years. People change, loving relationships end, and opinions get altered. There could be information out there now, or someone who's ready to speak, and new exposure on the case could help bring it out. A TV documentary about the case would bring it back into the limelight. The film crew should have been accepted here like royalty, but I get the impression they weren't welcome here.'

'These reporters and film crews who periodically turn up, do you really think they have justice as their primary motivation? It's money, detective. They turn up here, asking questions that tear open old wounds, and it's all to sell a product to a public that craves blood-soaked gossip, creates celebrities out of criminals, and wants to experience outrage that can be shut off by the flick of a TV power button. None of my people are willing to cater to those who sell the trauma of others, especially not a group of amateur film-makers who don't have the clout or the skills of the police. Ignoring these people was the correct thing to do.'

That reminded Bennet of Sally's mother's words along the same line. He'd been here too long and wanted to wrap this conversation up, go home, and forget this place... but a bug had him and he couldn't shake it. 'Sally is the Scottish King, isn't she?'

'What on earth are you talking about?'

'Shakespeare's *Macbeth*. Your people are like actors who refuse to speak the name *Macbeth* outside of the script, out of fear of getting cursed, and instead use the title the Scottish King. In Lampton, Sally is known as the *missing girl*, and speaking of her will bring disaster. If someone slips up, do you send them out into the fields to perform a cleansing ritual?'

Turner laughed, but there was loathing in his eyes. Then he got serious. 'If you hit a brick wall with your questioning about this subject, it's because people think poor Sally's mother should be left alone and not hounded. Sally's father ran away because he couldn't take the heat, leaving Anika all alone. It's because we care more for her well-being than the curiosity of morbid tourists and the bank balances of slimeball journalists.'

Bennet leaned forward, his face just inches from Turner's.

'Sally's mother wants to shout about her daughter from the rooftops. She wants to celebrate Sally's birthday, and plant a tree, and probably talk about her in shops, and she wants people to reminisce about her daughter. It would help her accept her loss. But she couldn't do those things, could she?'

Uncomfortable with Bennet's proximity, Turner shifted further down the sofa and folded his arms. 'Each and every armchair detective who comes here thinks they can solve the case and the word *murderer* is always bandied around. There is no murderer, Mr Bennet, I can promise you that. Yet every time that word is mentioned on TV or in a paper or in a shop by someone in this village, it fortifies the horrible notion that Sally will never return. And Sally's mother shouldn't be allowed to think her daughter is dead. She should believe there's every chance of Sally's return alive and well, and not upset herself by talking about death and planting silly trees to commemorate Sally's life. *That* is why my people will not talk about poor Sally, for it turns her into water-cooler gossip, as if she is nothing more than a soap opera twist.'

There was all sorts in that statement Bennet could have leaped upon. He chose: 'Shouldn't be allowed? She believes her daughter's dead, and I happen to agree. But everyone here seems to be trying to sell her a dream that's not feasible. I think the only way Sally's mother can properly move on is to accept that her daughter's gone and grieve the way she wants, even if it involves a tree, or a headstone, or talking about her in front of people. But she's been told not to, hasn't she?'

Turner looked puzzled. 'Told not to?'

'I think the Keys gave an order to the whole village: don't go around talking about the missing kid, because we don't like to be reminded of that. And people have become plugged into a hive mind that now sees Sally not as a vulnerable little girl, but as a dark cloud over this village.'

Now the councillor's puzzlement was replaced by anger again. 'An order to not grieve? Not accept her loss? We gave only advice, you fool. I care for that woman and I did everything I could for her, to help her get past this. Just ask the woman, for God's sake.'

'Oh, she sang your praises, Mr Turner. You were very nice to her after the tragedy. A good friend. You bought her a dress. But this is where my understanding falls short. You gave her some age-progression photos, for instance. Paid for out of your own pocket.'

'Convincing her that dwelling on her daughter is bad is one thing. I could hardly tell her to forget Sally altogether, could I? It was a nice touch I felt she deserved.'

'This is the first time I've known of age-progression photos being given in advance. When Sally would have been forty, giving the mother a picture of her daughter aged forty is fine. The way you did it says Anika will need it because she'll never see her again. Yet, in contradiction, the village doesn't accept that Sally is dead.'

'Sally is twenty now, and what if she doesn't return until she's sixty? And what if there are no photos of her in the interim? Anika will want to know how her daughter looked growing up, and I provided that.'

Bennet could hardly believe what he'd just heard. Either Turner was clueless and running himself in circles trying to get a handle on it, or he was too proud to admit and correct his mistakes. Or maybe there was something out of whack in his head.

Turner drained his glass and stood up. 'All I ever thought about was Anika. What I did helped her to avoid drowning in grief. Now, I've given you enough time, Detective Bennet. Your film crew came, got ignored, and left, and your business here is done. I'll bid you a safe trip home.'

Bennet went for the door. His time with Richard Turner; bachelor, vet, councillor, had left him as drained as the toughest interrogation-room conversation with a deranged killer. But he had to have the last word.

'You remind me of Kim Jong-il.' Before Turner could take offence, Bennet grinned and added, 'Big Hennessy fan.'

19

I t was a long shot, but he'd kick himself if he didn't scour the internet for Donald Ducke and later discovered it was actually the director's real name. So he did that.

He found numerous people on social media and whittled them down by photo – the guy was black and about fifty – and location – he lived in England – until he had a list of possibles. But there he got stuck. The possibles were only such not because of relevant details, but a lack of them. Some on Facebook had no profile picture, or no personal information, no posts, no hobbies list. Learning anything further would involve contact via message and he didn't have the energy or will to embark upon what would probably be a lengthy, dead-end endeavour. Who was to say all these Donald Duckes weren't also fake funny-name profiles? Why would anyone respond to his query anyway?

So he gave it up. All of it. He'd been desperate to find Lorraine, fast, but why? To give Joe a nice surprise after school? The kid had waited years and he probably didn't feel the rush his dad felt. It was unlikely Bennet wouldn't get hold of Lorraine within the next week or so, and Joe would be fine with that. So Bennet would be, too. It was time to end the chase.

Once on Lampton's main road, heading towards freedom, his eye caught a street on the left. He turned into the corner, figuring he could spare five minutes for old times' sake. Out of habit, he put the gearbox in neutral as he drove over the crest and down a road that fell away like a ski jump.

He'd played this game hundreds of times. Roll down the hill without power and see how far up the other side he could get. He'd never made it as far as the grit bin. He grinned as the truck gained speed, yet ran almost silently. So determined was he to succeed this time, he didn't even touch the brakes as a car started to reverse out of a driveway. He hit his horn and the car jerked to a stop, and a woman mouthed unsweet things as he blew past just inches from her bumper.

At the bottom of the hill, Liam bent forward and lifted his feet, as if somehow that would aid aerodynamics, and as the Pathfinder started to climb up the far side and began to slow, he coaxed it with soothing words.

The Pathfinder gave a good showing, but lost the battle ten metres short of the grit bin on the pavement. Not even close to his best. As the truck started to roll back, he put it in gear and drove the last twenty metres to his destination.

The houses on this street were all two-storey semis barely a few decades old, but many had ivy climbing the walls and trellises lashed to the red brickwork and ornate porches, as if to present the illusion of age. The house he sought had not subscribed to such trickery; it was plain, without bells and whistles, and the garden was easily the untidiest around. Unlike most, it also had no curtains or blinds, so Liam could stare right into the living room.

How it had changed since Lorraine lived there. He could remember all the little signs of her around the place. The slippers she always liked to leave by the front door, and the lampshade she'd made herself out of pigskin, Ed Gein-like. The hair bobbles she always left hooked over interior door handles. She had insisted on a nautical theme, with unfinished wood windowsills, seashells everywhere, and blue wallpaper contrasting with a sand-coloured rug.

'Good day to you all. I thought I'd let you know...'

Bennet wound down his window, at first sure he was hearing things. He wasn't. His eyes found a nearby telegraph pole, and the siren clamped to it.

'...so, this infection they're calling 2019-nCoV has now reached the USA, making it five countries with confirmed diagnosis and over five hundred affected...'

It was Turner's voice oozing out of the siren. Across the road, a front window opened and a woman looked over, also listening. The councillor had installed or commandeered a public address system to speak to his people. Bennet was surprised for all of half a second.

'...there's talk about this new infection becoming very large and very deadly, but I don't think we need to worry. Also in America, it's National Hug Day, so let's adopt it. If you're out and about and get a chance...'

When the announcement was over, Bennet felt his already low mood sink a little further. He'd had good times here, but they were gone forever. He wondered why he'd even detoured here. It was no longer Lorraine's house, and he wasn't the same person he'd been back when he used to visit. His home was miles away and it was time to head back there.

20

———

Bennet's phone rang as he was approaching the Panorama. Unknown number, so probably not Lorraine. Still, he cut a sharp turn into the Panorama's car park and answered with urgency. But it was a male voice.

'Former Detective Sergeant Ford,' it said.

It was the former detective Hooper had mentioned, once part of the investigation into the disappearance of Sally Jenkins.

'I hear some people are making a documentary. For the ten-year anniversary of a missing girl, Sally Jenkins. Up in the Peak District. As you probably know, I was part of the investigating team, and I'd like to help.'

For about half a second, Bennet didn't care to speak to the guy. But then he realised he'd spoken to the mother of the missing girl and a man who'd put himself centre of the investigation, and he barely knew a thing about the events of March 6, 2010. He was intrigued and to learn everything all he had to do was hold an electronic device against his ear for a few minutes.

'Thanks for your call, Mr Ford. Anything you can tell me would be great.'

'Happy to. Do you know if they pay? And will I be interviewed for the film?'

Bennet sensed the guy might open up more if he thought he'd get some glamour and cash. 'Could be. I'll pass your information and number on to them, then we'll see. But I need to know what you know. Start with an overview of the case. Everything you remember.'

'Sally Jenkins, ten years old...'

21

Sally Jenkins had been at a birthday party at a place called the Winding Wheel, in Chesterfield, about twelve miles away. The party was due to end at six thirty, but Sally wanted to leave at half five. She'd gone with a friend and that girl's mother, Kate, and they dropped her off. But not quite at home. Sally had exited the car at the end of Arton Place because her friend lived closer to the centre of the village; it was a short walk down the cul-de-sac, across the green, where children often played, and onto Grodes Place. It was a journey Sally had made myriad times without problem.

'Nobody saw Sally on Arton Place or crossing the green, but she never arrived home,' former detective Ford said. 'She was dropped off at 6.05, and a dog walker on the land saw nothing and no one at around 6.45. So we believe she was abducted or ran away in that forty-minute period. Our information is that no other children were at the park.

'Sally's mother, Anika, hadn't known that her daughter had left the party early, because Sally had said she wanted to surprise her, and so the friend's mother, Kate, hadn't informed her. When Sally hadn't shown up by about half seven, Anika called the police. Their response was rapid and within half an hour officers had invaded Lampton's streets, rapping doors and searching. By midnight, all manner of nooks and crannies had been examined and all Sally's friends and neighbours spoken to. As darkness rolled around the next evening, it was determined Sally wasn't in the village and the search boundaries moved outwards to include every home, farm and other building within a two-mile ring around Lampton. Roadblocks were installed to stop and question drivers. Nothing. The search widened.'

'What about the friend who dropped her off?' Bennet asked, transferring his phone to the other ear. 'Why didn't the mother or father take her?'

'I was getting to that. The party was hosted by someone Sally's friend's mother, Kate Harper, knew. Sally's parents didn't have an invite. But she offered to take Sally along.'

'CCTV of any of the journey?'

'Yes, I was getting to that too. CCTV outside the Tesco captured Kate Harper's car entering Lampton from the north, and it was slowing down, suggesting it did indeed stop at the end of Arton Place. Kate's car was on a neighbour's camera arriving home eight minutes later, just her and her daughter inside. No Sally. Unfortunately, there was only one resident on Arton Place with a camera, but it covered their garden and didn't show the street.

'Nothing led us to think Kate Harper had anything to do with Sally's disappearance; we accepted that she did, as claimed, drop Sally off at the end of Arton Place. We spoke to everyone present at the Winding Wheel party, but again we got nothing. The days and weeks rolled by.'

'Mr Ford, I know you want to tell this story, but for the sake of the documentary, I'd like to hear it by asking questions. Can we do that?'

'Sure, yeah, go ahead. As long as I get to say my version for the interview.'

'I just want to confirm that your team investigated the chance that Sally ran away? And did you suspect a local or a stranger? If she was taken from the green, that seems like a user-friendly zone that outsiders wouldn't know about.'

'Exactly. As soon as we got the call, our thoughts were on transients, Lampton being a tourist spot and all. We considered that the abductor could be passing through, or had left. We sought information on visitors who might have cut short a holiday, and anyone who seemed suspicious in the days before or after she went missing. But one look at that green area told us we probably had a local perpetrator, and that was our main focus.'

'I get the impression that the people of Lampton wouldn't take too kindly to being suspected. Any problem there?'

'Hell yes. Sorry, I won't swear on the video. Anyway, we got that same feeling, so at first we tried to keep the theory of a local perpetrator quiet and work on it on the sly. We sent undercover officers into the pubs and shops, just to gather gossip.'

'Let me guess. Nobody really talked about it.'

'That's right. Christ, you'd have thought a dog had gone missing instead. Sorry, I didn't mean to swear again. Anyway, when this tactic failed to get us anything worthwhile, we got a bit bolder. We sent out questionnaires to the womenfolk, hoping they'd feel guilty if they knew anything. We started visiting men of possible interest at home. Again, nobody stood out. Then, we upped the boldness. We announced our intention to hold a mass DNA screening of all males in Lampton at the village hall. We let out a rumour that there was DNA found at the playpark. It was a lie though. I mean, we weren't even sure that was a crime scene because we found nothing there to indicate a snatch. So it was a ploy to see if it prompted anyone to suddenly leave the area, or to try to avoid the DNA test.'

'Any takers? Or non-takers, I mean?'

'It failed. We commandeered the village hall to do it, but the people called their own meeting at the same time. Outside, one of the local big shots–'

'One Councillor Richard Turner, by any chance?'

'That's him. He rallied his people, condemning us for daring to accuse one of their own. He said his people would know if someone amongst them did this, and he would know if his people knew.'

'Hive mind,' Bennet said.

'Exactly. So, in front of a bunch of police and reporters, he proved his people had had nothing to do with Sally's disappearance. Ready for this? He asked his mass of people if any of them had taken her. And they all shouted *no*. And that was that. He gave us a smug look, as if to say, *there you go*. You believe that?'

Bennet did. Now it made sense why Turner had earlier mocked Bennet's claim that a child abductor would not admit to being so. Did this guy think his people worshipped him? He was just a councillor living in a tiny village.

Ford continued: 'So now the people insisted the police should focus on the perpetrator being a transient, some tourist passing through. They have a word for visitors...'

'Loper.'

'That's it. They were dead certain that if Sally hadn't run away, she'd been taken by a Loper. Needless to say, many of the local men refused to give their DNA because of this. Nothing we could do without a serious hue and cry, and it was a trick because we had no DNA, prints, anything. So our killer, if there is one and he was one of the Lampton locals, got a lucky break.'

'So Turner and his people were a hindrance? He told me the

police did a shoddy job. Sounds like they were shoddy only because they didn't follow his directions.'

'He was an obstacle for sure, but he didn't see it that way. When we were quite insistent that we needed to search the village, he organised searches. He got people to check their barns, sheds, to look in all the nooks and crannies. It took about an hour, tops, and then he came to my boss to declare it done. As in, look, we catered to your whims, and now we've proved it wasn't one of us, and now can you please stop thinking she's still here.'

'Richard Turner to a T. Did his people really just accept what he said? Nobody thought it could be one of them?'

'No, some people were worried. Kids were kept indoors. We would see that at night if we were about. Kids used to play in the evening all the time. Not after Sally went missing. But could you get a parent to admit they were keeping their kids close because there might be a wacko in the village? Good luck with that. His people knew not to spread gossip. But, you know, time favoured Turner. How often do we see weirdos like this snatch one kid and never do it again?'

A fair point. The kind of man who'd abduct a child, and possibly kill them, didn't satiate those urges forever with a single affair. 'I understand his people worshipping his every word. But not the police. You didn't listen to him, I assume.'

'Of course not. We couldn't just take the townsfolk at their word that they'd performed a thorough search. I mean, if Sally's abductor was in the village, he was hardly going to bring her out and say, hey, look what I found in my shed. But saying such a thing wouldn't keep the people sweet, so we went with trying to convince them that our searchers would do a better job. This meant we didn't just jump at their insistence we go search other towns and villages, and you want to know their response to that?'

'Mass protest in the streets?'

'Not far off. Turner complained to the media. They already had the story and they had people in the village, and he spoke to them. He accused the police of laziness and not accepting help from the locals.'

'Because you wouldn't effectively let him dictate how you did your job?'

'Yes. And you know how it is with the media, detective. They give you heart-shaped eyes that turn to daggers.'

Different police teams had other terms to describe this, but Bennet knew what the former detective was saying. At the start of a serious investigation, the police were given space and time to work the clues, gather the evidence, and arrest a suspect. In that honeymoon period, they got left alone to work. But a couple of days or a week or so in, the tone would change. The public and the media would get impatient and demand answers, and the police would come under fire, accused of failure. A man with Turner's clout could stoke this fire into an inferno with ease.

'I know what you mean, Mr Ford. Turner's a man who craves complete control and if you don't heed his counsel, you're wrong. Did it ever seem as if he was trying to deflect attention away from himself? Did you look into him as a suspect?'

'Of course. We were interested in him briefly because Sally used to spend time on his land, riding horses. But he had a cast-iron alibi. He was at a function some miles away until close to ten o'clock. Thirty people there. They were all cleared. We tracked his phone. It went from the function to his home and stayed there all night. He was very consoling and helpful to the mother. I think he paid for the funeral. But he also had an affair with her within weeks of the disappearance. Apparently he bought her a dress for press conferences, but she wore it out to dinner with him about ten days after, so who knows his real reason.'

'The dress, yes, but I didn't know about the affair. And you looked into the family? I know the parents drifted apart soon after.'

'I was about to say that. Yes, yes, we checked out all the family too. Always the first port of call. Only a mother and father anywhere close. They alibied each other because they were at home, but Turner was on their side and wouldn't let a bad word be said. The husband soon left her though. And the thing with the husband wasn't about drifting apart. A couple of years before, he'd been investigated by the Child Protection Service – a neighbour claimed to have witnessed him physically abusing Sally one day.'

'That's interesting.'

'It was. But the CPS investigation found nothing. However, we still had to question him, and we had dogs search their house for human remains. Again, nothing, but shit sticks. Some believed him to be dodgy – why didn't he pick his own daughter up from the club? The old abuse charge and our early interest in him and all the gossiping became too much. So he left the area. But that just raised more eyebrows, although it soon became the local opinion that he wasn't a likely suspect in the abduction. The police never had him as a person of interest, but he was never wholeheartedly ruled out, either. Apparently he's doing okay now, new family, new job, new life. Tabs were kept on him for a couple of years after, but nothing in his behaviour since he went to Germany raised any flags.'

'You keep using the word "abduction". Was this not upgraded to a murder enquiry?'

'We upgraded the scope of the investigation within a couple of days of Sally's disappearance, and treated it much like a homicide enquiry. Less emphasis on where she might have gone, more on who might have snatched and killed her. But we were basically told by higher-ups not to make it official. So it stayed a missing person's enquiry. Months later we were still getting reports of sightings of her all over the country, and we had to follow them up even though we doubted they were credible. Anytime anyone talked about murder, there was a complaint, so today Sally Jenkins is still a missing person.'

'Turner again?'

'Everyone. But he runs things behind the scenes. You and I and know Sally is likely dead, but saying it out loud would get a lashing. So I wouldn't go around talking about murder. That film crew should be careful, too, or everyone will clam up.'

'I've learned that. And I think the film crew knew they'd get the cold shoulder. It looks like they came in on the quiet to do their shooting, possibly under the guise of simple tourists, and didn't try to ask too many questions. Not sure they even spoke to people about that missing girl.'

'From the very outset, the village didn't welcome the publicity. The police and journalists were all over the village, but all for the wrong reasons. Journalists took all the hotels for the first few days, but even the extra money coming into the village annoyed the locals. Their cars were parked all over the place. But even after a few days, when we didn't find a body or arrest anyone and the story lost momentum and the reporters left, the village went through a change. The dark cloud over the village forced people out. Local businessmen with the ability to up and move did so. Some business enterprises cancelled. People sold homes and shops and left. Nobody wanted to be associated with the new infamy of the village. Tourists would come, but only to ask about what happened to Sally. Like the journalists, they all got told to sling their hooks. Basically, the village still has the wool pulled over its eyes about the whole Sally thing. I think they'd rather forget she ever existed.'

Bennet wrapped up the call when his phone beeped with another incoming. The screen said it was from a DC called Banks. One of his low-level workers, good at talking her way into homes to get information. It must be about the Pond Street case, although it puzzled him as to why a DC had gone straight to him, not to one of his sergeants or DI Todd.

When he answered, Banks was apologetic. 'I'm sorry, sir, I messed up. I've got Joe with me.'

It turned out that DI Todd had had an important call while en route to collect Joe from school, and had passed the task on to DC Banks. Banks got told Bennet was in Lampton. Banks then told Joe. Unfortunately, Joe had already looked his mother up on Facebook, now that he had her real name, and knew about Lampton. And now the kid thought his dad was bringing his mother back. Bennet was nervous when Joe came on the phone.

'Did you find Mum yet?'

He sounded elated, which made the bad news harder to impart. 'Not yet, Joe. I think I just missed her. Look, I don't think I can find her today. I won't be coming home with her tonight. Are you okay with that?'

'Where did she go? Back to Birmingham? Are you going there next?'

'Not tonight, Joe. She might not be there. She's got a job to do and she might be moving around. It might be for a few days. You won't see her today.'

Silence. Bennet could almost sense Joe's heart breaking. 'Patricia wants to take me to the cinema tonight and she'll make me dinner.'

Joe had changed the subject. Good. 'That's nice. You should do that. It'll be fun.'

'So you don't need to come home yet. You can carry on searching and go to Birmingham and other places. You can take all night. I can stay with Patricia again. Will you do that? Will you carry on looking? I won't stay up for you. I can wait till tomorrow. Please?'

'Okay.'

Joe whooped with glee. Had Bennet just made a bad choice? His promise to continue the search for Joe's mother might cause more pain in the long run, but he'd rather let his boy down face to face, where he had more control.

Joe talked about his school trip for a few moments and then told his dad he loved him and would see him later. After the call, Bennet sat in silence, looking out the window at the Panorama. He quickly got over his rising despair by focusing on his extended lease. He still had time to find Joe's mother and convince her to see her son.

Then he googled the Winding Wheel in Chesterfield, where missing Sally Jenkins had attended a birthday party, and called it. It had probably been the crew's next destination, and he hoped someone there would have information. The last thing he wanted was to stay in this place a second longer.

The conversation made his head throb a little more. The manager of the Winding Wheel confirmed he'd arranged to meet the film crew, but he'd been given no details. He didn't have names or contact emails or phone numbers. And the number he'd been called by had been withheld. But he confirmed an appointment at 10am that very Tuesday morning. However, no one had turned up or called to cancel.

Bennet thanked him and hung up. The Winding Wheel was about twelve miles away, a distance the crew could have covered quickly. Even if they hadn't been forced out of this damn village on Sunday, the director hadn't booked a second night at the Panorama. So where, between Lampton and Chesterfield, had the crew planned to bed down on Monday night?

23

No one was in the Panorama's lobby. Bennet rang the bell at reception and waited. His high patience level had taken a holiday. Waiting all night for a suspect to return to a dingy flat, no problem, but why wasn't Gemma answering her damn bell?

On the counter were a pair of newspapers, the *Peak Advertiser* and *Buxton Advertiser*. He idly flicked through one and, in the unimportant middle, found a Lampton story: the death of a 101-year-old man. It said he was a former quarry worker who'd survived an infamous accident at the Mill Close Lead Mine in Darley Dale in the 30s, when a slime tip collapsed and killed people. Died in his bed, surrounded by family. To some, the best way to go. At the end of the article was a note saying the story was covered in greater detail in the blog of a lady called Sandra Gingham. It was a name he recognised for some reason. A shop owner, maybe. Certainly someone with clout in the village.

He rang the bell again, this time almost slapping it flat. To pacify his impatience, he pulled out his mobile and googled the blog.

It was mostly drab personal stuff, given the list of contents, but he found PDF copies of every Lampton monthly newsletter going back seven years, one a month, every Saturday. Way back, he'd seen the newsletters pinned up in shops but hadn't really cared for what basically amounted to gossip. Now, he accessed random publications.

Each one's format was news followed by games such as a wordsearch and quiz, and finishing with minutes from a village meeting. The newsletters were not a captivating read. A councillor and deputy chairman of the Peak District Local Access Forum had gotten in hot water for not declaring hospitality from a contractor. A buried treasure competition at a fete had become a mockery when the organisers couldn't remember where they put the prize. Wider news seemed to be all about road closures, job losses, and the effect climate change would have on visitor habits. The big talking point at the latest meeting, this last Saturday, was that an old mobile paraffin van, eons ago used to sell paraffin for villagers' lamps door to door, had been sold at auction in London. Wow.

At the bottom of the minutes from each meeting was a hyperlink to an audio recording called KEY ADDENDUM, but clicking this brought up a login screen. Based on this secrecy, the Key Addendum files were probably notes from an additional summit, Keys only, not for mortal eyes. Sandra was probably one of the Keys. He disliked her already.

Where the hell was Gemma? Through a pair of batwing doors he could see another room with the back door open to expose the rear garden. He pushed through the doors, into a small sun room with three sofas, a TV, and large windows boasting a fine view of the countryside. There was a wall leaflet holder, from which he took a single copy of everything.

Upon reaching the back door, he saw Gemma in the garden,

soaking plants with a water pistol. There was a single iron gate at the bottom of the garden with a track running away from it through a field. He allowed a moment to chill before calling her name.

Gemma whirled her wheelchair around at Liam's voice and gave a big grin. She came his way, rumbling over the threshold ramp and into the sun room.

'Good to have you back at the Panorama. Couldn't wait to see me again, eh?'

'Of course.' He shook the mass of leaflets at her. 'And a bunch of your freebies, if you don't mind.'

'Go right ahead. Tea?'

'That would be nice.'

Once alone, Bennet grabbed a sofa and ran through the leaflets, ignoring local attractions and seeking hotels. He called the first he found, the Brockhampton Heights. It was answered by a woman who laughed, said something to someone nearby, and then introduced her establishment. How professional.

Liam said, 'Hi. I'm looking for my friends. They're on a trip, but there's a personal problem. They're film-makers and there's four of them. I need to speak to them, so can you confirm they're there? I don't want you to alarm them by telling them I've called. I'll come down when I find the right hotel. My friend sometimes uses the fake name Donald Ducke at hotels.'

It was a long shot in more ways than one. Years ago he'd had a case in which a man had called a hotel and asked if his sister and her boyfriend were there. Yes they were, and down he went. The sister turned out to be the caller's wife, the boyfriend exactly that, and Bennet's team found the illicit lovers sliced up in their hotel room. That hotel had gotten the message that giving out details to strange voices on the phone was a big no-no. Would this one be as cautious?

He killed the call ten seconds later, just as Gemma returned to the sun room. She put his tea on the table.

'No luck?'

'The Brockhampton Heights guarantees anonymity.'

Gemma nodded in recognition. 'That's Julie's place. I could have told you you'd get no success there. Here, let me help.'

She slotted her wheelchair next to his seat and got her own phone out. Fifteen minutes later, they'd called all the hotels, motels, guesthouses and bed and breakfasts within about ten miles, and gotten a mix of answers. Some careful owners, bless them, had refused to answer questions. Some had outright said they had no film-makers as guests. One landlady did have a director staying with her, but he was sixty and worked for the BBC. Others had claimed they had no idea of their guests' employment. In the end, the list hadn't been whittled down at all. Only seven had outright said no, even those couldn't be discarded. The film crew could have checked in separately or as a group of partying stockbrokers.

'Let me ask you something,' Gemma said. 'Why didn't you tell any of them you're a detective? I know it's not police business, but...'

Oh, how he'd wondered the same thing. On official police business, or pretending to be, he wouldn't have hit any of today's brick walls. Hotel owners would have been happy to help. Hell, he had a bunch of detective constables under his command and wouldn't have had to make a single phone call. And none of the Lampton lot would have been so antagonistic.

'It's not police business and it wouldn't be right to make people think it is.'

'That's very honourable, Liam. You're a good man so–' Gemma yelped as a fox appeared near the back door. Seeing the humans, it turned and fled. Gemma wheeled to the door and shut it.

'Isn't a fox that comes out in the daytime rabid?'

Gemma laughed. 'I don't think so... what are you staring at?'

Bennet was staring past her, at the back door. At something on the handle. Without a word, he left the table and headed through the lobby, to seek similar on the front door. He didn't find it. And that was unnerving.

24

When Bennet returned to the sun room, Gemma saw something had changed in his face. She asked what was wrong.

'The front door doesn't have one of these,' he said, tapping the back door's handle keypad. 'You said you had to give the director the code to get out on Sunday night. Why didn't you say he left out the back, across the fields?'

'Didn't I? I'm sorry. There's a path into the fields. That's why I thought he was filming a nature documentary.'

'You didn't think it strange that he wanted to go out the back way late at night?'

'Not really. My backyard leads into the fields and people like the walking trails. I have signs promoting it, and the landowner, Mr Crabtree, doesn't mind as long as they stick to the track and pass through his land without stopping. I'm sorry, did I upset you?'

'Well, this changes things. Now it looks like the director must have been meeting his people out in the fields. I'm sorry for snapping at you, but this was something I really could have done with knowing way before right now. Tell me the truth. You knew exactly what they were filming, didn't you?'

She said nothing.

'It's okay to talk to me, Gemma. I think that film crew came in here on the sly. They didn't waltz in with a fanfare because they knew exactly how they were going to be treated. They knew they were going to open old wounds. I think that's why all four didn't take rooms here. It's why they recruited a former resident instead of a current one. They wanted to try to film their scenes without alerting anyone. Because they knew it wouldn't go down well. But despite their caution, word got round. And word got as far as the Panorama, didn't it?'

Her eyes widened, as if her deepest secrets were about to unearth. He gave her a reassuring smile. 'Relax. It's fine. A dark time for the village, and nobody wants that brought up again. I believe the director didn't tell you why he was here, but you already knew, didn't you?'

Now she seemed to relax. Bennet had seen the same look on stubborn criminals at the very moment when overwhelming evidence left no choice but submission.

'I didn't know what he was doing at first, not until...' She wheeled to the batwing doors and had a look to make sure no one was around. Back she came. 'I got a phone call from a friend. She told me about them, said they were coming to Lampton. I think they'd emailed a former resident, wanting help, and he had passed the word on to someone here. I think they'd been spotted already.'

'Spotted by who? Doing what?'

'I heard that some people had said they'd seen people acting suspiciously. Two people, at least, had been seen talking together outside the village, but when they came in they pretended not to know each other. They just weren't acting like normal tourists. And one of them was on the green, where the police think Sally was taken from. Like they were doing secret filming. We were all warned to be on the lookout.'

'And then the director came here for a room? Carrying only, as you said, a satchel.'

'Well, by the time I heard all this, he'd already checked in. When he told me he was a director, I knew. We had been order— it was thought we shouldn't let them into our places, and then they'd leave. But it was too late for me by then. I'd already given him a room.'

She'd tried to cover herself, but the mistake had been made and Bennet hadn't missed it. And by her face, she knew it.

'Relax once more. You were about to say you were *ordered to*...'

She shook her head. 'I don't know what you mean.'

Bennet took a chair so they'd be at eye level. 'Gemma, relax and level with me. You won't get in trouble. The town meetings are once a month, every Saturday evening. But earlier you hinted that the last meeting the Keys had was on Sunday. An impromptu one, it would seem, and not listed on the latest newsletter. Like an urgent COBRA meeting when there's a nuclear attack, or the sort a council might have if a meteor destroys a city centre. Was this meeting the Lampton version of such a state of emergency? To decide to tell the film crew to leave?'

She couldn't face him. 'Yes. After word spread, a meeting was called. We get what you called impromptu meetings sometimes. My Proxy told me about the meeting. It was called in the afternoon. I didn't attend because not everyone is required to for the short notice ones.'

'Wait a minute. You didn't attend? So you could have? This wasn't a meeting for just the Keys? What they call a Key Addendum?'

'No, those come after. Usually after village meetings, the

Keys remain behind to have their own. No, this was a normal village meeting, where it was decided we should all band together and make sure we didn't allow the crew to feel welcome here.'

'There was a Key Addendum Sunday night. So that would have happened after the main meeting?'

'Yes. They normally rule on things the rest of us aren't supposed to hear. And we can't access those on the website because they're password protected. Sometimes, later, we can work out what they've decided based on changes in the village. But no, we don't get told the result of these meetings. I do recall, though, that the Keys left when we did. So their meeting must have been called quite a bit later, probably in the evening.'

Bennet thought. The Key Addendum might have been about discussing the events in the Lion, or an overview of how their give-the-silent-treatment programme had worked. Or something else. Curious. 'Okay, let me jump back a bit again. You said *Proxies*? I've heard that term, but remind me.'

'Well, they're important people. But they can't be Keys. They haven't been here long enough.'

'Okay. Like mafia men not of Italian descent, who can't become made men?' This point seemed to go over Gemma's head. 'And what do Proxies do?'

'They're responsible for sections of the village. A bit each. And each Key controls a number of Proxies to do their work and pass their messages on.'

'Okay. So you mean if a Key tells a Proxy he wants a giant pancake, that person goes out to their section of the village and tells everyone in that zone to bring all their flour and eggs? You're saying the Keys decided to ostracise the film crew and their Proxies rushed round and told everyone to give this Lopers crew the cold shoulder? And you kicked the director out of your hotel?'

'No, no, I wouldn't ever kick someone out in the middle of the night, unless they were violent and breaking things. And he was only staying that one night anyway. When the director came back to my hotel after the Lion, I confronted him. I told him he wouldn't get much out of anyone here and his best bet come Monday morning was to leave.'

'But he left that night.'

'I wasn't telling him anything he didn't already know. He told me he was sorry for hiding who he really was, but that he'd expected such cold treatment before he even came here. That was why his people were staying somewhere else, but he didn't say where. Or why he'd rented a hotel room. Then they'd met up and gone into the Lion, hoping to blend in and try to get to someone with a loose tongue. So I think he came to get his stuff because it was time for them all to leave. I think he was worried about further action from the people who threatened him in the Lion.'

'Blending in didn't work. And you honestly didn't meet the people he was with?'

'Honestly, I didn't. When he checked in, he didn't mention friends.'

'Did you suggest the back door so he wouldn't be seen?'

'No, no, he wanted to go that way. Maybe it was to avoid being seen, like you say, but he didn't seem that scared. In fact, I think he said something about a wall of silence being a good angle. I assume he meant for his documentary.'

Bennet wondered if he should hunt out more CCTV. He might witness a scene like something from *Frankenstein* or a Greek tragedy: the village folk marching the streets with torches and pitchforks, the Keys all robed and Richard Turner carried on a sedan chair. He wouldn't put it past these people.

'You've been here years, Gemma, and you run the only hotel. Why aren't you a Key?'

Gemma tapped her wheelchair. 'Not an all-commanding powerful look, is it?'

'Arseholes.'

She patted his arm. 'Do you want your girlfriend back, is that it?'

He gave a little laugh and shook his head. 'No, it's not that. It's complicated.'

'You didn't really fit in here, did you? Didn't want to be here? Did your relationship fall apart because you left?'

He shrugged. She got that he didn't want to talk about it. 'Wait here a moment.'

She wheeled off, subject forgotten. But not by him. He'd avoided every village meeting, never joined a local club or society, and, bar Gemma and the Argyles, had barely gotten to know anyone beyond the circle of Lorraine and her friends and family. Why? One foot out the door, dragged across the threshold by his career.

He'd met Lorraine at a Sunday market in Doncaster. At that point her parents had moved south from Lampton and she'd been renting it from them. Once she was pregnant with Joe they decided to move in together, but not here. He hadn't been willing to think about swapping his life to another city, but he'd expected Lorraine to do so. And she had. She had given up all her friends and the place she knew, to be with a man who lived his job even when not on the clock. How much had that contributed to their downfall, like Gemma had suggested? Bennet had always assumed they'd simply run their course. Sometimes he'd wondered if Lorraine had rapidly grown weary of being attached to a man who put more time into his job than into her. But one thing he'd never considered was that she'd resented his dragging her out of a comfortable life in Lampton that she'd reluctantly given up.

Something else Gemma had said worried him. He'd thought

he'd accepted the end of he and Lorraine, but had he? Had he really come to terms with it even now, a decade on? How much of this silly mission to find her was actually about Joe reacquainting with his mother? Was part of it a deep-down hope that they could be a family again? Even Turner had asked if he wanted Lorraine back.

No, that was stupid. He wouldn't have waited ten years to try to get her back. And she had another family now.

But why hadn't he ever found another partner?

He cut these silly thoughts as Gemma returned with a laptop, which she put in front of him at the table. She put her wheelchair right by him.

'If all four of the crew planned to have hotel rooms, it makes no sense for all of them to not stay here,' she said. 'Ground zero for their documentary. And if there were just four, it's doubtful they had a separate shooting unit somewhere. At some point between the Lion and my hotel, they split up. If the director went out the back of my hotel, it means his friends weren't waiting outside in a vehicle.'

He nodded. Very good. Maybe Gemma wanted to be a detective for real, not just writing about them in fiction. He watched as she loaded Google Maps and an aerial view of Lampton and a portion of the countryside.

'If they accompanied him to the hotel to check out, it would be hard for them to access the back field. It would mean going down a side street and through someone's backyard, and over a fence. So it makes more sense that they split up at the Lion. But if so, it means his friends walk a mile through the dark fields, to then stand around waiting for him out the back of my hotel? That doesn't make sense.'

She seemed pleased with her logic. He couldn't fault it.

'So they must have planned to meet at a specific place,' she continued. 'Perhaps where the other three were staying the night. Somewhere close, given they were on foot and it was cold and dark.'

Gemma shrank the map to a zone about the size of a half hour's walk. Various pins and icons showed places of intrigue and user photographs, as well as hotels. When calling hotels, Bennet and Gemma had worked outwards from Lampton, and he was certain they'd called all the displayed places, without joy. But just before he could remind her of this, she said, 'I've known farm owners to rent out their places to tourists. They're not officially hotels, but they'll be advertised on local noticeboards and shop windows, and sometimes on social media. Which means they might not be listed in those pamphlets you looked through, or on this map.'

Bennet looked closely. The map showed him plenty of shacks and barns and farm buildings. But without knowing phone numbers, he didn't have the time to visit each of these places, especially when there was no guarantee the crew hadn't already checked into a hotel in Chesterfield, or even finished their documentary and headed home.

She ran a finger in a circle around a portion of the map to the east and north of the village. 'All these nearest buildings here are on Ronald Crabtree's farmland. He's also got a residential ranch he built some years ago that people can rent. It was for his wife, but she died a few years back. I'm not sure where that is, but it's a mile or two from his home.'

The Crabtree Bennet had seen in the village centre had looked a wreck, and now he knew why. He looked closely at the map. As well as the main L-shaped farmhouse and various shacks and sheds and large storage bins, there was a wooden barn, an open-sided, steel-framed building, a trio of rocket-shaped grain silos, and a corrugated metal building that looked like a half-sunken barrel on its side. He zoomed out, hoping to see this ranch she'd mentioned, but within a two-mile radius there were too many to scrutinise one at a time, especially when he had no idea if the ranch was a luxurious getaway or a dilapidated wreck.

'One problem is that since he lost his wife, he's become reclusive,' Gemma said, 'and I doubt he'd answer questions, at least not on the phone. The other is that Google Earth isn't real time, so we can't see if any of these buildings currently have a vehicle parked outside. You would have to take a trek, but it could be a big waste of time.'

'I'm a police officer, Gemma. Ninety per cent of the leads I follow end up being a waste of time.'

25

About halfway along the track there from Benders Road, Bennet stopped at the PRIVATE. OUT. YOU. KEEP sign. The metal gate was chained shut, no code this time. But the chain was threaded through a large U-shaped nail hammered into the gatepost, and pressure from his Pathfinder easily yanked it free. Did a little more damage to the front of the vehicle though.

The new track disappeared over a small rise; beyond, the land slipped shallowly down and through a small wood. On the far side was Crabtree's farmhouse. It was starting to get dark now, doubly so out here where artificial light was scarce. Bennet had hoped to get home in time to give Joe some good news about his mother and then accompany him and Patricia to the cinema. None of that optimism remained.

The first thing Liam noticed upon exiting the woods was that the large barn shown on Google Earth had gone. In its place was a giant oblong hole and the beginnings of foundations for another building. Parked nearby was a front loader tractor missing its boom attachment, various kinds of which were scattered around. As well as a standard bucket, there seemed to be a tool for every farm task imaginable – including a giant steel spike reminiscent of a weapon in the TV program *Robot Wars*. The other buildings remained, although the corrugated steel edifice was rusted and had old farm machinery parts blocking the large roller door.

There were two other vehicles, both parked by the red wooden farmhouse. Crabtree's Land Rover, old and mud-plastered, and a family car that had no business out in the fields. It took another forty minutes bouncing across the uneven track to reach the farmhouse. Aware that an occupant at a window couldn't have missed his arrival, Bennet exited his vehicle and waved. Nobody came to the door, so Liam strolled to the porch, where there was a wooden two-seater swing-bench, footstool and table with a magazine weighed down by a rock and an ashtray full of cigar butts.

Police training urged him to look in the living-room window before knocking on the door. He saw Crabtree in the living room with a lady in an old dressing gown, on an old armchair. Their backs were to Liam as they watched a black-and-white programme on TV. So who was this lady, if Crabtree had lost his wife? Liam rapped on the door.

'Wait a minute,' Crabtree's gruff voice yelled. But it was almost three minutes before a shape appeared in the small window in the door. The old wood opened with a squeak from a draft excluder attached a little too low. Crabtree stood before him in grimy jeans and a blue pullover stiffened and crusted in places with thick splashes of ancient paint. The eyes were red and droopy, as if he'd been asleep. A sudden alertness in them at the sight of Liam said otherwise.

'Come on in, lad. Come on.'

The old man grabbed his wrist to try to drag him inside, which instantly raised Bennet's suspicions. He allowed himself to be led, but when Crabtree tried to shut the door behind them,

Liam turned to look outside. A moment before the door shut, he caught sight of a young woman slipping out from beside the house and scuttling towards the family car that had no business out here. Only it did, and Liam could make a good guess what that business was, based on the woman's short skirt and clearly young, smooth thighs.

Despite his urge to get Liam inside, Crabtree didn't move from the narrow hallway. He stepped past Liam and shut the door to the living room. Before it slammed closed, Liam got a glance inside, and he saw the ragged armchair where the old lady had been sitting. Empty. On the floor beside it was what looked like a grey wig.

Crabtree grabbed his coat off a hook on the wall and punched into it, but after that didn't move. The two men faced each other in the cramped hallway, two feet apart, each with their back to a door. Crabtree looked nervous, but Liam knew it wasn't because of their proximity. Bennet heard the car start up and make a sharp escape.

'I think I remember you,' Crabtree said. 'You used to date a woman that lived here.'

Crabtree remembered him from a decade ago? Or he'd heard the gossip that a nosey Loper policeman was asking questions? 'I'm looking for some people and I need information.'

Crabtree suddenly squeezed past him and opened the front door. Bennet thought he was about to be ejected, but instead Crabtree walked outside. The car was gone, but Bennet could hear it off in the distance. It wasn't lost on him that Crabtree had dragged him inside so he wouldn't see the escaping woman, then back outside so he didn't get to see the living space.

'You deal with vandalism?' Crabtree asked. 'I got some for you.'

'I'm not here about vandalism. There was a four-person film

crew staying in Lampton on Sunday. They left the same night. Tell me what you know about them.'

It wasn't a question. Bennet had no doubt Crabtree had heard about the crew: he knew of Bennet's visit from someone. Crabtree lit a half-smoked thin cigar that Liam hadn't noticed behind the man's ear because of thick, curly, grey hair. One such was stuck to the chewed filtered end.

'I know they're destructive bastards. It means you're here about vandalism after all. Let's go.'

Crabtree left the porch and stopped on the dried mud, waiting for Bennet. 'Vandalism?' Bennet said. 'Are you telling me the film crew destroyed some of your property? Where?'

'My ranch, my wife's beautiful ranch,' Crabtree spat. He stamped the ground in anger. 'They smashed it up for no damn reason. But now you're here, you're going to fix these bastards for me.' He pulled something from his pocket, and waved it, and then threw it on the ground and stamped on that too.

Bennet stepped off the porch and plucked it out of the mud. His heart skipped a beat.

It was a business card. Black with white text and a picture of a video camera. Along the top was a clapperboard image. There was an email address and website. And a name.

Francis Overeem, specialist in direction, production, casting and editing.

'Did the film crew give you this?' It seemed strange that Overeem would hand over his details when so much effort had been made to hide his reason for being in Lampton.

'Sure did. Which makes them idiots for trashing my ranch, doesn't it? Come on, I'll show you.'

26

Francis Overeem's website was a dot org blog, black background with white writing, heavy on the eyes. Top of the main page was a photo of the man himself standing beside a white motorhome in a field, grinning for the lens. A mini-biography beneath the photo said he had become a doctorandus at twenty-five, before a diagnosis of ME forced him to abandon a medical career. Then a chance encounter with a world-famous 1st AD – whatever that was – changed his fate; spin forward a few years and Overeem was now a director himself, with a popular YouTube channel, and a host of music videos under his belt.

The blog was a list of once-weekly links, posted every Thursday, so Bennet clicked the latest, from six days ago. It was a half-page paragraph of Overeem talking about his Weinsberg CaraHome, which was fixed now he had new high tension leads and a new exhaust pipe, and he was ready to roll. *Missing or Murdered?* would wrap filming in a few days in the glorious Peak District.

So, that was the name of the documentary he was shooting in sunny Lampton. The blog contained three pictures of the motorhome, its fresh parts, and a new piece of camera equipment he'd bought on eBay.

In the previous blog entry, one Thursday back, Francis discussed how his training was going for something called the Arrow Climb. A picture showed him scaling a tree half-naked. *Missing or Murdered?* had acquired some chap Bennet had never heard of, but he was an award-winning soundtrack composer. The film was on schedule for its March 6 posting to Dark Saint to mark the tenth anniversary of Sally Jenkins' disappearance.

Liam googled Dark Saint. It was a YouTube channel covering true crime cases. There were five films posted over the last three years, each forty-five minutes long, or the length of a one-hour TV show with advert breaks. This, then, was where Overeem's Lampton tale would wind up. Hardly prime-time TV, but each video had over a quarter of a million views and that wasn't to be sniffed at.

Bennet clicked on the latest entry, called *Don't Believe Her*. It was about the sister of a missing man accusing his wife of murder. Not a case that Bennet recalled making serious headlines, but the sound, narration, music and cinematography looked pretty professional. He wondered about the earnings of someone whose channel got a quarter of a million views every four months or so.

'Are you coming or what?'

Bennet looked up from his phone. Crabtree was standing nearby, watching, impatient. Bennet had told him to wait while he surfed the internet. Now, he put the business card away.

The CaraHome was a problem. If the crew had a motorhome, why did they need Crabtree's ranch? If they had the ranch, why had Overeem rented a room at the Panorama? If Overeem planned to stay at a hotel, away from his crew for whatever reason, why had he checked in with only a camera bag and a file folder?

'Hey, are you awake?'

'Watch your mouth,' Bennet snapped at the farmer.

'Well are you coming or what? I want these people arrested and charged and made to pay.'

Now that Bennet had the director's real name and an email address he could use, he didn't care to stay in Lampton. The film crew had a motorhome, which meant they were gone, and his entire day here had been a waste. He wanted to email Overeem, right now, and then drive home fast, right now. But he was intrigued by Crabtree's claim. He didn't know much about Francis Overeem or the others, but he knew Lorraine. Or had. And the Lorraine he'd known wasn't the sort to smash up a building.

Unless there was good cause.

'Did you know what they were filming?' Bennet asked.

'I only dealt with one man, a black man, him that gave me that card. He knocked on my door and paid cash and I handed a key and that was it. But I heard the gossip after that. News soon got round. We have our ways of knowing about people who come here. You can't hide anything here.'

'I know. Lampton has a hive mind. So people would have heard that you had the film crew staying at your ranch. And they didn't like it. The Keys ordered you to kick them out, didn't they? Is that why the crew trashed your ranch?'

Crabtree had been pacing in anger, eyes down as if seeking something new to stomp into the mud. He now stopped and stared at Bennet. 'Sir, no one orders me to do anything. I was one of those Keys once, you know?'

Bennet recalled hotelier Gemma's story about disability thwarting her chances of Key status. 'And when your wife died, you got ejected.'

Crabtree's expression confirmed it. 'I didn't care what they were filming. I don't care what their documentary does for this village. I don't live in there, I live out here. I would have been okay with them staying for however long they wanted. But I didn't want my Elise's ranch being on the TV, not connected to that missing girl thing. I didn't want morbid Lopers coming round. So I asked them to leave. Nice and polite. And when I came back to check later that night, oh, they'd gone. Gone and destroyed the place, the bastards.'

'Why didn't you call the police?'

'I've had my fill of people in there. No more guests, no cops. Cops won't do anything, anyway. I don't want anyone else traipsing around my Elise's place. I'm going to put it right and then lock it up and leave it, like I should have done in the first place.'

'But you want to show me?'

'Only cos you're here right now, and I heard you're after that crew. I don't know what they did to get South Yorkshire cops coming all the way here for them, but now you can add thousands of pounds of vandalism. So I hope you're serious about arresting them. Now let's go.'

27

———

Crabtree said his Land Rover needed a starter motor and that Liam's Pathfinder would get stuck, so both men rode in the loader. It was half a mile and the land was indeed rugged, but the Pathfinder could have made it because they followed a clear rutted track created by the loader on some prior day.

As they rode, Crabtree gave him the tale. He had built his wife, Elise, a ranch for when she had episodes and needed space. He didn't elaborate on these 'episodes', but hinted that they required Elise to be away from people. To rekindle the love they'd shared as teenagers fifty years ago, Elise had wanted them to dump modern amenities like the car and the TV and the phone. So they walked everywhere, and they spent time reading together or playing cards, and when an episode forced them apart, they tried to develop a retro communications system between the ranch and the farmhouse. Carrier pigeon, but it died. Morse code, but Crabtree could never get the hang of it.

Elise had died at home while Crabtree was out shopping. Neither did he explain what caused her death, except to say it wasn't quick. There was enough time and coherence for her to have picked up the phone and called for help. Except Crabtree, upon her wishes, had ripped the phone out of the farmhouse. She was found in her car, engine running, having tried to drive for help.

After her death, Crabtree had kept the ranch pristine and untouched, but in the last year or so had outfitted it to cater to families and made it available to rent. Big mistake. Never again.

The final part of the journey was in silence, except for the tractor's engine. They turned around a collection of man-high rocks and the ranch came into view, sitting all alone out here in a shallow valley, perhaps three hundred metres away. Two minutes later, the tractor pulled up. The loader's tracks ran to an area out front of the ranch where the grass and mud had been churned into chilled solid micro mountain ranges and valleys, clearly the result of the loader performing manoeuvres.

The ranch was single-storey, all old logs painted brown. Nursery-rhyme quaint. Very much the kind of place someone would honour his wife with. And the sort tourists would love to rent. But never again.

Liam hopped off the loader and watched Crabtree slowly dismount. The farmer stared at his own ranch, as if fearful. His mouth moved silently. Liam thought he got the word *sorry*. Did the farmer believe bringing a visitor here would offend his wife's soul or something? Days after strangers had stayed at the place? Strange.

Crabtree found a key amongst a set and walked to the door. He took a deep breath before inserting the key. Liam noticed that the handle and lock were heavy-duty, and shiny as only the brand new can be. Another deep breath, then the farmer pushed open the door.

Immediately the emptiness hit Bennet. Like that cold aura you get upon entering your own home after being away on holiday, but amplified. There was little furniture. The painted wooden walls were bare, floors too. Except for the graffiti.

Red and black and green swirls, twists, lines and curves, everywhere. The floor, the walls, the ceilings, all ruined. No words or pictures, just chaos. There were streaks and bare spots and smears and translucent areas where attempts had been made to scrub the paint away, and cleaning materials were in every room, reeking of it. In each room, Crabtree ranted as if seeing the carnage for the first time.

In the living room, Bennet noted an oblong section of the wooden floor that was a little less scuffed than the rest of the room. Where a sofa had been. Crabtree was quick to explain: 'They ruined my sofa. And it was the first sofa me and my wife bought for our house. Vandals.'

In the kitchen were a set of four wooden chairs against a wall. 'Kitchen table, oak. Lovely. Someone gouged a load of swear words into it. My wife's mother gave us that table, and I had to smash it up and burn it.'

There were two bedrooms, one with a single bed and one bearing a double. Both were just metal frames. 'I burned the mattresses and covers. Dirty scumbags shat on them. I couldn't use them again. How could I? I burned all the stuff, and I burned everything they left behind, all their nasty trash. There was loads of it, like squatters had lived here for months. Doesn't this make you angry?'

No, just confused. He tried to picture Lorraine here, a maniacal grin on her face as she smashed and graffitied, but it wouldn't come. Too far-fetched. Had she watched in horror as the others, in revenge for being snubbed by the village, let loose their inner wild child? It was the only answer that made sense.

Unless Lorraine was no longer the woman he knew. Did he want such a person reunited with Joe?

Crabtree grabbed his arm. 'Come see their stuff.'

Bennet shrugged the hand away. 'No. I don't know what I'm

doing here. I need to be leaving. Call the damn police about this.'

But outside, he stopped, and when Crabtree turned to walk around the back of the ranch, he followed to a brick annex with a heavy iron door that was fire-blackened on the inside, like the bare brick walls. The space had no lighting, so Crabtree used the torch on his phone to light up a concrete floor covered in ash and survived paper fragments, twisted metal and springs from a sofa, blackened nails and pieces of metal from other items. It all still gave off heat.

'You burned it inside after all. Hardly a shrine now,' Bennet said, aware that he was lashing out at the farmer unfairly but unable to prevent it.

'Piss off,' Crabtree spat. 'There was nowhere else. Look, this is all the shit and trash they left behind. Maybe you can get something from it, some evidence these scumbags did this. Cos I know they'll just say the ranch was fine when they left.'

Bennet strolled through the mess, kicking at things, turning others. He bent in amongst the ash and burned wood and spiky metal and paper that disintegrated under his shoe. He bent down and picked up a sliver of white paper with the typed letters 'EXT – STR'. He figured he knew what it was. 'EXT –' was movie terminology for *exterior*, meaning a scene shot outdoors. Possibly on a STReet. He'd found a piece of a script. The film crew had definitely been here. But it didn't prove they'd caused the destruction Crabtree was blaming them for. Maybe the ranch had been fine when they left.

Or was that his brain trying to defend his son's mother?

Bennet's ears pricked up at the sound of an approaching vehicle.

28

It was a Mercedes G-class four-by-four, coming at speed and dancing on its suspension. Clearly recognising it, Crabtree ran ahead to greet it. Liam knew the farmer planned to say something in secret to the driver, but he didn't care.

The driver was Councillor Richard Turner. When he exited, he was careful not to get his fine shoes dirty. It seemed obvious that Turner had heard about Bennet's visit to Crabtree, possibly from the man himself, and rushed over. Just like when he'd learned of Bennet's meeting with Anika Jenkins.

'I told him I'd cleaned the place of their foul memory,' Crabtree told the councillor. Turner gave a slow nod and threw his arms wide.

'Now, detective, what do you think of your film crew?'

'A little over the top, but I understand their reaction. If they'd been carried out of town on a rail.'

Crabtree looked puzzled; Turner didn't. An educated man, he knew what Liam referred to. Riding the rail was a form of punishment popular in the USA in the 18th and 19th centuries, in which undesirables were carried about town on a rail, parading them before they were evicted. Liam had read about it in *The Adventures of Huckleberry Finn*.

'If these people felt unwanted,' Turner said, 'that was on them. We've had this discussion and I have no mind to repeat it. As you can see, your girlfriend and her people have gone. My village would relax, but there's an annoying off-duty policeman slinking about, asking questions.'

It was as good as an admission. Bennet had come to suspect that the film crew had suffered more than just a wall of silence. They'd been run out of the village.

'Wait a minute,' Crabtree said, staring at Bennet. 'Girlfriend? I thought you said they were criminals.'

Turner grinned. 'Ah, our friend here is on a personal mission, not police business. Look, detective, your film crew were bothersome, here for nothing but selling a story. No one here cared and they certainly have no interest in where these people went. They came, they vandalised this pretty home, and then they left. Good riddance. I'm sorry you're having problems with your girlfriend, but that's no reason to cause trouble. And that's certainly what you're doing.'

'Ex-girlfriend,' Bennet said. 'I'm just trying to do right by my son and find his mother–'

'Enough,' Turner cut in with a flick of the hand, as if dealing with a pesky fly at a picnic. 'You're not here on official business and we don't have to answer any more questions. I've had to interject twice now, to make sure you're not harassing my people, and it's tiresome. I suggest you head home and continue your enquiries without interrupting our lives any further. Otherwise, I may make a call to your superiors about a harassment charge. Do you understand my meaning, detective? Game over with the monkey business. If you want to do right by your son, buy him a Lego set.'

Turner was awaiting a response, with a slappable grin on his face despite claiming to be upset. The response Bennet gave was to start walking. The loader's tracks offered a route to chase back to his car.

'Goodbye, detective. You should report this vandalism, by the way. Now that you know about it.'

Bennet wanted the last word. As he passed the G-class, he said, 'Idi Amin was also a Mercedes fan. Have a good day.'

29

The rush-hour traffic thinned when he got out of the boondocks. Once free of the Peak District, Bennet turned his mind to the Buttery Park case, which he'd neglected for his personal mission. He was still on a pair of days off, so the investigation hadn't suffered without his input, but that didn't stop him feeling he'd mired it in mud with his absence. On the drive home, he made some calls with an eye to directing some angle or other, but his team had fared well without their decision maker. No forward movement, though, which was a growing cause for concern.

After that, he found his thoughts again turning to Lorraine. He checked her Facebook and Twitter, but she'd made no updates today. He pulled in at a lay-by and composed a text to Hooper, requesting him to trace the unknown number she'd called his landline from. But he couldn't send it. Today he might talk to Lorraine, and tonight he could watch her and Joe have a good old time, but tomorrow the Independent Ethics Panel would come down on him like a ton of bricks. There were easier ways, like messaging Lorraine's husband, but that felt just as wrong.

He emailed Francis Overeem instead and saw a chance to give his contact a semi-official mask. His lie: he'd gotten wind of a vandalism accusation and wanted answers before he reported it to Derbyshire police. He then scoured the director's blog again and found the names and pictures of the two unknown crew he'd visited the Peak District with. Betty Crute, sound engineer, was a petite girl in a tank top with red dreadlocks and tattoos all down both arms. John Crickmer, cameraman, was a guy who looked like a grunger, with shaggy long hair and a heavy-metal jacket. Bennet sent both of them the same email he'd written to Overeem.

Which made him think. Turner had been right: Bennet now knew about the vandalism and had a duty to report it. His mind made a leap from that to an image of Lorraine in court to answer such charges, with Joe crying as he watched her get sentenced and taken into custody. Unlikely, but he couldn't shake the idea. He decided he would get the story from Lorraine and the others before passing its details to Derbyshire police. He sent Lorraine yet another message via Messenger – this one asking her to urgently get in contact – then tossed his phone onto the passenger seat and rubbed his face. What a goddamn day.

He was home soon after. Stepping in the car to stepping out again: seventy-three minutes. Joe and Patricia were eating dinner before heading out to the cinema. He'd already called Patricia to explain his plan and she had some cottage pie left over for him. The lengthy return journey for a trip of about twenty miles had included a McDonald's stop, but he found space for her cooking.

Perhaps because Patricia filled the void, or he didn't want to mention her in front of the neighbour, Joe didn't bring up his mother that evening. But Bennet didn't fool himself that it meant Joe was over her. As they queued to park, and bought popcorn, and squeezed past legs to find their seats at the cinema, Bennet debated his next move. Joe's nonchalance had cut the urgency Bennet had felt all day, and with time on his hands, and room to think clearly, he came up with a plan.

If she hadn't called him by tomorrow morning, he would get hold of her husband by Facebook. An innocent little note to a man who surely knew about Joe's existence. Just a prompt: *hey, do you think Lorraine would consider seeing Joe for an hour or two?* Her husband probably wouldn't mind, unless he was an immature bastard, and his blessing might convince Lorraine it was a good idea. No more of this silly chasing her, and no need for guilt-trips. He just had to hope the snarky message he'd left her didn't mess things up. He would also liaise with Crabtree to find a resolution not involving the police. The farmer didn't want police traipsing through his ranch, and Lorraine's husband was rich, so maybe there was a fiscal route through this mess.

Knowing he had a way forward if necessary, Bennet relaxed a little. He even followed the movie. But the worries came back at close to midnight. While heading upstairs to bed, he checked in on Joe and saw something unnerving as he bent to kiss his sleeping boy's cheek. A portion of his pillow by his nose was puckered, and there were dried streaks of fluid on his cheek. Tears. Joe had been crying in bed. And the culprit, his phone, was in his hand.

Bennet took it and, out on the landing, hit the wake button. The device immediately opened onto Facebook Messenger. Top of the list of message recipients: Lorraine. Joe had written HI IT IS JOE HOW ARE YOU? Seven hours ago now, but no tick to show she'd read it. What if Joe didn't know what that tick meant? Maybe he believed his mother had ignored him. Maybe she had.

Was this Bennet's fault? Had he promised too much, too early? Had he made a mistake by giving Joe his mother's new name, thus allowing him to find her on social media? Had he already ruined any chance mother and son had at reconciliation with that stupid message he'd sent, warning her to stay away?

He felt like crying into his own pillow. This entire day was one he wished he could erase from history.

30

———

His phone rang at four in the morning, but he was already awake. A dream had roused him minutes earlier. Not quite a dream, but a memory.

I can't help you. I'm sorry.

His last words to Anika, mother of a missing, possibly dead young girl. He'd investigated missing people before, perhaps two dozen, and in every single case he'd performed as a police officer bound by duty. That meant consoling a worried family member and promising to provide them with answers, good or bad. Sometimes the missing turned up and his team backed off, but often a body was found and the investigation hit turbo boost. Sometimes there was glorious success and sometimes there was nightmare failure. But the constant was always that pledge to do everything in his power to right the wrong.

Until this last time. That he wasn't attached to the Sally Jenkins case, or even there in a police capacity, didn't matter. He had still stood before the girl's traumatised mother and as good as shrugged her off: *I can't help you.*

The memory burned him because he had never experienced it before. Even if Sally rode home tomorrow on a golden horse, twenty years old and beautiful and rich, he would experience this nightmare for days to come. Somehow, it was worse than if he'd agreed to help Anika and then delivered her a corpse.

The ringing phone cut into his thoughts. Unknown number. He snatched it up, sure it was Lorraine. For the moment, Anika's hellish world was forgotten.

'Have you seen Lorraine?' a male voice said. 'I just finished my night shift. She's not at home. I called people, but no one's heard from her.'

It took Bennet's sleepy brain a moment to orientate. He realised he was speaking to Lorraine's husband. 'No. You haven't heard from her?'

'No, I said no one has. I know you two had history. I thought she might have told you what she was doing. We didn't argue, so I'm worried.'

Bennet sat up, instantly fully awake. 'She tried to get my help. I left a message on social media, but I've not heard back. She went to Lampton? She didn't return? There's no evidence in the house that she came back?'

'No, she hasn't been back. She went off to do a documentary with some people. She was supposed to be away Sunday and Monday, back Tuesday evening. She didn't come back.'

'She never contacted you at all while she was away?'

'No. Sometimes we go days without, you know? It gets like that after you've been with someone a while, doesn't it?'

Bennet wouldn't know, at least for the last decade. 'Do you know who the film crew are? Any contact numbers? Did you meet them?'

'No. She dealt with all that. She drove off to meet them, down in Oxford. But after that I didn't hear from her. She was looking forward to the trip. I've been working nights, so I was asleep when she went, and I wouldn't try to call her at night while I'm working.'

Bennet put the phone on speaker on the bedside table so he could talk as he got dressed.

'Look around the house, look for a note or something to do with the film crew. When she contacted these people, she might have written something down. Look for a name or a number, perhaps on a flyer, because that's how she contacted them.'

'I know that someone called Joe contacted her on Facebook. I saw that. There's been no activity on her account since I last saw her, though, which is also strange. She posts a lot. I'll go look at this Joe's profile and see what's what.'

Bennet was dismayed, and not just because a simmering fear about Lorraine had now ignited into an inferno. He'd always wondered how her *new* family felt knowing an *old* family was out there. Now he had his answer: they didn't feel anything, because they didn't know. Lorraine's daughter didn't know she had an older half-brother. Her husband had no clue his wife had had a child years before she met him.

'Joe's nothing to do with this,' he said, his voice cracking. 'He's someone I know. Look for that note. Stay by this phone. I'm going to call you again within half an hour. Okay?'

'Should I report her missing? This just seems bad. Did that film crew do something to her?'

'Just do what I said. I'll get back to you.'

He hung up, his head a muddle. He'd spent a day hunting Lorraine, without success. He should have had more answers for her husband. He should have found her.

But now he had no shackles, and he *would* find her. He called Detective Constable Hooper. No answer at such an hour, so he left a message: Call me the moment you get this.

Dressed, he got a key from one of the kitchen drawers, then headed into Joe's room. He lifted him, still in his duvet, and carried him from the house. The cold wind outside didn't stir the boy, nor did he wake when Bennet almost dropped him while unlocking Patricia's front door. He put Joe on the sofa and sent Patricia a text saying he had to go out and Joe was downstairs. As he was climbing into his car, he saw Patricia's bedroom light flick on. God, she was great.

Churchfield Police Station was closed until 8am, so he let himself in with his key fob and sat behind the reception desk. Data protection meant the PC was password protected, but nobody broke into a building full of police and the password was on a sticker on the monitor. He loaded up CONTACT, the system used to file a Misper – a missing persons report. He called Lorraine's husband back.

An initial report needed such details as name, age, description, address, location missing from and locations frequented, as well as information regarding concerns the reporter had about the Misper's likelihood to be sexually exploited, if they'd been missing before, were likely to harm themselves or others, or travel out of the country. He didn't need all that. He asked Lorraine's husband for the names and contact details of close friends and her vehicle registration, and then he hung up without a goodbye.

Initial report done, it was due to be reviewed as part of a Vulnerability and Risk Assessment, and someone would decide just how much effort should be put into finding the Misper. No risk meant doing nothing and reassessing the situation at another time. At the other end was high risk, which the Home Office had defined as *A risk which is life threatening and/or traumatic, and from which recovery, whether physical or psychological, can be expected to be difficult or impossible.*

Bennet marked Lorraine as high risk, which would allocate the immediate deployment of police resources. The case would be appointed a high-ranking investigating officer. As a DCI, Bennet counted: he put his own name in the box.

Usually, the Missing Person's Bureau should be contacted if a person was gone for seventy-two hours. Now that Lorraine's disappearance was noted as high risk, this action was required immediately. Bennet logged the details with them and also with the Major Crime Investigative Support unit of the National Crime Agency. Finally, he updated the Police National Computer, so that police across the country would know that finding her and her vehicle were a priority.

Within two minutes of making it all official, he got 'pricked' – the unofficial term South Yorkshire police used for receiving an automated message sent by its private SMS network, *Holding Hands*. Sure enough, the message asked him to urgently report to his immediate superior. No need, of course, because he knew exactly what the case was. And now it was official.

Because he'd designated Lorraine as the highest risk, senior managers would also be contacted. These people usually only got pricked for major events, like the kidnapping of a royal child or a terrorist bombing, and they weren't going to be happy about being woken for a missing adult nobody.

So what? The ball was rolling. Bennet would deal with the backlash when it was time.

31

On the way home, Bennet called the Red Lion in Lampton, but got no answer. Unsurprising at little past six in the morning. As he was pulling into his driveway, Hooper returned his earlier call. Bennet quickly explained: missing woman, we've got the case. 'I need you to put aside what you're doing on the Buttery Park case for today and work this.'

He gave Hooper the names Francis Overeem, Betty Crute, John Crickmer, and Lorraine Cross, wanting them checked out on the Police National Computer. He gave his DC a rundown of events since yesterday, but didn't mention that Lorraine was his son's mother. He didn't talk about his personal life to his team, even though he'd worked with some of them for years, and wasn't sure how much they knew. Probably a lot, being detectives, but they knew better than to talk about it. He told Hooper to chase up Lorraine's car and liaise with her husband for further information on her habits and friends and known haunts. More than likely, the husband would inform him of Lorraine's connection to Bennet, but he could do nothing about that.

'I also need you to get someone to drive down to the Red

Lion public house in Lampton and... scratch that. Stick with what I gave you. Get moving, keep me updated.'

The action he'd been about to give Hooper would crawl its way through him to someone else, who would have to sanction the journey... too much time wasted. He had another job planned in that area, so he would take the Lion task as well. Better if he kept busy and cut down worrying time. He sent Patricia another message, now asking her to take Joe to school. Then he slid his car out of the driveway.

This time he had more urgency, and an early morning lack of traffic, and a warrant card to show any police who pulled him. Stepping in the car to stepping back out: thirty-three minutes.

He laid his Pathfinder in the secret car park behind the Lion and jogged out front to rap the big oak door. Publican Jonesy appeared at a first-floor window, sleepy-eyed. Bennet aimed his warrant card up.

'Down you come, open the door.'

Damn, that felt good. It was a relief to finally not have to pussyfoot around this fool. It took Jonesy a few minutes, and he opened the door with obvious distaste. Bennet walked past him. Jonesy flicked the lights on. 'So what's this about? At this bloody hour. Not your film troublemakers again, I hope. You know as much as I know.'

'I want to see your CCTV of Sunday night, when the film crew came in.'

'Still at it, eh? What do you hope to see? Your people upped and offed. Place was heaving, so I don't know what you think you'll find.'

Bennet could have told Jonesy that the film crew were now officially missing and he was investigating it. He didn't bother. He just stared at the landlord until the man wilted.

'Okay, whatever. Come on. Let's make this quick.' Jonesy led him behind the bar and the curtain at the back, where they took uncarpeted stairs to the first floor, where one of the rooms had a foldaway bed and a table bearing the CCTV system. It was a clunky box with a joystick and various buttons, clearly old, and Bennet wasn't optimistic it would provide a jackpot. He wasn't even sure what he hoped to find.

'You can probably figure out how to use this,' Jonesy said. 'Only look at Sunday, okay? Don't be noseying at other days. Come down when you're done. Don't take ages.'

When Jonesy left, Liam sat at the desk. At the moment all four cameras were displayed in quad screen, and all were black and white. One picture was an obsidian square of nothing, one watched the beer garden, and the other two covered the lounge from front and back.

He worked out how to make one feed fill the screen and chose the interior camera above the entrance, which gave the best view of people standing at the bar. He then got his head around how to fast-forward, rewind, and to jump backwards in segments of ten, fifteen, thirty and sixty minutes. Some digital CCTV systems employed trick mode, which meant the playback in fast-forward included only certain frames, but this ancient analogue set-up didn't. If that sounded like a benefit over modern equipment, it wasn't: the synchronisation quality would be worse than the live feed. He took the recording back to Sunday gone, 6pm.

The lounge was empty except for a young woman behind the bar and an older male sitting before it. The low resolution made it hard to connect her face to the one displayed on the wall in the lounge, but a large blot of colour on her cheek, a birthmark, told him he was watching Barmaid Vicky.

And her sole customer? Unbelievably, it was Dog Man with his pooch under the chair, trusty cup and newspaper before him. In the sandwich shop, Dog Man had said the film crew *came* into the Red Lion, instead of *went*. Liam now understood why: Dog Man had watched the quartet enter the pub. A little detail he'd neglected to mention.

Bennet fast-forwarded until customers started to enter. Because the camera was above the door, Liam's view was mostly of heads and shoulders. They filed in fast, zipping here and there like electrons as the lounge filled. An anomaly was Dog Man; as if by camera trick, he barely seemed to move. The effect was fractured only when he took a sip of his tea or turned a page in his book. As people came in, Dog Man didn't even look – but he'd looked when Bennet came in, hadn't he?

So Bennet focused on him, not the customers, and when the timestamp read 2051, Dog Man turned his head towards the door. Bingo. Bennet rewound a minute and pressed play, to watch in real time as the people who'd intrigued the old dog lover entered. Only Lopers could garner such scrutiny. He knew he'd found the film crew.

A woman entered first. Real time, the blonde girl floated up the screen as she walked away from the camera. She grew a body and arms and legs with the changing angle, and he made out double denim. He knew it was Lorraine, even without seeing her face.

Next came Betty Crute and John Crickmer. Bringing up the rear, in a suit and blue trench coat, was the man known as the director; then Donald Ducke, and now Francis Overeem.

They were a bizarre-looking group, like something out of a video game. Lopers were one thing, but this group stood out like a sore thumb. If they'd hoped to sneak around the village under the guise of tourists, secretly filming, they'd gone about it the wrong way.

As the director followed his colleagues to the bar, a young guy angled their way and bumped him, on purpose. The director raised a hand in apology, which the young thug didn't care for. Liam saw no other black patrons and wondered if this was a race thing. Maybe these backwater bumpkins thought black people were invading extraterrestrials. Or the pair had had a run-in earlier.

The crew looked around, then sat at the bar. They seemed to be minding their own business, but local heads were watching, fingers occasionally pointing. Only Barmaid Vicky spoke to them. Just doing her job, perhaps, or, as an out-of-towner herself, maybe she was not so closed-minded to strangers. She stood right across the bar from the director, doing a good job of paying attention to him. The camera didn't have the resolution to catch moving mouths, but Liam could tell they were talking.

Overeem looked around again, then back at Vicky. She tiptoed and moved her head, also scanning the room. She shook her head and said something and looked at her watch.

Intriguing.

When the crew moved to a table at the back of the lounge, Bennet switched to the other interior camera and got a much better view. The director was indeed about fifty, as hotelier Gemma had claimed, his wavy hair shiny black apart from a scattering of grey around the ears. Tattoo was no older than twenty-five, he guessed, with piercings in her nose, above her left eye, and a bunch in both ears. Grunge was a nerdy-looking guy despite his wild hair and heavy-metal outfit. Lorraine had her back to the camera, so he couldn't see her face. But he wanted to.

The crew didn't seem to be in the pub to interview, and nothing about their demeanour said they were 'mouthy'. Others were. Bennet watched a young local approach, say something, get ignored, slip out of shot, and re-enter it with three mean-looking older cronies. Words were said. One kicked the table, spilling a drink. Lorraine got up, tugging at the director's arm. He seemed willing to stand his ground, but she got him moving and his comrades followed. It was 2121. As the film-makers headed for the door, a bag of crisps entered stage left and hit Lorraine on the head.

Bennet clenched his jaw as Lorraine and the film crew were hounded out of the pub.

He was really pissed off. He'd suspected the crew had been ostracised from the village, but seeing it on tape made it real. They had come to highlight an old abduction case, to remind the public in the hope of a breakthrough, and the entire village had taken offence. And made it known. Idiots. It explained why Overeem had gone straight to the Panorama to check out. And, later, Crabtree had ordered them to leave his property. Bennet would have probably trashed the place if he'd experienced such hate.

32

Downstairs, Bennet slapped the curtain aside. The landlord, Jonesy, was right before him, his back to Liam as he cleaned the till with a small towel. He turned.

'Find what you need? Only looked at Sunday, didn't you?'

Liam ignored him and passed through the bar hatch. He went to the framed picture of the staff and jabbed Barmaid Vicky's photo. 'Get me her phone number.'

Jonesy pulled his mobile and recited it. Bennet typed it into his own phone.

'That it, we done?' Jonesy said.

'Everyone in this village is an idiot. You included.'

Jonesy threw his towel on the bar hard enough to make a slapping noise. 'Police or not, you're now barred. Well done, because I've never barred anyone in my life. Maybe you should just not come back to Lampton at all.'

'Don't you need the Keys to make that judgement?'

Back in his Pathfinder, in the secret car park, Bennet called a number and, despite the early hour, it was answered quickly.

'Vicky, from the Lion? My name–'

'Jake? I told you I wasn't interested. And it's like the crack of dawn.'

Yet it sounded like she was in the midst of a party. Oh, to be young and wild. 'Not Jake. Maybe Jake got the message. Detective Chief Inspector Bennet, South Yorkshire police. You were working in the Lion last Sunday night, Jan 19th.'

A pause as she yelled at people behind her to keep the racket down. 'Yes. Why?'

'Lopers who upped and offed. Four members of a film crew. They got kicked out.'

'Yes. But not by me. Mr Jonesy runs the place, so he–'

'I know it wasn't you. Keep calm. I saw the CCTV of that night and you spoke to one of them, a black man. His name is Francis Overeem. Was he looking for someone?'

'I'm not sure. I don't know. Who?'

'You tell me. He looked around, spoke to you, then you looked around and shook your head and checked your watch.'

'Oh, yes. No, he was asking if we would get busier, that was it.'

'For sure? You'd need to check the time for that? Because it looked to me like he asked you if a certain someone was in, and then you had a look and said this person wasn't there.'

'No, nothing like that. I think the time thing was to see if we'd reached our peak yet. And they didn't stay long. So what have they done?'

'Keep this phone nearby, Vicky...'

'London. Vicky Anna London. Look, am I in trouble or something?'

'Another officer will call you, and they'll want to visit, so stay where you are and talk to the officer when he calls.'

Bennet deflected more questions and hung up. He then sent another of his team a text with Vicky's name and number and details of her less-than-convincing answers, and an order to perform a follow-up, face-to-face interview. After that, he set out on the job that had brought him to this neck of the woods.

Because now he had a good idea where the film crew might have stayed on Monday night.

33

During his calls to various hotels, he'd found one just a couple of miles from Lampton whose name now popped back into his head. Name: the Arrow Hotel. In his blog, Overeem had mentioned training for something called the Arrow Climb. Coincidence? Not to a copper.

The website listed the Arrow as a small pub/hotel, dog and family friendly, with great food, four-star average reviews, and thirty years in the Good Beer Guide. It was on a cliff overlooking Lake Stanton and had once been home to the Stanton family, whoever they were. There was a rumour that marauders had tried to scale the cliff wall by firing arrows and using them like a ladder; today, iron arrows had replaced them and an extravaganza saw visitors attempt to make the climb for a hefty cash prize – only those who'd a room at the Arrow Hotel, of course. The three-day event had been hosted once a month for fifteen years, and there had been 'NO FATALITIES YET!!' Liam had never heard of it during his residency in Lampton. Ten years ago it would have been something he'd have given a shot.

The last Arrow Climb had been Saturday, Sunday and Monday. If Overeem had been planning to enter the competition, it would explain why he'd stayed at the Panorama on Sunday but scheduled an appointment at the Winding Wheel in Chesterfield for Tuesday. Monday night: a room at the Arrow Hotel.

Lake Stanton had been created by a quarry company forty years ago, but part of the land adjacent had recently been purchased by a large supermarket chain that was hoping to open a giant store within the next few years. Locals were arguing against it at the moment, so there wasn't much movement. Before everything stalled, the supermarket had re-tarmacked an old road along the western side of the lake for their construction traffic. Google Maps showed Bennet a track running between the new service road and Benders Road at a location north-east of Lampton. That sliver of the world belonged to Ronald Crabtree, and now it all made sense.

From the ranch, Overeem's CaraHome could have reached Benders and found the unnamed track, then the service road by the lake. At whose northern end lay the Arrow Hotel. Barely four miles.

So, Bennet would go to the Arrow Hotel. With luck, Overeem was still there or staff would have a location for him. Last time, the receptionist at the Arrow had blown him off. Not this time.

34

———

'Your director, Francis Overeem, has also been reported missing. Thames Valley Police got a missing person report on Tuesday night from his girlfriend, down in Oxford. No contact, phone dead, no bank activity. They logged the vehicles parked near his home and one of them is registered to Lorraine Cross. Also, they tried to locate two other people he went to the Peak District with, a John Crickmer and Betty Crute. Their vehicles were also parked near Overeem's house. No one knows where they are, either, and their phones are also out of action. There's a watch out for Overeem's motorhome, but it hasn't been clocked by a camera since entering the Peak District early on Sunday morning. That was just outside Rowsley, about five miles south-east of Lampton.'

Bennet had pulled into the side of the service road by Lake Stanton to take the call. Tall, thick shrubbery lined the right side, while the lakeside woodland towered above him on the left, condemning the road to eternal gloom. The two-lane tarmac road had indeed been newly laid, but the surface had been torn up in places even more recently: two staggered lines of holes, much like a movie might have employed to show the footsteps of a passing tyrannosaur. Bennet had to drive down the centre line to avoid them.

The lakeside trees lurked beyond a chain-link fence and, behind it, the remnants of a brick wall. He figured the wall, far more ancient than the road or the fence, was something left over from a land boundary. In places the brickwork was stubs and towers poking up like a line graph; in others giant jigsaw-piece shapes remained. Bennet had no idea how high the wall had been until he parked to answer his phone. There was a whole segment that had endured the passage of years, with arches ten feet high. This location had no chain-link fence, but portions of such material had been used to block the arches. In places the woodland was thin and the sparsity behind the arches allowed him to see flashes of the lake, some fifty metres away. A peaceful site on any other day, when he hadn't just taken a call that chilled his heart.

He'd been fighting his own brain since yesterday, but now the battle was over. And paranoia had won. How could he now deny that something terrible had happened to Lorraine? Four people had met at Overeem's place in Oxford on Sunday and taken his CaraHome north, and after being run out of Lampton they'd vanished. Four people out of contact, phones dead. It was fruitless to try to continue hoping there was an innocent explanation. Bennet was very worried now.

He continued driving. A little further on, there was a break in the shrubbery on his right. A stone cottage sat about thirty metres back in a clearing filled with garden ornaments hung with price tags. A sign on a stake said, 'Anders Gardens'. The fairy-tale aura of the cottage was marred only by a big CCTV camera on a pole on the roof and a sporty Audi convertible out front.

Bennet's phone rang. It was his boss, Superintendent

Hunter. Bennet pulled up across the garden centre. He'd been waiting for this call, but not in a good way.

'Liam, what's going on? I got a prick. And now I find out one of my DCIs filed his own missing person's report, about his own ex-partner no less, and designated it of the highest urgency. And then made himself investigating officer.'

'I did it for my son. That's his mother,' Bennet said. 'Look, David, I know what I did was off protocol, but I have good reason to think something bad has happened to Lorraine and the film crew she was with. I cut past the basics because I've effectively been investigating this for a day and a half, and I know something is badly wrong. Four people, all missing, all with their phones dead and no activity on social media or at their banks. We needed to get boots on the ground as soon as possible and mine have been there all day.'

'This is totally out of order. If anyone finds out Lorraine is your son's mother...'

'I know. Look, Thames Valley Police have their own missing person's investigation running, and you can allocate another officer to ours. But not yet. I just need a couple of hours.'

'No, Liam. You're running a murder investigation, and you can't just gallivant off to look for your ex-partner.'

Bennet could have argued that he was off the clock, but knowing this didn't halt the guilt. Most of the senior detectives he knew didn't turn off just because they weren't on duty. He could have spent his free time on the Buttery Park stabbing, same as every other moment since the start of the investigation. Nor did it help to try to convince himself that this missing person's enquiry was also important: he'd been chasing Lorraine down way before it became a matter of urgency. The result of his tumbling emotions was frustration.

'Article two of the European Convention on Human Rights

gives her the right to life, and I as a police officer, am obliged to safeguard these rights.'

'Oh, come on, Liam. You say something like that? To me?'

Bennet took a breath, ashamed of himself. What had come over him? 'I'm sorry. Look, David, I let bad events get a head start on me. If I'd known more information yesterday, I could have had a proper head start, or even fixed this by now. I was delayed by... I didn't do this as an officer of the law, and I wish I had. You know the last thing I said to Lorraine? *Stay away.* She might not have if I'd not said that. She might have come to see Joe. And now it's too late. If she's dead.'

Hunter paused. Bennet waited. He knew what came next would either kill or promote his mission. 'Liam, I'm going to downgrade the missing person's–'

'I don't think–'

'Stop, Liam. Just listen. I'll downgrade it and say the high-risk designation happened by error. But I'll dedicate some resources to this. Okay? Including you. For today only though. Given your connection to Lorraine, I don't think your head would be on the job anyway. So, the rest of the day. And that's it.'

'Thank you.'

Hunter hung up. Bennet got his mind back on track. He was about to drive on when he spotted a man in the garden centre, coming his way. He had wild long hair and, somehow in winter, a deep tan. When Liam put his window down, the guy yelled a hello and then put his gloved fingers to his temples, as if thinking. Then he pointed at Liam.

'Early and eager. You look like a water-feature man to me.'

Liam shook his head. 'You get much business out here?'

Anders pointed at his flash Audi, which made Liam laugh. 'Exclusively no riff-raff.'

That explained why Liam had seen no signs advertising the shop: you came here if you knew where it was and had the intention to part with cash. Not that it would ever draw much custom; it was probably this man's pet project of a retiree rather than a legitimate business.

'Seen anyone in the last couple of days in a white motorhome? Probably Monday. Four people. A big black guy with them. And a blonde woman in her early forties?'

Anders lost his smile as he realised there was no sale to be had here. 'No. Anyone comes this way, they're probably coming here. Until that sodding supermarket's up and running. I tell you, if they have a garden section, I'm gonna kick off, and no one wants to see me kick off.'

'That Audi'll have to go back. Hey, why is this road full of holes?'

'Oh, that's the Stanton Beast, ain't it?'

Anders had a grin on his face, like someone eager to be asked to explain his shocking statement. 'Of course, silly me,' Liam said, and crushed the accelerator.

35

At the end of the lake, the service road turned right then arced left, all of it a sharp climb to meet a small roundabout at the front of the Arrow Hotel. The building looked as if it had once been a stately home. Three storeys, a turret at each front corner, and tall windows. A high, ancient stone wall blocked the view of the ground floor and front garden; the sliding gate across the driveway was a solid panel just as impenetrable.

As he took the exit towards the hotel, Bennet saw a traffic camera on the roundabout. Its bright-green casing pegged it as a Highways England Automatic Number Plate Recognition camera. He hoped that wasn't a bad omen. He pulled up by an intercom and pressed the button. He expected to have to state his business, but this was a hotel, not a secret government installation: the gate immediately started to withdraw.

The driveway split a mown lawn with parking area with bays outlined with white paint. Bennet drew to a stop in the turning circle before arched oak main doors, which were wide open. A sign reckoned the proprietors were *absolutely thrilled* to have him here. Bennet reckoned they'd soon change their minds.

All doors bar one in the dim foyer were shut. That one put him in what looked like a pub lounge. Mostly empty, apart from a barman and a couple of early-starters in suits drinking tea and working on laptops, and a technician fixing a fruit machine. There was a mammoth corkboard with some darts tournament scores, and leaflets promoting local events, and a BARRED list with two photos of young men on it. At the back, long windows offered a tremendous view of the sweeping Peak District landscape.

Beside the corkboard was a recessed reception like a ticket booth. An old guy sat there, cleaning the room-key fobs. He looked too old to be the receptionist Liam had spoken to earlier; probably a manager. Liam approached the window. On the counter was a register, just like at the Panorama, and he got a good look at recent guests' names before the old guy spotted him and flipped the book shut. Four rooms currently taken, and seven used since Sunday.

'That's private, I'm afraid,' the man said, standing. His badge said: TONY. He had a stoop that shortened him about ten inches, lush brown hair and perfect white teeth, both obviously fake. Liam pulled his warrant card. It felt like a breath of fresh air.

The old man gave a smile and a salute and flipped open the register. It took Bennet just a blink to note no name of Overeem or Dark Saint or Donald Ducke. And no Cross or Taylor, in case Lorraine had made the booking. Didn't mean the film crew wasn't here, or hadn't been.

Bennet shut the book and showed his phone. First a screenshot of Overeem from his blog, then a photo of Lorraine from a Facebook album.

'These two might have been here on Monday. I believe the male was interested in your Arrow Climb.'

Bennet swiped back and forth between the two photos,

giving Tony a good look at both. And he took a long look, as if really trying to help. He even leaned closer and squinted and furrowed his eyebrows in thought. Ultimately, though, he shook his head.

'I remember all the pretty girls, and I don't recall that blonde girl, and we had no black people in that night. Or any night I remember in the last few weeks.'

'How about your CCTV of Monday? Can I see that?'

'Can't say no to the law. We've got a camera on the car park. But I'll save you some time. Me and my girls run this place and I don't take days off. Been every night for months, and I can promise you them two didn't come in.'

Bennet had suspected this. DC Hooper had told him that Overeem's CaraHome had last been captured by ANPR a few miles south-east. If the camera on the roundabout hadn't flagged it, it hadn't been this way.

Or maybe it *had* travelled the service road... just not all the way.

'Can I look out back?' he asked, pointing to the long windows. Tony told him to go right ahead. Bennet opened a door and stepped out onto a veranda with small tables and stackable aluminium chairs. He approached a chest-high railing and stared out. The view was indeed fabulous, but his attention was caught by a metal gibbet-like scaffold off to his left. He walked over to it. It had a winch with a mass of wound cable and a safety harness dangling over the fence.

'That's for the Arrow Climb,' Tony said from behind him.

The lake was some seventy metres below, its tip just a couple of metres from the bottom of the cliff. It spread out in an oval, ringed by trees. Beyond the lake in all directions: fields and urban areas. Bennet leaned over the fence to peer straight down. On the ground, the trees had been cleared in an area the size of a basketball court and a wooden platform laid. Dozens of metal rods staggered down the smooth cliff face in a line, all the way to the platform.

'Kind of seems like cheating,' Bennet said. 'The marauders way back didn't have a winch system.'

'Wasn't allowed to do it without. Can't have my customers smashing to a pulp. Especially not the ones with a tab at the bar.' Tony laughed at his own joke.

Bennet saw that the nearest 'arrow' was eight feet below. 'How do you reach the top from there?'

'We have to remove the top two and bottom two when the event's over. Stops people sneaking here at night at trying to make the climb.'

'Anyone ever done it? Won the test, I mean.'

'A few. On Sunday I had to bar a guy though. Turns out he was a professional rock climber. Against the rules. Anyway, these people you're after. What they done, robbed a bank or something?'

'Or something.' Bennet immediately regretted his mockery and explained: film crew, visiting Lampton to make a documentary. He didn't mention Sally Jenkins.

'Nah, I haven't had anyone like that here. Sorry. Why do the police want them?'

'Routine enquiries on another matter.' Bennet returned his gaze to the lake. The ring of trees was perhaps fifty metres thick. By their left arc he could see Anders' garden centre and fragments of the service road through the canopy. But he couldn't see any roads or tracks whose entrances weren't visible from the service road. A little way past the garden centre there was a kind of seam in the ring where trees weren't as densely packed. Inside this line across the width of the woods, was that stone he saw?

'What's that?' he asked Tony. 'Just past the garden centre.

Where the trees look thinner. Looks like remnants of a building in the woods.'

Tony didn't look; too busy preparing a wad of phlegm that he loosed and watched plummet to the wooden platform. 'That's the old boathouse and slipway from the Stanton Estate. Just a shell now, and the slipway is overgrown. The owner doesn't want to sell or restore, even though he gets visitors about the Stanton Beast.'

'I used to visit someone over at Lampton. But I'd never heard of the Stanton Beast until today.'

'Well, it's all a bit silly. Thing's supposed to be twenty feet tall, yet it lives in these woods? Couldn't miss a dog in there, never mind some monster. It started life as a rabid horse Stanton let loose, and the rumour mill gave it horns and fangs and made it five times as big. If you go down that service road there, you'll see holes that are supposed to be its footsteps.'

'You're joking. You believe that?'

Tony laughed. 'No one sane believes it. Some fool pissed about the new supermarket tore the road up with a drill. But it's a good line to give the tourists. Mind you, the other night I was in here after we shut up, on my own, and I swore I could hear the thing crashing about in the woods down there.'

'What?'

Tony laughed again. 'The boathouse is a magnet for yobbos and hikers and partying teenagers and stuff. The Stanton Beast gives this place a sort of Blair Witch feel to some Lopers and they camp out in the building, hoping to see the Beast. I can hear their whooping and shouting late at night sometimes.'

Intriguing. 'Was this on Monday night?'

'Nah. Last night. Noisy sods. Go see Albert at the garden centre. He'll tell you. He's got that CCTV with sound. He's got loads of recordings of it. But don't let him trick you into believing it's the Beast. Hey, this film crew, are they doing a piece on the monster? That why they're here?'

Bennet shook his head.

There were no roads, paths, trails or tracks big enough for a vehicle leading off the service road. Overeem had planned a visit to the Arrow, but he hadn't followed through. His own visit had been a waste of time. He was done here.

36

Liam took the roundabout exit back onto the winding road that led to the service road, and drove to the garden centre.

Albert Anders was tending to a water feature as Bennet turned into his forecourt. Perhaps remembering his failed sale earlier, he didn't look happy to see his visitor return. Bennet showed his warrant card.

'Can I get a look at your CCTV?'

'If you like. What's it for? I didn't see those people you asked about.'

'You've got recordings of the Stanton Beast, is that right?'

'Tony tell you that? Up at the Arrow? It's not really the Beast. He tell you that?'

'He did. You've got recordings of people, shall we say, partying at the boathouse?'

'Yeah, but not on video. This camera here, it's got good audio, picks up stuff all around.'

'Do you check your video? Any chance it caught a motorhome going past late at night?'

'Possible. But didn't you just say you wanted partiers at the boathouse? There were some sods early this morning.'

'I'll take what I can get.'

Anders was happy to show him. They entered the cottage. The showroom was downstairs, all four walls papered with life-size trees to make you think you were lost in the woods. Upstairs were the living quarters: a kitchen, bathroom, bed-sitting room. Here, amongst games consoles, a giant curved TV, pinball machine and treadmill, was a desk with the CCTV control panel.

This was state-of-the-art, not the clunky box used at the Red Lion. Playback was done by either picking a time and date, because the digital storage went back weeks, or by rewinding time with a dial. Digital also meant no quality loss at increased speed, and it didn't have trick mode, so Liam would miss no frames. The camera covered the forecourt and the slice of road visible in the gap in the shrubbery.

Also unlike at the Lion, this owner refused to leave Liam alone with his gadget. Anders created a racket on the pinball machine as Liam found the recording for Sunday night, when the film crew had left Lampton. He spun the dial to speed up time. Out here nothing happened, and that didn't alter for hours. The timestamp whizzed, but nothing else moved. The first blip, a long time coming, was a light washing across the forecourt as Anders' Audi turned in and the man got out, all taking place within half a second in fast-forward.

A real-time hour later, a small van turned into the grounds. Obviously not the CaraHome, but Bennet played the video in real time in hope of a clue. As promised, there was audio. Really good audio. The microphone not only caught the noise of the van's engine, but also registered the slap of its driver's door closing after the driver got out. Bennet even heard it over the damn pinball machine. Anders approached the guy, said '*Hello, you look like a water-feature man to me.*' So, just a customer. Bennet spun the dial again.

This little portion of the universe remained inert thereafter. The light sluiced rapidly from the sky, and the picture turned black. Then green, as night vision kicked in. Wow. Bennet almost jumped out of his skin when something flashed on the screen at about 1am. Monday morning. The CaraHome?

But when he rewound, real time, three motorbikes zipped past backwards, trailing their headlight beams like comets' tails.

'Joyriders,' Anders said from the pinball machine. 'Little shits wake me up all the time. Should hear how loud they are out here in the middle of the night. You'll see when you get to early this morning.'

The sun came up with cartoon speed. Bennet spun through Monday. The sky got bright and then dark again, but the picture otherwise didn't change. By the time night fell and the world turned green again, Liam was buzzing with frustration. He had hoped that the CaraHome had indeed taken the service road to the roundabout, and somehow avoided being snared by the camera there, perhaps because it tailgated a truck or... whatever. But Anders' camera wouldn't have missed it.

Bennet was sure he was wasting time, but he continued to watch the video. Tuesday was more of the same nothingness. The only break was when a pair of girls in a small car turned into the forecourt. Customers. They snapped a few photos of each other standing by large garden ornaments, but bought nothing and were gone twenty minutes later. Anders' Audi was definitely going to have to go back.

Tuesday night became Wednesday morning. It was just after 2am on-screen when Anders stopped playing his pinball machine and said, 'About here's where you want to press play. If you want to hear the Stanton Beast.'

Bennet slowed the video to twice real time, and dropped the

fast-forward altogether when he saw a green-lit Anders come out of his home. It was obvious why. The microphones caught the faraway crack of wood, and the roar of a throaty engine. The sounds were barely there, which added to the eeriness.

'I came out because I wondered if the road was being fixed,' Anders said, leaning over Bennet's shoulder to watch the screen. 'The supermarket people, they re-tarmacked early so their suits could ride on down to see the site for the new store. But some people reckon they were planning to start building on the sly, get some momentum going while this thing got argued in court. I was ready to start shouting, what with them doing that stuff at that time of the morning. But then I wondered if some people were pretending to be the Beast, you know?'

If the noise had been a flash, there and gone, anyone might have guessed at a car crashing into the woods. But the sinister sounds continued, a steady mix of throaty growl and crack of wood, reminiscent of the sound effects in horror movies. The faint noise certainly sounded intentional.

'I didn't want to get involved if some gang of yobbos was larking about,' Anders said. 'Vicious bastards these days, carrying knives and all. So don't think I'm a wimp for not rushing down there.'

The Anders on screen went back into his building. The mega microphone even caught the sound of bolts being slammed into place as the man who wasn't a wimp fortified his stronghold. A floodlight came on, lighting up the garden and shutting off the camera's night vision. The strange noises continued.

But it got no louder or fainter, so whatever it was didn't move closer or further away from the camera. No vehicle went past. There were no lights out there in the woods.

'Where did the noise come from?' he asked Anders.

'Down to the left. Not close, but I couldn't tell how far. But I figured it was at the boathouse. Yobbos mess about there all the time.'

The boathouse. Anders was the second man to state that it was a location sightseers liked to visit. If Overeem wanted to fully explore Lampton for his crime documentary, and inject a few unnecessary thrills, and pad the runtime, there was a chance he'd chosen to cover the Stanton Beast myth.

So, the boathouse. A long shot, but all Bennet had left. Besides, just like he'd told the Panorama's manager, Gemma, ninety per cent of a copper's work was a waste of time.

37

Bennet returned to the spot on the service road where he'd parked earlier to take a call from Hooper. The intact portion of wall, with a complete arch barred by mesh wire, didn't interest him this time. A couple of metres to the right, he saw the old stone boathouse in the trees. He was surprised he'd missed it last time. He approached the mesh-covered arch, and got a surprise.

This was where, from the Arrow, he'd noticed a thinness to the trees from road to lake, and now he understood why. From that remote, elevated position, the tops of the trees had hidden what lay below. The ground was clear of trees in a ten-feet strip from the archway to the lake, lined on both sides by a border of mossy stones, many of which were missing or askew. Once it had been a concrete slipway for a boat, but it was virtually gone. Nature had spent years reclaiming it. Underground life, pushing for the surface, had ruined it. Trees crowding its sides had expanded the reach of their branches to smother it. It made Bennet think of a healing wound.

But something had happened here.

Bennet walked around the section of wall and entered the

woods. Ahead of him was the boathouse. If the stone building had once stood in a clearing, that was gone. The boathouse was headed the same way. It had only three walls, so one side was open to the elements, and he could see all he needed to without getting close. All that remained of the roof were a few joists. Nature had claimed the floor. There was litter all over the ground, but the cans and crisp packets and bottle labels were all faded with age. Although it looked as if people had been here, there was nothing that looked as recent as Monday night. He doubted the film crew had stayed here and nothing suggested they'd been here to shoot a film scene.

But something had happened here.

He moved left, emerging onto the old slipway. Now, closer, Bennet could see definite damage. Branches to the side and above the slipway had been snapped and shorn. Some hung loose. There was a carpet of busted wood on the ground, where only smaller plants had been left untouched, everything else having been uprooted; but the remaining flora was bent towards the lake, as if straining to reach the water. Locals might have blamed the rampaging Stanton Beast, and Anders might have blamed supermarket engineers working on the sly. But one had no evidence and one was stupid. Liam knew what he was looking at.

But he needed to confirm it, so he walked back to the wall, and around, and approached the wire-mesh archway. Again, proximity equalled enlightenment. He could see a groove in the interior lining of the brick arch where the edge of the chain-link fencing had been slotted. But not with care, for in places it had slipped its housing. The people who engineered this barrier hadn't done that; clearly the mesh portion had come free at some point and been sloppily reinserted.

He gave a push. The fencing yanked free easily and fell away. Bennet stepped into the arch and looked up. Double his height, at least. Ten feet wide. Big enough to fit the CaraHome. The damage to the tree branches and undergrowth looked like the work of a vehicle of similar dimensions.

If the film crew had entered the woods in their vehicle, why? There was no room to turn on the slipway, no path off it they could have taken. The CaraHome would have suffered scratches from the broken branches, and it would have had to reverse out again. It made no sense.

Unless they had been hiding...

He walked down the overgrown slipway, stepping in clear spaces where he could, and brushing aside long, thin branches that had flexed with the passage of a vehicle and sprung back into place in its wake. Now out of the woods, he could see the whole lake stretching away to his left. It was still. The treeline held a position a couple of metres from the water's edge, creating a clear border around the lake. But it was not wide enough to permit a vehicle and the rocky earth would have posed a problem even for a bicycle. His eyes returned to the water. It was clear on top but faded to black just a few feet down, as if a film of water lay upon a mass of oil. But in that silver skim he saw another colour, specific to a point directly before him, and as his eyes soaked in the details it took a shape. Oblong, perhaps seven feet by ten.

Bennet took a step into the water, sinking his foot a few inches, leaning forward, staring at what appeared to be a submerged white floor, and his heart started to thump. But upon his next step, to lean ever closer and confirm a growing suspicion, solid ground evaporated. As if he'd stepped off a ledge, his entire foot sank and he pitched forward.

He felt his torso strike the cold water, but stop dead as if it was a sheet of ice. But it was his hands and knees that had broken his fall. This close, his eyes an inch above the water, he saw the white floor all around him, but directly beneath his hands was a square black abyss. He raised a hand and slammed it down, and felt the impact of his flesh against an invisible barrier across the black hole. But he was confused no more.

Glass. A black window in a white floor that was no such thing. Right then he knew he knelt upon the flat back end of the CaraHome, nose down in the lake.

PART II

38

———

'Did you find Mum?'

Bennet had to wipe an eye and it took a few seconds before he responded to his son. Thankfully, the boy couldn't see down the phone.

'No,' Bennet said. He thumped a fist into his own leg. 'Look, I need to go. I'll call you soon.'

He hung up and turned. The uniformed police constable held his hand out for the phone. Bennet shook his head. 'I'll be keeping this.'

The constable hadn't expected that. 'I was supposed to take your phone back after the call.'

'Go tell your superior I refused to hand it over. It's my phone and it's staying with me. And the statement's done.' He pointed at two sheets of paper on the bed. 'And I haven't had any breakfast yet. And find out if Superintendent Hunter is here yet.'

The constable didn't press it about the phone. Different police services or not, Bennet was still a DCI. The uniform took the sheets and left.

Bennet approached the window of the hotel room. Outside, police cars seemed to fill the grass car park, and beyond the closed gates were more vehicles. Not police though. These belonged to people with cameras and microphones, all eager to talk to someone in the Arrow Hotel. One of the reporters saw Bennet at the upper window and aimed a camera. Bennet shut the curtains.

There was all sorts of noise from outside the room. But not from traditional guests: the eight present had been kicked out to accommodate the abrupt influx of Derbyshire's finest. The Arrow Hotel had been commandeered as a police command centre/incident room, a welcome change to a tiny room in a police station or a truck rolling around the village.

And because it was close to a major crime scene.

Bennet lay on the bed, stared at the ceiling, and waited. He'd been here for about three hours. Earlier, he'd been debriefed, here in this nice room with a cup of tea. Just one copper unloading info to help another. They'd given him his phone back and some of the hotel manager's old clothing to replace his sodden gear. And they'd politely asked him to remain on-site in case they had more questions.

But Bennet knew the game and he wasn't fooled. His chat with the other detective hadn't been recorded, there had been no mention of a solicitor, but Bennet knew the 'debrief' had actually been the first of many interviews. He had his phone, but they'd taken it away for the first hour to scrutinise recent activity. His wet clothing was going for analysis. The door wasn't locked, but a uniformed officer was stationed outside. His chief inspector status got him the sweet treatment, but he knew they hadn't yet ruled him out. They were fifty–fifty on whether he was a witness or a suspect.

Such was the honour of those who discovered dead bodies.

The officer came back a few minutes later. Bennet didn't even look away from the ceiling. 'Superintendent Hunter arrived a few minutes ago. He will see you soon.'

Bennet said nothing, but he rose and headed for the door. The officer looked concerned.

'No, you shouldn't leave yet, sir. I'll come get you when it's time. You should stay here.'

Bennet had spoken to four different policemen and each one had used *shouldn't* instead of *can't*, but Bennet didn't see the difference. However, the officer knew he couldn't manhandle his charge, and Bennet stepped out of the room.

He was followed down the stairs, to the foyer. Immediately, he saw two suited men amongst the casually-dressed detectives and police officers. Seeing him, they approached. One was a middle-aged man, quite bland, with a bald head. The other was the dapper Superintendent Hunter. Hunter got there first and stepped into a quiet corner with Liam.

'I was coming to see you,' Hunter said. 'Liam, are you okay?'

'I seem to be being treated more like a suspect than a witness, sir. Did you read my statement?'

'Yes. And I've spoken to people at the scene. There are inconsistencies, Liam.'

'They think I lied?'

Hunter looked disappointed. 'What's going on? What happened out there? I mean, what *really* happened out there?'

Inconsistencies. Bennet's thoughts turned to Joe, and the lie he'd told to his own flesh and blood.

39

This statement (consisting of ...2...pages each signed by me) is true to the best of my knowledge and belief and I make it knowing that if it is tendered in evidence, I shall be liable to prosecution if I have wilfully stated in it anything which I know to be false or do not believe to be true.

I am a police officer of the South Yorkshire Police...

(page 2)

...I entered the woods. At the end of an old slipway, I looked into the lake and saw something two or three feet beneath the surface that looked white. I waded in, but the land slipped away after just a few feet and I fell forward. I landed on the object below the surface, which I realised was the flat back end of a vehicle with a window in it. My assessment was that the vehicle was a Weinsberg CaraHome belonging to Overeem. The vehicle had gone into the water, dropped over the submerged edge, and sunk nose down.

I ducked under the water for a closer look, using my phone torch. I could see a human body pressed up against the back window. I also saw three more bodies, sitting in the front seats with their seat belts in place. At this point my weight broke the back window and the body against the glass floated out and up to the surface of the water. Because she was face up, I visually identified the body as that of Lorraine Cross, my son's mother. She floated to the shore and lodged there. I got out of the water and called the police...

175

40

Bennet and Hunter stood on the veranda, staring out at Lake Stanton. At the activity taking place at the crime scene. The treetops obscured the slipway and the service road, but amongst the green Liam could make out the white of vehicles and the shimmer of police officers moving around. By the shore, divers entered and exited the water. Heavy machinery was en route to remove the CaraHome. It pained him that he was here, not there.

The bodies, according to Hunter, had been retrieved and were already at the mortuary for urgent post-mortems. The CaraHome would be out before nightfall. The scene had been cordoned off by simply blocking both ends of the service road and the entrance to Anders' garden centre, but in such a wide open area it was impossible to prevent prying eyes. Bennet could see people in ones and twos and larger groups scattered around the far shore of Lake Stanton, and even some creeping closer on the off-limits side. Lampton locals eager to learn news, and journalists eager to sell it. Lorraine lay dead, and these bastards were loving the break in backwoods monotony. He wished he had a sniper rifle.

'Why did they take over this hotel?' Bennet asked.

'Closer to the crime scene,' Hunter replied. 'I think one of the locals arranged it.'

Bennet had suspected as much. And he had a bad feeling he knew who. 'That someone called Councillor Richard Turner, by any chance?'

'I think I heard that name. Who is he?'

And there it was. Lampton locals didn't want a police invasion of their little enclave and Turner had worked his magic, just like he had way back when Lampton hit the headlines because of a missing girl. Maybe he'd heard the news from a fox-hunting detective buddy, and had called his Freemason friend the chief constable. But he'd failed to stop word spreading, given the bastards amassed at the gate like a hungry zombie army.

'Has anyone contacted Lorraine's husband yet?'

Hunter was staring down at the Arrow Climb. 'For ID? Her driver's licence was found in her purse. We did it by photo. He confirmed.'

'How did he take it?'

It might have been a silly question to some, but not veteran detectives. In their time, both men had seen every imaginable reaction to news of a dead loved one. Hunter had often told a tale from his detective days when he was dumped with a death knock. Informed of her husband's death in a traffic accident, a wife had excused herself and ran to the bathroom, but it wasn't vomiting or distressed shrieking he'd heard. And when done laughing, she'd asked Hunter out for dinner.

'Numb,' Hunter said. 'Are you going to go see him?'

Bennet shrugged. He really didn't know. At the minute it seemed wrong to. And wrong not to. 'Am I going to be arrested?'

It was the second time Bennet had asked the question. After the first, Hunter had brought him out here, for privacy. But he hadn't answered it.

Now, he avoided it again. 'Clear some things up for me, Liam. Then we'll get you out of here. The SIO on this case, a superintendent called Sutton, told me about some inconsistencies between your story and what they've found so far. Are you ready to tell me the truth?'

'What inconsistencies?'

'You said the window in the back of the motorhome broke and Lorraine's body floated out. DCS Sutton thinks you made sure to mention that you got fully submerged, to explain your wet clothing. He thinks that although the window was big enough to get a body through, it's doubtful Lorraine's would have floated out. Primarily because the bodies haven't been dead long enough to enter the bloat stage. None of them would float yet. Next, he doubts your ability to have seen other bodies. The divers indeed found three more, seat-belted in place in the cabin. The motorhome is nineteen feet long. The divers said that even with their lights, the water was so murky visibility was only about ten feet. They were halfway into the vehicle before they saw the three other bodies. Not possible from the vicinity of the back window.'

'So what does he think happened?'

Hunter grunted in frustration. He held up the two pages of Bennet's official first statement. 'Liam, old friend to old friend, is this bullshit? Did you go inside that motorhome?'

'That's a preposterous suggestion, sir. Of course I didn't.'

41

———

Superintendent Hunter arranged for him to be allowed to leave the Arrow Hotel. Bennet's Pathfinder was in the car park, but DCS Sutton had wanted Bennet to be driven home because he was under strain and in no condition to drive – or so he'd said. But when Bennet refused an escort, the truth emerged: given Bennet's relationship to one of the dead, Sutton didn't trust him to stay away from the investigation. Only upon a promise to Hunter had Sutton relented.

Bennet was required to go 'straight home and stay there', compassionate leave beginning immediately. Eager to get out of the hotel ASAP, Bennet promised to obey this order. And he would. But he intended to be a little fuzzy on the definition of *straight home*.

He entered Lampton via the north end and immediately noted that the village had changed. Police officers were everywhere, and the few locals he saw on the main road looked like shell-shocked war survivors. Four dead bodies as opposed to one missing girl this time: the village might not survive its new infamy.

Doubtless there would be a village-wide canvass for

information now that four bodies had been found. As he turned down a side street deeper in, he found evidence of this. From his elevated angle he saw a number of police cars and their officers knocking on doors.

He drove past. At one house, a female officer was talking to a woman on her doorstep, and the homeowner was crying. A little further on, a suspicious constable stepped into the road to block him. Bennet showed his warrant card and was waved on. The officer didn't seem to recognise him as the man who'd found the bodies and who was supposed to be on the motorway by now.

He turned off the street, onto another, and parked outside a semi-detached house with a pond in the garden and a stack of cuddly teddies in the living-room window. A single police car here, but no officers in sight. They would be in another house, asking the resident if he or she knew of a raving lunatic in town. Bennet wanted this task done and dusted before he was spotted by a fellow blue.

The gateposts were house-brick towers with stone lions the size of cats atop. One, at least. The other was a jagged shard where the lion was missing.

The door opened. A craggy old lady appeared on a tiny three-wheeled mobility scooter. She had curly grey hair with red tips, as if long-ago dyed, and eyes sunken and cloudy. Combined with a droop to one side of her face, as if from a stroke, she looked little better than a zombie. He'd never met her before, but had heard from Lorraine that the lady had been a professional diver who'd nearly gotten a medal at the '56 Summer Olympics.

'Lorraine Taylor,' he called to the old lady. 'She was once a resident here. You never met her. But she's very sorry. She was coming home a bit drunk one night and fell into your stone lion, and broke it. She was always very sorry about it. She just never got the courage to come here and apologise.'

His words didn't seem to register. She just stared.

'She was a very nice person. I think I loved her. I might still do. It's all very weird for me at the moment. She's dead now.'

Knowing the lady wouldn't really understand had made it easier to say those words aloud. But voicing them made it more real for Bennet. He *had* loved Lorraine, he realised. Because she had given him Joe, he still did. He had not once been in her company in the last decade, having followed her life via digital words and pictures, but he would miss her immensely.

'I want to kill the person who killed her,' he told the old lady. Thankfully, those words didn't seem to register, either.

42

———

Partway down the hill into the main road into the Well at Lampton's centre was a terrace of convenience stores converted from houses, including Hughes' News. Hughes and his wife had run the little newsagent's since 29th July 1981, the day Prince Charles married Lady Diana. The last Bennet knew, ten years ago, the old pair had been saving for relocation to the Isle of Man, where they had family. When he saw a young woman behind the counter, he knew they'd achieved that dream. She put down her newspaper and stood with a smile.

'Janine, isn't it?'

She lost the smile. 'I'm not supposed to talk to reporters. Are you one?'

'No. So, is it Janine?'

She seemed to take a moment, looking him up and down, before speaking again. Clearly, she'd decided he didn't look like a reporter. 'How do you know my name? I don't recognise you.'

'You're the Hughes' daughter, right? You lived on the Isle of Man.'

She nodded. 'My parents emigrated over there, about two months ago now. They gave me the shop to run. I'd just got divorced, so I thought, why not have a change of scenery? But I thought I'd met everyone who lives here. They like to introduce themselves. I don't remember you.'

'We never met. I left Lampton ten years ago. I lived with a local girl called Lorraine Taylor. She used to come in on Thursday mornings to collect the *Buxton Advertiser* for her dad. She taught your mother a knee-strengthening routine.'

'Oh, wow, yes, Mother told me about some knee exercises. She said they worked so well she could get up the stairs without the handrail. I don't think she mentioned anyone called Lorraine, though. I'm sorry. So, that's why you're here? To visit? You picked a strange old day. Have you heard what's happened up at Lake Stanton?'

'I sure did. I bet the rumours are flying already.'

'No one knows anything yet. The police are interviewing everyone. God, what a thing. And then we had that missing little girl that other time. People won't like that being brought up after so long.'

'Out of respect to the mother, right?'

'Yes. Best if she is just allowed to move on, in her own time. Poor woman. Every time I see her in here, I just want to hug her and ask if she's all right.'

'But it would open old wounds, break her healing process, right?'

'Yes. Poor woman. I don't mention it.'

So it wasn't just visitors who got sold a line. Even residents who hadn't been part of the world back then had been brainwashed by Turner's bullshit about respect and compassion and doing the right thing. 'Are people talking to the police?'

'Sure, why wouldn't they? Look.' She picked up a leaflet from the counter. It announced a meeting tomorrow at 9.30am at the village hall, which everyone was invited to and expected to attend.

'The police say they'll give us updates then. God, this is so shocking. Too much for such a little place. To think we might have a killer in the village.'

'Yes, it is. And Councillor Turner hasn't tried to veto the meeting yet? Or called his own?'

'Richard? Oh, he's meeting some high-ranking police today, I heard. He rushed off to do it. He's going to try to get the journalists kicked out. He's warned us they'll be all over the town once they've finished taking photos up at the lake. There's a few hanging round. I thought you were one.'

Liam put a pound coin on the counter. 'About Lorraine. Your dad undercharged her one time, years ago. A bag of Maltesers missed off the bill. I'd like to pay it. Lorraine always wanted to pay it, but never got round to it.'

Janine looked puzzled, then amused. 'You mean ten years ago?' She laughed and pushed the coin away, but he shifted it right back towards her.

'She felt bad about it. Please take it. You're going to hear her name a lot over the coming days. I just don't want people to... please just take it.'

He left her looking a little shocked. Missing young girl, quadruple murder, and now shoplifting. Welcome to Lampton.

43

———

All the village centre shops had shut early and few people were around. Of that scattering, most were police, but Bennet also saw journalists and tourists. Locals were by far the minority. The police had parked a large white van near the green, with a stall next to it, and this was where most of the activity took place. The stall had a police officer behind it and it was loaded with personal panic alarms, which a sign claimed were free to all residents. Two teenaged females were being shown how the alarms worked, while other folk queued or talked to other officers or the reporters.

If the free alarms didn't make it obvious the police were worried that a madman was still about, nobody could fail to get that message from a display stand near the van:

HELP US HELP YOU. LOOK AT YOUR FRIENDS, AT YOUR NEIGHBOURS. DO YOU KNOW OF ANYONE WHO HAS BEEN UNCOMMONLY ABSENT RECENTLY, OR ACTING STRANGE? HAVE YOU SEEN ANYONE WITH BLOOD ON THEIR CLOTHING? REPORT ANYTHING SUSPICIOUS IN CONFIDENCE TO THE POLICE.

Bravo. No pussyfooting around this time. A young girl had

gone missing, and ten years later a film crew documenting the crime had been murdered. Only a fool would connect both events by coincidence, or believe that the same criminal had snatched a girl, left town, and then returned to murder a team that might expose him. Bennet had overheard detectives at the Arrow saying the very same thing he thought, and which that sign effectively announced: Lampton was home to a vicious killer. A decade ago, mass-autohypnosis had convinced these folk their little enclave was safe and secure despite a child-snatching. No magic trick would bury the truth this time. Councillor Turner was going to have his work cut out sweeping this one under the carpet.

Bennet found a space amongst the police and media vehicles to park. Nobody saw him exit and run down an alley beside the library.

The first time he'd visited Lampton, on his third date with Lorraine, she had shown him the village centre and led him round the back of the library, where there was a small garden and the town's only actual well. The well hadn't been active in years and now was nothing but a circular rock wall with a rusty grate. But it provided a handy step for Bennet to climb into one of the two winter-naked small ash trees. A curved bough created a handy seat and there, hidden by thick green leaves, Lorraine had sat on his lap, and they'd done the sweet nothings thing new couples practised.

But there was one thing couples did that they hadn't: carved their names, at least in entirety. Lorraine had scoured hers into the wood, above a heart, but the old proprietor of the library, on a cigarette break, had ordered them down and out before Liam could immortalise his own name. They had planned to return and finish the job another day, but it never happened.

Now, over three thousand days later, Bennet stared at a blank space beneath that heart shape, and prepared to slice his name into the bark with his car key. But he couldn't do it. En route here, the idea had appealed as a reminder of their history, of their creation of Joe, and a way to honour Lorraine's death. But now, sitting here, it seemed silly. She was dead, and they hadn't been a couple for a decade, and she had had a new family, and what kind of grown man did that anyway?

He moved on. A path out of the garden snaked its way to the village hall, which had been built as a free church school a century and a half ago. There was a small graveyard behind it. Here he found the mossy, cracked grave of a man called Dunn, part of the Durham Light Infantry in the Great War. Lampton had ceased burying people here decades ago, but the families of those already in the ground had objected to the removal of any remains. They got their wish; however, as the village transformed around the boneyard and the surviving kin left or died, the dead were abandoned.

The gravestone he sought was down on the ground, flat, hidden from a distance by unloved, long grass. Liam was annoyed that nobody had picked it up in the fifteen or so years since it had fallen. Now, he dug his fingers beneath and pulled and pushed and lifted it. He got it upright in the rent it had opened when toppling, and stamped grassy soil down to lodge it in place. A stiff breeze might undo his work, but intent and action were what mattered to him.

'Lorraine is deeply sorry, Mr Dunn,' he told the air.

As a teenager larking about, Lorraine and a friend had stumbled into the gravestone and sent it crashing to the earth. When she'd shared the story with Bennet, he had suggested they right her wrong, but their promise to never materialised. Now, with the task completed, he felt a sense of finality.

The people of Lampton had mostly forgotten him, but he didn't want that for Lorraine, who'd been born and bred in this corner of the planet, and then hounded out of it, and then slaughtered by one or more of its citizens. And because she'd been part of that reviled film crew, no one would care. He knew he couldn't make the village folk honour her death, but he could make sure she got, if not respect, then zero *disrespect*. Amends had been made to all those Lorraine had slighted in her time here. It wasn't much, but he hoped it was enough.

And it was done, so now he was done with this damn hellhole.

Actually, no. There was one more job to do.

44

─────

No answer at Turner's front door, so Bennet looked around the back, as any copper would. In the dusk, he saw light emanating from the former stable across the field. He started across the cold-hardened mud.

Without knocking, Bennet put his face to the glass in one of the stable doors. Just like Turner had said, the building was now a workspace, with carpet and wallpaper, but the stalls remained. Above the first was a sign that said REEVE – former home of the filly Sally Jenkins liked to ride. It was now an office.

But Turner was sitting at a desk in the other stall, formerly for B'fly, the Clydesdale Sally had dreamed of riding, and what Bennet saw there made him forget all about knocking. Turner's back was to Bennet, so he turned the door handle quietly. The door was well oiled and opened without a sound. As he cautiously stepped inside, he heard the councillor speak.

'Lana, stop right there.'

Bennet stepped closer. Turner's desk was before a laptop and a curving bank of monitors, five columns of three, each with two camera feeds minimum, some with as many as eight. Atop the bank was a larger screen displaying the view from CAMERA 85.

189

Bennet had seen streets he recognised, and the exterior of the Panorama, and the interior of Jenny's sandwich shop, and so much more. The sirens scattered about the village weren't just for audio: they had hidden cameras.

Camera 85 showed a typical street and a woman on the pavement with her dog, both staring up at the lens. The dog wore a coat and she wore a woollen hat. Turner spoke into a microphone by his laptop.

'You left a stain, Lana. Get it up.'

As Bennet watched over Turner's shoulder, the woman called Lana turned away and squatted on the pavement before a brown stain. In one hand she held a small plastic bag that she put down. Dog poo. She pulled disposable tissues from a pocket.

'No, Lana,' Turner said. 'Use your hat.'

She obeyed without question. Bennet watched the middle-aged woman yank off the hat, spit on it, and scrub at a dog-poo stain on the concrete. He couldn't believe what he was seeing. This was worse than just spying on people.

Bennet took another step closer, but his foot creaked on a floorboard. He froze, but Turner hadn't heard. Below him was a barely visible trapdoor. Another step put him two feet behind the councillor.

'Hitler had a secret bunker too. He would have loved this bit of kit at the Wolf's Lair.'

Turner almost jumped out of his seat at Bennet's voice. 'Bennet. How dare you just walk in here?' he snapped as he hit a kill switch somewhere and the screens went black.

'Now I know why certain people don't want their CCTV fixed. You really do run this place, don't you? Like your own little toy.'

Turner's shock became outrage. His fists clenched as he stood. 'You shouldn't be here, Bennet. You were told to stay away. Get off my property and out of my village.'

So, Turner knew that DCS Sutton had ordered Bennet to go nowhere near the village during the investigation.

'I'm going, Turner, right after I leave here. But I had to come. As you well know, my son's mother was one of the four found dead in that lake. Tell your people whatever fantasy you want, blame aliens, blame the Illuminati, whatever. But you need to treat these victims with respect. Lorraine Cross once lived here. Don't pretend she didn't mean anything to the people who knew her.'

Turner gave him a long look, as if unsure there wasn't a trick afoot. And he relaxed. 'Okay. Whatever. Is that it? You can go now.'

'No, one more thing,' Bennet said as he turned to leave. 'Let Sally Jenkins' mother plant a goddamn tree for her daughter.'

45

On the way home, Bennet made a call to Hooper for an update on the Buttery Park stabbing. It had only been a couple of days, but it felt as if he'd been away from that investigation for weeks. Hooper at first was reluctant to talk. DCS Hunter had taken over the investigation and warned the team that they weren't to contact Bennet while he was on leave. Bennet had to remind Hooper that he was still the man's boss and the investigation was hardly eyes-only, top-secret. And when that didn't work, he had to promise he'd not say a word to Hunter. After the call, Bennet sent a mass text to the main members of his team to explain that he was still available at the end of a phone if they needed advice.

From Hooper he learned of only one new development: the Turtons, parents of the murdered boy, Mick, had called the station to complain. Some thugs had been causing trouble: revving their car outside the parents' house way past midnight, posting trash through the letterbox, and egging the windows. The Turtons wondered if it was to do with their son's murder, as if they had done something wrong by seeking justice. They wanted to know if there were any suspects yet.

Bennet knew no one had told the parents that the police had indeed found a suspect, and arrested him, and then released him due to lack of evidence. He had no doubt Don The Man and his teenaged crew of thugs were behind the harassment of the Turtons, and it upset him deeply. Those vicious idiots had killed the couple's son and were now causing them strife, and the police would do nothing about it because Don The Man was officially still innocent and egged windows weren't a priority.

Bennet arrived home in time to take Joe swimming, but made an excuse why they couldn't go. Instead, he told Joe he could have the new UFC game, and son and father could play it all evening. He could barely meet his son's eyes, knowing the secret he held from the boy. The quadruple murder in Lampton was already a big story across the internet, but the media had scant details thus far and Bennet hadn't found Lorraine's name mentioned. Or his own. The major news outlets would save it for their scheduled programmes and publications later today and tomorrow morning. At the moment Bennet had time to work out the best way to tell Joe about his mother's murder. But he would have to keep the boy in a bubble until then.

While the purchase downloaded, Joe did his homework in his room and Bennet went downstairs to try to get the hang of Backup Buddy, a mental health support app for South Yorkshire Police. Hunter had certainly been busy, having already allocated Bennet a meeting tomorrow afternoon with a member of TriM – the Trauma Risk Management team. The lady had emailed him half an hour ago to say he should download the app. It had advice on coping strategies, stories from other officers who'd gotten through heartache, and numbers and emails of people who could help. He tried an audio segment on meditation, but it only increased his urgency to do… something else. He closed the app and called the number the TriM representative had put on the email. It went to voicemail.

What if I was right now about to jump off a bridge? he almost yelled at the phone, before he was urged to leave his message. 'Joan? DCI Liam Bennet. I'm supposed to meet you tomorrow. I just wanted to know if I could pay you privately to talk to my son. He needs this more than I do. Call me back as soon as you get this.'

Next, he called DCS Hunter. Again he got voicemail and left a message: 'Boss, I can't sit around, I'll just dwell on things. Take me off compassionate leave. Make it adjusted duty and I'll work from home.'

His next call was to Liz Miller.

The detective was still in Spain, still hanging around waiting for her target to do something juicy so he could be arrested. Bennet didn't even allow her to speak before he launched into a synopsis of his day and finished with his current setting: waiting for the optimum moment to deliver crushing news to his son.

'Sooner the better,' she said. 'Before he hears it on Facebook.'

Bennet had worried his kid might come across a news banner ad embedded in a website. He hadn't considered social media. 'I'll make an excuse to get his phone away from him.'

'Good luck with it. I hope he's okay.'

'He will be,' Bennet said, with no clue if he was going to be right.

'And what about you? Is adjusted duty the right thing? Perhaps you should take the compassionate leave. Maybe go on holiday.'

Hunter had suggested the same thing, because Lorraine's murder was going to be in the air for a while. 'I'll be okay. I mean I *am* okay. I don't need leave. They don't understand. I'm not traumatised. I'm not burned out.'

'You might be and not know it. Take the advice and stay away. Don't even take phone calls about your cases.'

It sounded like she was saying he was in denial. 'It isn't about me. Lorraine was long gone from my life.'

'Are you sure?'

No, he wasn't. 'This is about Joe. He's just lost his mum, and he can't remember her because he was too young. And now he'll never meet her. Hell, he doesn't even know yet. He's up there in his room, oblivious to the fact that his world has just been crushed. And I'm sitting here with that knowledge.'

'You're angry.'

'The anger is because I caused this. I knew where Joe's mother lived, and did nothing to reunite the two of them. If I'd gone after Lorraine earlier, years ago, when I should have, this would have been avoided. Or, if not, then at least Joe would have met her.'

'You couldn't know. It was the right thing to do at the time.'

'And I'm pissed off that I held back. I know it wasn't police business, but I could have pretended it was and got answers sooner, and this could have been avoided.'

'But there was no investigation, she wasn't reported missing, so the police couldn't have done anything.'

'Then that's part of the problem too. Rules. I'm getting sick of having my hands tied. So sick that I... I did something bad.'

'What?'

'She was my son's mother, and I couldn't... waiting for people... forms to fill in... permission... I hate it all and I couldn't...'

'Liam, I don't understand. Are you saying you broke a rule?'

'I've changed. I was the straight-laced man, known for it. But that's not me anymore. Maybe it never was. Remember Pond Street?'

'Liam, this doesn't make sense. "Never was?" Did you do something wrong? If you did something wrong, it's understandable. You'd just found Joe's mother dead and–'

'No. No. Pond Street. I took a suspect to a crime scene, remember? No solicitor, no recorded interview. That was wrong. There was no dead mother of my son back then.'

'Liam, stop. You're doubting yourself and you shouldn't. You're a good man, a fine police officer. But with all this, I think you need help.'

He didn't agree, but it would do no good to make Liz worry about him. 'You're right. I'm attending an appointment tomorrow, and hopefully that will... let's say cheer me up. Get me straight. Look, I need to go see Joe. I'll call you tomorrow maybe.'

He didn't need help at all. And he wasn't really concerned about getting in trouble for police misconduct. He was worried about the kind of man he'd become. Even now, knowing he had heartbreaking news to give Joe, he couldn't shake the anger he felt towards himself. He had failed Lorraine and Joe, and he had failed the Turtons. Trying to be a good man had allowed two killers to remain free.

46

As Bennet and Joe were playing Xbox, a call came through from a lady who introduced herself as a detective constable and immediately launched into a volley of facts. She got two sentences out before Bennet, surprised, realised what was going on.

The last thing he'd asked of his boss, back on the veranda at the Arrow Hotel, was to be kept abreast of the quadruple murder investigation. DCS Hunter had said he'd see what he could do, and what he could do had been to sway DCS Sutton into allocating a woman to play envoy. Bennet had expected a call from Hunter, not someone attached to the murder investigation. He paused the Xbox game so he could slip out of the room to talk. Not that he got to talk: Envoy Lady gave a lecture, asked no questions of him, and hung up rather abruptly when her task was done.

Bennet had informed the police of Councillor Turner's extensive CCTV coverage of Lampton and they'd visited his stables with watering mouths. There the good news ended. Turner's many cameras covered most of the village, but they didn't automatically save what they saw. A control box's trigger had to be depressed to record. Turner's reason for such a set-up: privacy. He would watch his people, but only record activity he found suspicious. So, nine tenths of the cameras in Lampton were useless and the police couldn't track the CaraHome or the film crew. What few private CCTV cameras the residents operated was still being collected, but nobody was holding their breath. If Bennet thought Turner wouldn't be able to piss him off any further...

The last known place of visit for the film crew, Crabtree's ranch, had been searched, but nothing of worth had been unearthed. A more specialised team would be returning soon for a detailed sift through the building, especially the annex where items had been burned, for bloodstains, DNA and the like – the place had been scrubbed clean and dedicated mega tidying affairs always raised tec eyebrows. Another team was working its way along the supposed route the CaraHome took from the ranch to its final resting place at Lake Stanton.

An investigator's first port of call and best chance of finding a killer: the victim's background. So far, police had found nothing suspicious about any of the four dead except for John Crickmer, the cameraman. He had a four-year-old conviction for drugs, so that was something to explore. People got their drugs somewhere, and drug dealers could be or could know vicious bastards.

So, Bennet found himself wondering about Lorraine. He'd been asked by the Derby boys if he knew of anyone who would want to hurt her. He'd said no, which was the truth, but he didn't know much about her life over the last decade. He'd learned his information from social media, and she was hardly going to post about her criminal activities or those of friends. He prayed that, if the killer was connected to one of his kills, it wasn't on her side. Her murder would be easier to digest if she was someone simply in the wrong place at the wrong time, like so many thousands of others. Better for Joe if she wasn't blamed in the media.

The CaraHome had been retrieved from Lake Stanton, and a search of it had provided a possible motive: robbery. No mobile phones or expensive movie-making equipment had been found. Right now the CaraHome was in a vehicle lab for a more detailed examination.

And on to a new shocking twist. From the veranda at the Arrow Hotel, Bennet had witnessed people sneaking close to the crime scene for a nosey. There had been some more creative attempts since: folk had tried to get inside the cordon by moving through treetops like Tarzan, swimming across the lake, and even flying drones. Someone with a long lens had managed to capture video of the moment divers retrieved something from the water. It was a trunk that had been squashed into the lakebed, and thus hidden, by the nose of the CaraHome.

Inside, a human body. A small one. Word quickly spread: little Sally Jenkins, missing now a decade, had been found.

47

Following the discovery of Sally Jenkins' body, things exploded. The crime scene virtually came under siege by reporters and extra police had to be pulled in to keep them at bay. Curiously, though, the locals had backed off, as if ashamed. They should be, Bennet figured. They had pulled the wool over their own eyes for ten years.

The story raced across the country far faster than that of four bodies found in a motorhome. Bennet was more interested in Lampton's response to it. On YouTube, he found various short videos posted by users with untraceable names. He figured some of these people might be locals independent of Lampton's hive-mind denial. Drone footage. Mobile phone footage. Even reaction videos, some whose creators' voices and faces were obscured – could the latter be locals wary of Turner's wrath for speaking out?

One video caught his eye because of the title: *Moment Dead Girl's Mother Hears The News.*

It did what it said on the tin. A reporter was outside Anika Jenkins' house on Grodes Place in Lampton. His cameraman stood back as the reporter banged the door. When Anika answered, it was with a pair of headphones in her hand. It seemed she must have been busy indoors and missed the furore. Shock as a microphone was thrust at her.

'Have you heard about the body found in the lake? Did you know it was your daughter? Have you tried to get to the scene to view her body?'

What a moron. Anika reeled back, as if punched, and grabbed keys from the hallway wall, and fled out the door, knocking the reporter out of her way. As the cameraman turned to follow, the street was exposed. Many people, neighbours and friends, standing on the road or their doorsteps, and more reporters. Another turned up and his car almost hit Anika as she stumbled to hers; instantly he was out, microphone first, machine-gunning questions.

Anika ignored him, but not the growing crowd. To those living on the street, she yelled, 'You all knew already, my God, and you stand there watching? You bastards.'

As she got in her car and it screamed away, and reporters turned their own vehicles to follow, Bennet shut down the website. He couldn't watch any more. Not because of Anika's distress, but due to the slimy reporters. He hoped the bastards rotted.

Other slimeballs had focused their attention elsewhere. After his daughter's disappearance, Sally's errant father had been unable to cope with the scrutiny and had fled to Stuttgart, Germany, where his brother owned three restaurants. Now, Alan managed one of the establishments and had remarried and done a fine job of forgetting the past, but it had reared its ugly head. In no time at all, the story had travelled overseas, been picked up by the media, and a journalist had tracked him down.

Bennet found an audio file of her attempt to engage Alan in interview. She had called his restaurant, claimed to have a complaint for the manager, and when he got on the line she said, 'Have you seen the news from your home city? Your daughter's body has been found.'

'What? Who are you?'

'You were investigated by the police about her disappearance, weren't you?'

'Are you talking about Sally? Sally's been found? Look, who the hell are you?'

'Why did you leave the country if you had nothing to do with it?'

Here Alan hung up, as might anyone who desperately needed to verify a piece of information. The reporter announced that she'd give him time to read the news and would call him back. She did that an hour later. She'd recorded their second conversation, again over the phone.

'You again. Listen, I had nothing to do with my daughter's disappearance. The police wouldn't have let me leave the country if they suspected me. Your information is bullshit. I left the country to get away from soulless bastards like you, hassling me every day. Now, please, piss off.'

The reporter didn't piss off. 'Are you going to return to England to help the police? To go to the funeral? Will you meet the mother and–'

'No, okay? No. If Sally was alive, sure I'd go back. But she's not, and so what's the point? Just to face idiots like you and go through all that again? If they catch the killer, I'll go to his damn trial. Don't call me again.'

Alan hung up. The same story reported that Alan had been living in Germany all these years and nobody knew about a daughter, never mind that she'd gone missing a decade ago. Shades of Lorraine there. There was more: the reporter had then visited his restaurant for another confrontation, and this time there was video. But Bennet had seen and heard enough already.

Lorraine's husband knew of her death, and doubtless the family and friends of Francis Overeem, Betty Crute and John Crickmer had received a death knock. And now, all these years later, Sally Jenkins' mother and father knew the truth. Joe was the only one still in the dark, still living in a painless dreamworld, and it was wholly down to his selfish, stupid dad. He punched his own thigh.

When Bennet went back into the bedroom, Joe immediately unpaused the fighting game and, laughing, started pummelling his dad's character. Bennet turned the Xbox off at the plug.

'Come on, Dad, it was just a joke.'

He sat by his son. 'I have to talk to you, Joe.'

Joe looked a little shocked and scared, which gave Bennet the impression he'd done something bad at school and thought his dad had just learned of it.

He would have gladly swapped a telling off for what he was about to do.

48

―――

The murk makes it hard to see even his outstretched hand in front of him, but he pushes onward through the cold water fast, against a clock that will kill him if it wins. His fingers catch something hard, protruding, and in the next moment he is close enough to see it is a shiny silver tap in a sink.

Onwards. Paper and various other buoyant debris waft past him, ahead of him, all around, into the beam of his torch and then gone as he moves past, downward. Three shapes loom ahead, framed neatly in the oblong of the windscreen, somewhat like rounded triangles in a line. His hands latch on to the back of a seat, and he pulls himself closer. He knows the shapes are the upper bodies of people sitting in the cabin seats, trapped by their seat belts. He sees the backs of their heads in his light, as if they're staring at the lakebed just feet beyond the dark windscreen.

Three shapes, but not four.

The shockwave still pounding through his head now fights against the thump of his airless chest for dominance. But he pulls himself closer still, until his body floats between two heads, and then he sees it. The fourth body.

It is Lorraine. She shimmers before him, sideways, laying across the legs of the others. He sees her face: the obsidian canyon of the open mouth, the jet holes of the open eyes, the dance of her hair. Resting on her stomach is the rock he used to smash the back window and gain entry.

The clock immediately starts to tick down faster as his heart thumps and a portion of his breath detonates in myriad bubbles. But onward he moves, both hands outstretched, and one delves into the rippling cloud of her hair, and clutches, and pulls, and the rock tumbles off her stomach, and Lorraine comes to him, weightless as a ghost.

49

The dream woke him in the early hours. He had expected it. He didn't doubt it would be back for many nights to come. But he didn't class it as a nightmare. He had experienced the events of the dream for real and survived, so how could images in his head hurt him?

He went into Joe's room, happy to see his boy asleep. Joe had taken the news of his mother's murder well, or well compared to how it could have gone. He hadn't said much, so perhaps he'd been numb. But he'd performed as usual for the rest of the evening, although he'd put toothpaste on his brush, and that was a task he still always got his dad to do. Did that mean something?

He had also said 'thankyou', and it was this that still created turmoil in Bennet's gut. He'd been unable to tell Liz, his closest friend, the truth about finding Lorraine's body, and he'd lied to his boss, to the Derbyshire murder squad running the investigation. Joe was a kid, didn't need to know, might even be better off with oblivion, yet Bennet had willingly told him.

'It was a crime scene, Joe,' he said. 'I should have known better. I knew she was dead, but it didn't matter. Down there, in the cold, in the dark... I couldn't leave her there. I just couldn't. I had to get her out. Out of that vehicle, out of that lake. And now I'm going to get in big trouble for it. But I don't care.'

'Thankyou,' a ten-year-old boy with little life experience had said to him, before pulling him into a hug. 'Thankyou for getting my mum out.'

Bennet sat at Joe's desk, staring at his boy but not really seeing. Joe had been a toddler when he learned that his mother had left him, which was too young to fully comprehend in one bite. He'd had time to adjust as he grew. Not so with this. It was the first, real, devastating, life-changing twist in his life, and Bennet wasn't sure how it would change the boy as the days rolled by. So far so good, but like any disease or cancer, mental fracture could have an incubation period. He was a little scared of the outcome.

Bennet didn't try to get back to sleep. At the kitchen table, he wrote notes in a thick, old pad he used for murder investigations. It was half empty because those torn-out pages were in the files at the station. Just like when running a murder investigation, he listed things to do, but found this harder. His mind was a blank beyond calling Joe's school.

So he returned to the news, which had had time to ferment. Still the country seemed more intrigued by a ten-year-old body than four fresh ones. Shockingly, Sally's mother had identified her daughter's body on a main road. Alerted by the slimeball reporter, she had raced to Stanton Lake, found the body already en route to the mortuary, and set off in pursuit. She cut in front to stop the coroner's vehicle and bellowed until she was allowed to see the body.

Sally's corpse was still in the tartan skirt and butterfly T-shirt she'd worn to the party on the night she disappeared, and her butterfly hair-claw clip had been found at the scene. This made the police ninety-nine per cent certain who they'd found, but they still needed official identification. The body had been found in an old steamer trunk, designed to be waterproof and survive the flooded holds of ships, and had been well-preserved. Anika had stared at her daughter's still-intact face, poking out of a body bag zipped up to the neck, and collapsed, yelling. There went the final one per cent.

Visibly, a cause of death wasn't obvious, with the body displaying no stab wounds or lacerations or clearly broken bones. A post-mortem might divulge horrible news for the mother, including whether or not she'd been sexually assaulted, but at least she had set eyes upon her daughter without seeing the damage her killer had done to her. Bennet's heart went out to the woman.

And here he saw the first mention of himself, although not by name – the police had managed to keep that secret so far. Sally's mother had been willing to speak to a reporter who'd followed her following the ambulance, but only to thank the policeman 'who came looking for the film crew. Without him, I would never have gotten my Sally back'.

But he hadn't helped at all, had he? His impotence had failed to help anyone, especially Lorraine. He still felt useless, but carried that itchy tension to do something.

Hours later, he made the school call: Joe would be off for at least the rest of the week because of a death in the family. He waited for the receptionist to blurt that she knew all about it, but she simply said okay, and that was that. When it was done, and Joe was awake and fed, Bennet answered the bugging call to action. Father and son got dressed and took a drive. Joe had no idea where they were going.

En route, Envoy Lady called with another update, this time about cell site analysis. The police had found the phone numbers for all four dead people and traced their devices. The phones were all dead currently, but historical data put them in and around Lampton and showed their trip beforehand. As Bennet already knew, Lorraine had travelled to Overeem's home in Oxford in her own car, then all four members of the crew took the CaraHome north to the Peak District.

In built-up areas cell towers are more densely packed, allowing for greater location pinpointing. Their phones were pinged at various places, including near a café in Eggington on the A38, where calls were made, and close to the Red Lion at the correct time.

Unfortunately, in remote areas the number of cell towers decreases, but they have a greater range. Once the crew entered the countryside to stay at Crabtree's ranch, cell site accuracy dropped from pinging their phones 'within metres' to 'within a kilometre'. Finding those phones, especially if they weren't in a building, would be next to impossible. The only certainty the police had was that a tower in the grounds of the Arrow Hotel hadn't registered the devices, which meant they hadn't travelled with the owners to Stanton Lake. Not that this helped much.

Upon arrival at their destination, Bennet parked and heaved Joe onto his shoulders. He felt his age, or he felt Joe's, and could only carry him halfway before his lower back turned to fire. Father and son walked the rest of the way. Because he thought the park itself was their destination, Joe didn't ask where they were going as Bennet led him down a grassy hill. Soon, they arrived.

The thing Bennet wanted wasn't where he'd expected. On a hunch, he looked at a nearby bin, which had overflowed and scattered some of its trash. He followed a trail of rubbish laid by the wind, and under a bush, near a pop bottle, he found it. It was sticky with a splash of sugary drink and a food stain.

'What's that?' Joe said as Bennet wiped it clean. Bennet handed the laminated A5 sheet to his son. Joe read its words aloud. 'To our loving son, Mick, taken away too soon. Rest in peace, and we will see you again. 03/10/2003 – 02/01/2020.' He looked at his dad. 'This Mick was sixteen. Was he killed here? Are you solving his murder?'

'Yes. He was killed in this park. And yes, I'm trying to solve the crime.'

'Do you know who did it?'

'We have a good idea.'

'Is he arrested?'

'Was. We had to let him go.'

'Why?'

'Rules, Joe.'

'I don't get it. Even though it was him, you let him go?'

'It was the right thing to do.' It wasn't lost on him that others, including Liz and Councillor Turner, had used that very same line. 'According to the rule book.'

Joe handed the laminated dedication back. 'Why was it in the bin?'

'Rules, Joe. Always rules. It was stapled to the bench, but the parents had no permission to put it there. So, to some, taking it off was also the right thing to do. But not to the people who actually matter.'

Joe looked at the bench, at the existing bronze plaque there. 'Why is Mick's paper and not metal? Is he not as important?'

'The boy's parents don't have much money. And no, to some he's not important.'

'Are you going to put it back?'

In answer, Bennet folded the sheet, put it in his pocket, and they left Buttery Park.

50

Around midday, Bennet got another update from Envoy Lady: the pathologist had finished the autopsies on all four victims found in the CaraHome, working virtually through the night. Of course they'd fast-tracked that, delaying some other post-mortem and making a poor someone with a dead soulmate wait for answers and justice.

All four had been smashed about the head and then their throats were opened, and post mortem had suffered massive blunt force trauma from head to toe, resulting in myriad fractures and breaks of various bones. Pushed for a guess as to the weapon used for the neck injuries, the pathologist had suggested a kind of hook knife, although there was tearing as well as slicing. When asked about the body trauma, she had surprised the investigators by comparing the injuries to those of a man who'd laid dead on her table two years ago. 'That fellow was a rock climber and he fell three hundred feet, bouncing all the way.'

Intriguing. The Peak District had mountains. A search had begun. But there was another surprise in store.

Although the time of death was sometime Sunday evening

or Monday morning, there was evidence the bodies had been moved afterwards, and only submerged in water since Tuesday evening. Also, they had been buried at some point before being transferred, along with soil, to the CaraHome. This was a shock to Bennet: he'd visited Lampton early on Tuesday, which meant the bodies had been dumped into Lake Stanton *after* he'd started making enquiries about the film crew. It meant that the bodies had been dug up sometime *after* Bennet had visited Lampton. It was possible his presence in Lampton had spooked the killer or killers and they'd made additional efforts to smother the crime.

Bennet hadn't yet informed Patricia, his neighbour, of the horrible news, but when she banged on his door, he knew she knew. After hearing his tale, and offering her support if he needed it, she insisted on seeing Joe. Joe was eager and invited her into his room – and he shut the door. Bennet suspected his son might want to tell her things, perhaps his feelings, that he was uncomfortable sharing with his dad. Or the animosity in the boy that Bennet hadn't discerned. Either way, it gave Bennet time for another task. In Birmingham.

The house was in an urban maze, but stood out from the others because of a large extension to the side and rear which more than doubled its size. Bennet parked by a high fence alongside. Through slats of wood, he saw into an expansive games room, where a five-year-old girl was zipping about on a hoverboard. Ian, Tessa's father, was by the pool table, sorting through papers that covered the baize. Bennet knew the terrible news had been delivered; perhaps Ian was looking for life insurance papers, or an address for Lorraine's mother.

God, he hadn't considered Lorraine's mother, cousins, aunties. Had they heard the news yet? His own father, living in the countryside down south, also deserved a phone call.

The little girl seemed happy, but it was harder for children to understand, wasn't it? Or it was harder for adults to understand the mental processes of kids. Despite the smile on Tessa's face, he felt for her. Through no fault of her own on this occasion, Lorraine had for the second time left a father alone with a child. Bennet had often wondered if she would return, if his remaining single was in preparation for such a day. But the father he watched knew that would never happen.

As the daylight slowly relinquished its turn, Bennet wondered why he had come here. Had he planned to console the man? Tell him that coping alone was possible, because Bennet had done it? Had he hoped to make moves towards bringing Tessa and Joe together because for too long Bennet had kept them apart?

All those ideas had run through his head as he drove here, but they had felt wrong, and especially so now he was here. Lorraine was the only connection between the two families, and she was gone. Nothing biological connected Tessa and Bennet. Tessa and Joe were half-siblings, but too young to understand such a bond yet.

Some day in the future, if they chose, they could seek each other out. It wasn't Bennet's place to force that. All Bennet could offer right now was a promise to Ian: he would catch Lorraine's killer. But that was the worst of all things he could do. It wasn't Bennet's murder investigation, and solving it was no certainty anyway. Many killers died years after snuffing out a life, free and happy in their own beds. Lorraine's murderer could even be one of the dead film crew, beyond the reach of justice before a soul knew of his crime. Police officers were cautioned never to make such promises to grieving relatives, and it would be a bad, bad idea to get out of the car, knock on that door, and say those words. He should just go home to Joe.

He got out of the car.

51

———

All day, something Sally Jenkins' mother had said had been revolving in his mind: 'Such a contrast. A mother who knows exactly where her child is, but doesn't want to see him. And a mother who would do anything to know where her baby is.'

And now there would be no happy ending for anyone.

But there was another mother in suffering. Someone who had experienced the ultimate horror of murder of a loved one, and who had so far been abandoned by those who were supposed to help her. Tonight, right now, he couldn't help Joe, and he couldn't kill Sally's mother's pain, but he could get justice for someone.

The house was a semi on a street with high hedges bordering the front yards. When Bennet knocked, a rake-thin man answered. He had messy hair and sunken eyes. Anyone's first guess as to his appearance would probably be grief, and spot on.

Without a word, Ralph Turton gave a nod at Bennet and led him in. Sophie Turton, a large lady with an equally sad face, was at the kitchen table, absent-mindedly peeling potatoes. Her

214

husband didn't introduce Bennet, and she gave him the same blank look. In the early days, each visit by one of Bennet's team had been met with a look of expectation, but no more. They were used to no good news. Or no news at all. Clearly, they expected the same tonight.

Ralph sat by his wife. Bennet took a chair opposite and took something from his pocket. He laid the mugshot on the table and the Turtons stared at it.

'Donald Ashcroft,' Bennet said. 'He's sixteen. A drug dealer and all-round thug known as Don The Man. This is the little shit we think killed your son.'

Ralph turned his head away, disgusted, but Sophie bent closer to get a really good look. Ralph got up and went to the kitchen window. The man seemed to be watching his own reflection. Sophie was mouthing something to herself, eyes locked on the face in the photo.

Bennet showed her a picture on his phone. She almost had trouble dragging her eyes off Don The Man, on to a Google image of a black Citroen Saxo. Sophie nodded. 'The car we've been seeing around. His?'

Bennet nodded. He saw both Turtons deflate. Now they knew the bastard who'd killed their son was the same man taunting them about it.

'Why hasn't he been arrested if you're so sure?' Ralph demanded.

'He was. We had to let him go, lack of evidence. Someone higher up than me decided not to tell you. It was deemed not right to condemn him since he's not been charged. It would just get your hopes up. But this Don The Man, he's not out of the woods yet. We're still hunting evidence to arrest and charge him.'

Ralph almost spat. 'But he's not in a cell. He's out, having fun, laughing at you. Laughing at us.'

'Ralph, watch your mouth around Mr Bennet. He's trying to help. Who would help us if he didn't? They'll get him one day.'

'One day,' Ralph mocked.

'And now watch how you speak to me, please.'

'I'll get him for you.' The way Bennet said it made both Turtons wake up a little. Ralph forgot his black reflection and Sophie looked up from the mugshot. 'I'll make sure he doesn't come round here again. I'll go mess this idiot up. Or I can plant evidence. I'll do it tonight, right now. Just give me the word.'

Sophie gave her husband a look and got up. 'I need air. I need to go to the shop.' And she grabbed her cigarettes from the table and left. Bennet heard the front door open and close.

Ralph took his wife's place at the table. There was a new wakefulness in his eyes. Bennet realised that Sophie might not have fled in disgust, or confusion. Perhaps she had left the room to give her husband the floor. To give him permission.

'I want you to do it,' Ralph said, turning the mugshot face down. 'Plant blood or fingerprints, whatever, and get this bastard locked up.'

Bennet nodded. Ralph got up and returned to the black window, and his gaunt image in the glass. Bennet understood it was time to leave.

As he was about to open his car door, a voice cut into the silent darkness.

'You never did promise.'

He turned. Sophie hadn't gone to the shops: she was by her high front hedge, barely more than a shivering silhouette with a burning cigarette.

'To find my son's murderer. I asked you to promise, and you never did.'

'I do everything I can. Saying that word, it doesn't really make anything different.'

'To me it does, and things are different now. So, do you know where that monster lives?'

Bennet realised his error. Sophie hadn't left the house to allow her husband to act on his anger. She had come out here, away from him, to act on hers. He nodded.

'Then hurt him for me. Tonight. Hurt him bad. Tell him it's from my son. I want you to swear you'll do it.'

For the second time, Bennet made a promise he shouldn't have.

52

S at in his car outside a chemist's, with a packet of painkillers and bandages, Bennet wondered what the hell he was doing. His boss, Superintendent Hunter, called with a warning. 'SIO Sutton is about to call you. Be honest with him, okay? I don't know what it's about.'

He looked at the painkillers and bandages he'd bought. So, Don The Man thought he was funny for buying Liam sleeping medicine? Well, the idiot was going to need what Liam had bought for him. 'It's about the theory that I entered that motorhome and dragged my son's mother's body out. I did, David. That's exactly what I did. I messed with a crime scene. I couldn't leave her in there. I'm sorry I lied.'

'I know. I'm just glad you admitted it. We'll deal with that. I got your message about wanting to be on adjusted duty. Let's leave it as compassionate leave, and maybe that will help with how this whole thing plays out for you. I'll say no more about it here, on the phone. Tell Sutton the truth when he calls.'

'Thank you.'

Bennet was driving to Don The Man's flat when Sutton's call came. He pulled in to take it.

Sutton immediately said, 'I've reviewed that garden centre CCTV you told us about. That engine noise we can hear from Tuesday evening? I think you're wrong about it being a motorhome engine. Far too aggressive.'

'The CaraHome's exhaust had been repaired. If it wasn't done correctly, a damaged silencer would make the noise louder.'

'Well, we have doubts.'

'I recently heard the autopsy results. The pathologist said there was trauma she thought might have been from a fall. Francis Overeem was planning to do something called the Arrow Climb. You know what that is?'

'Oh, yes. You're wondering if our victims were pushed or fell off the cliff, up at the hotel? Forget that. We looked at that scene and there's no evidence anyone fell. And CCTV of the Arrow car park at no point shows that motorhome, so it wasn't there. It was a nice theory, given the proximity of the lake and the cliff – you know, the victims take the tumble, and then our perp brings the motorhome down from the Arrow to the lake, drags the bodies and puts them inside, and dumps the vehicle in the water. But we ruled it out. Besides, the pathologist came up with the big fall notion because, well, this is the Peak District. Lots of rocky hills. Since then she's reassessed. Nothing definitive, but she would say the injuries are more likely from a high-speed car crash than a tumble down a mountain.'

'Okay. I just thought I'd mention it. I should also mention that it's time I told the truth. You were right, superintendent. I did go in that motorhome. I broke a window and went inside.'

Bennet repeated his reasons, as given to Joe, but without emotion: a straight blast of facts. He didn't really care to get the DCS to forgive him. He just wanted no more part of lying to people.

'I knew it all along. Thank you for telling me the truth. We'll deal with that another time. Now, do you recall the woman I was with when I arrived at the scene? She's a principal consultant for the Forensic Collision Investigation and Reconstruction group. I was at a seminar with her when I got the call, so I brought her along because a vehicle was involved.'

Bennet recalled a snooty lady with the superintendent, and that she'd looked disgusted seeing Bennet soaking wet, knelt by Lorraine's body at the shore of Lake Stanton. 'What about her?'

'She had something intriguing to say about the scene. The undergrowth, the tree branches overlapping the slipway. All thick enough that quite some speed and momentum would be needed to punch that motorhome through. It was scratched to hell by branches and broke some big ones.'

'I saw the slip road. I figured as much.'

Sutton continued: 'Tight space to enter through that brick archway at speed. Very thin service road. Thirty miles an hour, minimum, she says. That's how fast the motorhome would have had to enter that slipway, to force itself through. Any slower and it would have jammed up with the mud and the branches and undergrowth. And she doesn't believe the motorhome could have made the turn at that speed.'

Bennet's heart started to thump. 'Pushed? By another vehicle?'

'Yes. Something big enough to–'

'I know what,' Bennet cut in. 'I need to come down there, DCS Sutton.'

'What do you mean, you know what? You know which vehicle did this? Tell me.'

Of course, Bennet should have told him. Sutton was leading the murder investigation, and Bennet had no authority to be part of it, even if he hadn't been barred by his relationship to one of the deceased.

'No. I want in. I want the arrest, DCS Sutton.'

'Bennet, don't piss about with me. If you have information that–'

Bennet hung up. He stared at his phone as if it were a weapon he'd just attacked the DCS with. Of course, he should have called back. He'd just refused to divulge important information to a superior investigating the most high-profile crime of the last few years. On top of his contamination of the crime scene, this would destroy his career, might even result in criminal charges. He could have made that return call, apologised for the dropped connection, and told what he knew. The phone was still in his hand, awaiting that move.

He didn't make it. With shaking hands, he removed the battery and SIM card from his phone, so nobody knew where he was.

Or, more important, where he was going.

53

The land around was quiet, the field and sky black. The only illumination apart from the moon came from a porch light attached to the nearby building. The only building out here. Where he had business tonight. It was just past midnight.

The moonlight bounced off something metal in the dirt, which he picked up and examined. He approached the building and tried the front door. Surprisingly, it was unlocked. He slipped in and waited for his eyes to adapt to the darkness. The house was silent. Ahead was another door, open, and his eyes picked out the dark hollows of doorways. But he ignored them and turned to the stacked horizontal lines of a staircase. Slowly, he climbed, heading for the owner's bedroom. Where he had business tonight.

Three doors on the upper landing, two shut. He crept through the open door, into a bedroom. He saw the square of a double bed, and a single figure lying on one side of it. He flicked on the light, and watched the sleeping figure slowly rouse, trying to shield its eyes against the sudden brightness. Then, when the man in the bed saw the man in the doorway, he yelled in shock.

'Ronald Crabtree, I am arresting you for the murders of Francis Overeem, John Crickmer, Betty Crute, and Lorraine Cross, on or about the 19th of January.'

Still squinting against the light, Crabtree looked around, as if for help, or a weapon, or just because his brain had been jolted awake and was still working out what the hell was going on. 'What? How did you get in here?'

Bennet slammed the door behind him, and the thunderous bang seem to whack the final remnants of sleep from the farmer. 'That's how you honour your wife's memory, is it? The brutal slaying of four people in her shack?'

'No, no, the police searched it. I didn't do anything like that. Look, you can't just bust into my home–'

'Don't lie to me,' Bennet yelled. 'That shack is the last place their phones were active. You scrubbed it clean and burned their belongings. The police searched it again and found blood traces.'

That was a lie, but it seemed to work. Crabtree said nothing for a few moments. He clutched a pillow like a baby comforted by a teddy.

'You buried their bodies, right here on your land.'

Crabtree shook his head. Bennet walked to the foot of the bed. 'You panicked when I turned up, asking questions. You dug those bodies up to go dump them somewhere else.'

Crabtree made no movement this time, and said nothing. He just stared.

'You used your tractor loader. Oh, it came in very handy. It scooped those bodies out of the ground. Admit it.'

Crabtree's eyes dropped to the garden fork tine Bennet wielded, found in the dirt outside. They were loaded with fear. There was a long pause, as if the farmer weighed up his options here. But his muscles weren't tense; this wasn't the tension of a nervous system debating fight or flight. A more calculated, conscious analysis: trial or funeral? Coffin or cell?

Crabtree seemed to deflate a little. Bennet had seen killers react like this upon finally confessing: the sudden unburdening of all the massive tension that came with holding a terrible secret; with ceaselessly fearing capture. But this was different. Crabtree's sudden calm was that of a man released from the gallows at the eleventh hour. Bennet was appalled by the weapon in his hand and he dropped it. But the anger persisted: Crabtree had admitted nothing.

'And at Lake Stanton that tractor came in very handy. You used it to push that motorhome down the slipway, into the lake.'

Crabtree had seen the weapon fall. But the threat was still in Bennet's face, so it changed nothing: the farmer just watched him. Still, he had not admitted a thing.

'You knew about the ledge in the lake and the deep drop, perfect for making a vehicle disappear. You knew about it because you'd killed and disposed of Sally Jenkins there ten years before.'

'NO,' Crabtree yelled, instantly out of his subdued state and into rage. He jumped out of the bed, fists clenched, and the shock and speed of it made Bennet take a step back. 'Don't you dare blame that on me. I had nothing to do with Sally. I don't know anything about Sally. I was as shocked as everyone to hear she'd been found in that lake.'

'That's the only thing you deny? Sally?'

Crabtree sat on the bed, suddenly breathing heavily, as if his adrenaline burst had exhausted him. 'It makes me sick to think I was there, just metres from her body.'

Those words, a backroad admission, hit Bennet like a punch. Now it was real. Here, before him, stood the man who snatched Lorraine away from Joe, and parted them forever. Bennet kicked the rusty fork tine under the bed before he crossed a line there was no way back from.

'But we didn't kill those people,' Crabtree said. 'We went there to give them grief, but there was no need. They were already dead.'

54

Crabtree had said, 'I know you won't believe my words right now, under accusation. So try my words from back a way.'

It was intriguing enough to give Bennet pause, and to trust the man. Bennet followed him downstairs, where Crabtree flicked the living room light on and went to a desk for his laptop. Bennet noted how ancient and dirty the room looked, as if Crabtree hadn't tended to it since his wife died. The grey wig he'd seen the other day, along with a dress fit for an old lady, lay on the armchair. Where Bennet had seen a prostitute sitting.

Seeing Bennet stare, Crabtree called out, 'You're here to see this, not gawp at my house.'

The farmer hit some keys on the laptop, then stepped back. Bennet stepped forward. He took the seat at the desk. Such was his curiosity, and a belief that Crabtree didn't have a trick planned, Bennet didn't object when the farmer moved out of sight behind him.

There was a Lampton village newsletter on the screen, scrolled to the bottom, where there was a KEY ADDENDUM link. Bennet clicked it and was asked for a password. He'd been here before and hit a wall. Now there was no wall: Crabtree recited the password.

And it worked. Either Crabtree was still a Key, or nobody had updated the security since he was ousted.

There were two audio files titled with the time and date of creation. Crabtree told him to pick the earlier file. Bennet clicked it. A female voice spoke.

'Minutes of the Lampton Keys' meeting, held in the chamber on Monday January 20th, at 0147am. Present are Richard Turner, Arnold Mabledon, Pearl Vacari, Jason Ness, Iain Lockaton, and myself, Sandra Gingham. On the agenda is the sole subject of four visitors to the village and reason for their presence. Chairman Turner played a recording from local farmer Ronald Crabtree. We heard this live, but let me just refresh our memories. As follows...'

A crackle of static as, Liam assumed, Sandra started playing a tape. Crabtree's voice filled the air.

'On Sunday I rented my wife's shack to those four film-makers. A black man came to my door and paid cash, and I handed over the key. He was alone. I didn't see anyone else. He said he was a businessman in the area looking for property to buy, so I didn't know who they were at first. Not until Councillor Turner told me they were using my ranch. I wanted them out. I travelled to the ranch, knocked on the door. No one came to the door, but the same black man called out, asking what I wanted. I said I wanted them to leave. I didn't lie to them. I told them I knew who they were and they had to leave. The black man refused. He said he was going to solve the Sally Jenkins murder and I was wrong to stop him. I only had the one key to the door, so there was no way to get in and evict them. I called Councillor Turner about it.'

Back to Sandra, who outlined that Chair Turner had called the meeting to discuss action against the film crew. Turner opted for a confrontation: the film-makers would be told to leave the village. The motion was seconded and Sandra put it to a vote. All present were in favour. Turner then proposed to send Ronald Crabtree and his own son, Lucas, and he would accompany as an observer. Turner then ordered another meeting at 9am the next day, Monday, to discuss action if the warning failed. Sandra then adjourned the meeting.

The audio file ended. Bennet had learned nothing new. 'Is this supposed to be proof of something? This doesn't mean things didn't get out of hand when you went there and–'

'Just play the goddamned next file.'

The second file wasn't from 9am Monday, when the next meeting had been planned. It was dated just a few hours after the first, in the dead of night on Monday morning, suggesting the Keys had been urgently recalled. Despite that, Bennet didn't expect to learn anything shocking from this file either.

He was wrong.

55

As before, it began with Sandra Gingham's voice: 'Minutes of the Lampton Keys' additional semi-meeting, held in the chamber on Monday January 20th, at 0245. Present: as before. Additional: Ronald Crabtree, Lucas Turner. On the agenda is the discovery recently made in the ranch owned by Ronald Crabtree. Chair Turner wishes for Ronald Crabtree to describe what they found. Mr Crabtree? You may speak.'

CRABTREE: 'A playwright – I forget who – once said something about forgetting regret, or you'll miss life. Well, life is mine to miss.'

GINGHAM: 'Just tell us what you found, Mr Crabtree, please.'

CRABTREE: 'We go there in my tractor. We wanted noise, to make sure they were awake. They were. I saw that black face at the window. But then they ignored the knocking. And us calling for them. We had weapons, so I thought they'd seen we were tooled up and ready for action and thought they could pretend they were asleep. The funny thing is, we're there, shouting for them, banging on the door and windows, and not one of us thought to try the door, not for ten minutes or so. Door's unlocked.

'Inside, in the living room, that's where we found the first one. Buff young man in just shorts. He's on my sofa, and it's ruined. Ruined by his blood. His neck's been gashed wide open. Man's dead for sure. Councillor Turner can't bear to go on, I'm sure he won't mind me saying that. Lucas and me move on. Kitchen next.

'In there, that's where we find the black man. He's laying across my Elise's kitchen table. He's in shorts as well. This guy's neck is just ruined. His blood's covered the table, pooled round his feet and the table legs. Lucas's legs are going, but I'm fine. I'm an old man and I was more worried about having to throw down with these youngsters.

'Just the bedrooms left, and there's two in there. One in each room. Both the women. A redhead girl and a blonde. Blonde's a bit older, a bit prettier cos the redhead has that dreadlock hair thing going on, and she's got tats all over her arms. None's pretty at that point though. Both their throats, gone, blood all over the beds. Redhead is kind of peaceful-looking, tucked up in bed. Blonde girl, though, she's hanging half out her bed and some of her blood is on my walls, right across the painting Elise's mum did for her. Looked like the blonde one woke up or something while it was happening. Put up a fight. A scrap she lost.

'And that was it, really. We went back out, out to where Councillor Turner was waiting. We drove away. I was going to call in the law, but Turner said he'd call another meeting first.'

GINGHAM: 'Thank you, Mr Crabtree. So, as you all know, Councillor Turner called us here in order to work out what to do next.'

TURNER: 'It's obvious. If we let the world know what happened here, it kills our village. The disappearance of Sally Jenkins almost ruined us. This certainly will. Local business owners will shift out, just like last time. Genuine tourism will dry up and we'll cater only to journalists and the morbid.'

MABLEDON: 'What do you suggest?'

VACARI: 'I think we all know what he's suggesting.'

MABLEDON: 'Yes, but for real? How would we hide this? There's four bodies.'

NESS: 'You can't be serious. Hide this? How on earth could we do that? These people have friends, family, and they'll be missed. People will come looking for them. Including the police, when they're reported missing.'

MABLEDON: 'That's right. They would have told people they were coming here.'

LOCKATON: 'But did they? I mean, do their friends and family know anything for sure? The film crew tried to sneak about. Maybe this was a secret mission. Secret from everybody.'

NESS: 'Preposterous. This wasn't a witness protection programme or a clandestine military mission. They would have told people.'

TURNER: 'But it doesn't matter, don't you see? Most of our village didn't even know they were here, until they visited the Lion last night. And we all thought they'd left, didn't we? Only Crabtree knew otherwise, because they stayed in his ranch.'

GINGHAM: 'So we pretend they moved on? Is that what you mean?'

TURNER: 'Exactly. The film crew said it themselves. Their slang term, what was it? When they were done, they'd "Alt F4 this joint". Exit, in other words. So we pretend they did that. They exited. If any of their friends or family ask, we tell them they simply left our village and we don't know where they went.'

VACARI: 'And if the police ask?'

TURNER: 'The same. Is it any different for any other tourist we've ever had? Pearl, the Italian woman in your shop the other day, the one who knocked over a shelf. Do you know where she went when she left? No. And that's all you could tell the police if they turned up and said she'd gone missing.'

LOCKATON: 'I agree that would work. The film crew left, and that's all we know. And I can live with that to save our world.'

MABLEDON: 'Live with that? Simple lies are, well, simple. But there's another problem, isn't there? Something I alone seem to be considering. We have four bodies sitting out there. What about them?'

NESS: 'Are you serious? Really? You're talking about getting rid of four bodies, aren't you? We can't do that. We couldn't keep that secret.'

GINGHAM: 'They say two people can keep a secret if one of them is dead. Well, as long as nobody outside this room speaks of it, not even to our Proxies, that secret would die with us.'

NESS: *(inaudible)*

TURNER: 'Oh, we can if we want to save this village. If this murder becomes world knowledge, the police will invade our world. And this time they're not looking for a young girl who could have run away. This is a major crime that will go into the books. The police will delve into everything, everyone's background. Dr Ness, I know there are aspects of your life you don't want going outside this room, never mind across the globe.'

MABLEDON: 'Please, ladies and gentlemen, whether we do this or not, we still have four bodies sitting out there.'

TURNER: 'Arnold, just hold your tongue a moment. Dr Ness isn't convinced yet and we need a unanimous vote.'

NESS: 'And I can't vote on that.'

TURNER: 'The good doctor here is missing a point. We all know that Sally Jenkins ran away, but nobody else does, do they? The proof is in the fact that a film crew came here, that the police still stick their noses in our business every half year or so, asking the same old questions. To the naïve wider world, Sally was kidnapped and killed, but nobody is a hundred per cent certain. So what do you think will happen to that theory when the world learns of a quadruple murder in our village?'

GINGHAM: 'He's right. The world will firmly believe Sally was killed here. The pressure will be intense. The police will come back with a vengeance. We'll have a hundred film crews here. Everybody important will move away. I don't want that. Heck, I vote yes. We get rid of the bodies.'

TURNER: 'Not so fast, Sandra. We need the doctor to vote with logic, not because he's the odd one out. Jason, think about this. When the police come back and start to open up our lives, some dark secrets might be exposed. They're hunting the killer of a child, so what do you think they'll make of a man once rumoured to have–'

NESS: 'Okay, okay, just stop. If we did this, how would we get rid of the bodies?'

TURNER: 'We use Mr Crabtree's tractor to dig a hole. On his land. He's renovating and there's turned earth and deep holes and soil mounds everywhere. It's the perfect place, and a year from now those bodies will be under tons of metal and concrete. Mr Crabtree has already agreed, because he knows this will work. He'll be sworn to secrecy, as will my son, who will help. I think those two men alone can do the job. Tonight.'

NESS: 'Already agreed? Did you have this worked out before we even convened this meeting?'

TURNER: 'Of course. I knew it was the right thing to do the moment I saw those bodies. But you are my friends and I wanted your blessing.'

NESS. 'Jesus Christ. Look, I want it noted that I objected to this. But I agree, okay? I agree to do it, under duress. And I don't like that we've recorded this meeting. This of all meetings.'

GINGHAM: 'No one is forcing you, Jason. Yes or no, of your

own free will. Yes, and we do this, and we save our village. We tell our people the crew upped and offed, and that will be the truth, no matter who or whatever evidence tries to say otherwise. No, and announce the presence of four dead people out in a field, and we deal with what comes.'

NESS: 'Whatever. Okay. Yes.'

GINGHAM: 'Good. And we record everything, always, Jason. You know that. I'm on tape admitting that thing up in Scotland.'

MABLEDON: 'And it's on record that I–'

NESS: 'I said yes, didn't I? Can we just get this over with?'

TURNER: 'Of course. So we'll vote. But let's reverse it. All in favour of honesty and having our happy, blessed lives ruined in one fell swoop, keep your hands down.'

56

If Crabtree's story was true, Lorraine's colleagues had probably been dispatched in their sleep, or so fresh out of it they'd offered minimal resistance. But Lorraine had fought her attacker. There was little comfort in knowing she'd made it hard for the killer though. How must she have suffered in those final moments?

It was best not to dwell. She was suffering no pain or terror now. He slapped the laptop closed and got up. He started to pace in Crabtree's living room. It was better to burn energy this way than... by a more terrible method. 'What did you do with the bodies?'

Crabtree gave him a look like he was stupid. 'You know what? We put them in Lake Stanton.'

Bennet clenched his fists, and Crabtree didn't miss it. 'Don't piss me off. I want to know what you did.'

'We put them in their motorhome. Drove that here. Then we cleaned the ranch and burned all the stuff they'd left inside. We hid the motorhome in one of my buildings. I was going to dismantle it over the coming weeks. But we buried the bodies and the gear that was in the motorhome.'

Crabtree said his last sentence with caution, as if knowing the images it would throw up. Bennet tried not to think about this man, or Turner's son, or even Turner himself, kicking Lorraine's bloody corpse into a dark hole, and throwing soil across it. But he saw her face, half-submerged in the dirt, one open eye the last piece of her to vanish. He sat down. It felt like putting an extra obstacle between his hands and the old bastard's neck.

'The graffiti? The burned items? All part of the plan?'

Crabtree nodded. 'Turner told me to. He said there was a chance the police might eventually come and they'd look inside the ranch. We couldn't just clean up. It would look like we'd cleaned a crime scene. He said if the police see evidence of a clean-up at the last known place of missing people, they get suspicious. He said we should actually trash the place and cover it in graffiti, spray it where there were bloodstains. And then only half-clean it up, so the police could see the damage, and then they'd believe our story. So we left the ranch half-cleaned so you could see it.'

'Overeem didn't give you that business card at all, did he? That was part of the plan too?'

'We found that when we found their bodies. Turner told me to act as if I had been about to call the police about the vandalism. I should insist on showing you the ranch and hide nothing. I should insist on wanting the film crew arrested. The card was so you'd know who I suspected, yes.'

The trick had fooled the seasoned detective in Bennet, but Crabtree's smart and scary competence wasn't his biggest concern. 'You retrieved those bodies when I arrived in the village. Tell me.'

'I hadn't started on the motorhome yet. We thought we'd have longer, since the crew had only been dead two days and probably not even reported missing yet. Turner wanted the bodies moved. We thought Lake Stanton would be a good idea because we knew it was deep and had a ledge. The motorhome still drove, but we would have to take the loader to push it down the slipway. So we dug the bodies up and put them in the motorhome–'

'No,' Bennet snapped. 'You don't just get to say you dug them up. This is a story, isn't it? Show, don't tell, and use some elegance. Say that you used the loader, and rammed that heavy metal bucket into the soil.'

Crabtree looked frozen.

'All that power and weight,' Bennet continued. 'You stabbed that loader bucket deep into the ground, smashing bones, gouging flesh, and hauled those destroyed bodies from the land. You dragged those ruined, dirty corpses into the motorhome. Was my Lorraine's mouth full of dirt? Were her eyes still open?'

'What are you going to do to me?'

Bennet was surprised by the question, until he caught sight of his face in a wall mirror. He looked ravaged, like a zombie, or a lunatic, and a far cry from a father and police officer. He hung his head. He had broken into this home, with a weapon. What had he become?

Bennet dropped onto the sofa, suddenly drained of energy. 'I told her to stay away. I warned her. Stay away from me and my son.'

Crabtree was staring, unsure how to react. But Bennet wasn't speaking to him: these words were for himself.

'I sent her that horrible message. I hated her at that moment. But she would have come to see Joe, if she could. I know it. But she couldn't. She was already dead.'

57

Bennet leaned on his car outside Crabtree's farmhouse and turned his phone on. While it loaded, he turned his eyes to the dark sky. It felt weird knowing this was his last night as a police officer.

Missed calls, a lot of them. Patricia, Joe, Sutton, Hunter, other colleagues and even some of his friends. Sutton had been in contact with a lot of people, trying to track Bennet down. He wondered if the Derby cops were planning to trace his device. He wondered if anyone suspected he'd returned to Lampton. For the final time, he hoped.

He called Patricia. She answered with desperation in her voice: police had been to the house, looking for him. He told her to calm down. 'I'm fine, don't worry. I'll explain everything later. I just want to let you know I'll be back in about two hours. Is Joe awake?'

'No. But he's worried. I can wake him for you.'

Joe was worried. Father of the year. 'No, I'll wake him when I get back. If he wakes before, tell him I'm sorry I didn't leave word. I'll be back soon. Thank you and I'm sorry.'

After that call, he made one to Sutton. Past midnight, but the superintendent answered immediately. He was worked up and Bennet had to cut him short.

'I'll explain everything later. Right now you've got something bigger than a rogue detective to deal with. I'm going to send you an audio file. Get your people ready for a bunch of raids.' Bennet listed the names of the Keys, plus Crabtree and Turner's son, Lucas. 'The Keys should be at home. I'll get Turner. You'll have to find his son. Crabtree is waiting at his home, dressed and ready to go to the station. He'll show you where he buried the bodies. There should be some treasure there still.'

'Bennet, what the hell is going on?'

'You'll know after you listen to the audio file. I'll email it now.'

'Again, detective, where are you? And I don't want you going near Richard Turner until I know what's going on.'

'I'll see you at Crabtree's farm. Here comes the file.'

Bennet hung up, emailed the file, then separated the components of his phone again. He'd broken so many orders and rules recently, and one more wasn't going to matter.

58

Screen 13: the video feed from the lamp post outside the car park of the Panorama, showing forty metres of the dark main road. Parked directly in the foreground were two cars, nose to nose and connected by jump leads. Four teenagers present, one in each driver's seat, two watching.

Screen 72: the turning circle of Arton Place. Quiet at this time of night, with a scattering of bedroom lights on and just a single living room illuminated.

Screen 46: the camera in the centre of the Well, showing various establishments, including the Red Lion. The pub was the only place open. People moved past the window periodically and two women were smoking just outside the doorway.

Screen: 1: Turner's house. The camera was on the far side of the street in order to capture his home, driveway and the road directly outside. This camera was all about security, not snooping. All the lights in the house were off.

Bennet turned his attention to the laptop, which had a portable speaker attached. When he stroked the mousepad, the screen saver vanished and, thankfully, there was no password security. He needed two minutes to work out the system and another to plug in and access a flash drive he'd gotten from Crabtree's house. File loaded, play button pressed, he leaned back in Councillor Turner's comfy desk chair to watch his work.

'Minutes of the Lampton Keys' additional semi-meeting, held in the chamber on Monday January 20th, at 0245...'

Screen 13: as the audio of the Key Addendum meeting washed across the four teenagers working on their cars, they looked up and round, directly at the camera. On their faces, pure shock. On the road behind them, an approaching car slowed. It stopped dead centre of its lane, and the driver's door emitted a man in a McDonald's uniform, probably heading home from a work shift. He stood by his door, staring at the camera.

'...find the black man. He's laying across my Elise's kitchen table. He's in shorts...'

Screen 72: like a machine starting up, lights appeared in bedroom windows all around the turning circle on Arton Place. Then hallway bulbs illuminated glass in front doors. One opened and a woman in a dressing gown stood on her doorstep. Across the way, a man exited his house, just in pants. Bedroom windows open. Hypnotised faces stared up at the camera and its speakers, as if at a hovering alien craft in the sky.

'...let the world know what happened here, it kills our village...'

Screen 46: The Lion had emptied as if a fire drill had sounded. Nothing of the sort, of course. Recorded words from trusted village elders, admitting a ghastly crime and, far worse, a secret pact. Perhaps a dozen people milled outside the pub's front door, in a puddle of light spilling from inside. Publican Jonesy was amongst them. They stared, they listened, and like all others they wore faces of disbelief.

'...be considering. We have four bodies sitting out there. What about...'

Screen: 1: Turner's front bedroom light clapped on. Bennet

turned his chair from the bank of screens and stood. Beyond the open door of Turner's stable workspace, across the black field where horses once galloped, the rear of the house remained dark. And then it didn't. The kitchen light came on. The back door opened. A figure emerged at a run across the grass. Bennet heard Turner yell, 'Who's there? How dare you? Get out of my property. You'll regret this.'

'…as long as nobody outside this room speaks of it…'

Turner was in tracksuit bottoms and a T-shirt, probably his preferred sleeping outfit, and his face was red from a panicked sprint. He stopped in the stable doorway, panting and angry, and wide-eyed upon recognising the man who'd infiltrated his ultra-sacrosanct realm.

'You? You bastard. Turn that off, now.'

The councillor stepped forward, swinging an elbow to bash Bennet aside so he could reach his console, but Bennet grabbed the man's arm, kicked out a leg, and slammed him face down on the carpet. Turner immediately tried to thrash free, but Bennet ground a knee hard into the man's back. The older man gave it up.

'You're under arrest, Turner. That means game over with the monkey business.'

Turner laughed. He actually laughed. 'You're an idiot, detective. This won't change what my people think. They'll know we were only protecting them. And I'll be going nowhere. Perverting the course of justice? Preventing the lawful burial of a dead body? And whatever other niche crimes you people come up with as safety nets in case people beat charges? They're nothing. What, five years suspended for those charges? I won't go to prison, and you won't damage my power in this village. So, you fool, what exactly do you think you've achieved here?'

'…our happy, blessed lives ruined in one fell swoop…'

59

———

Bennet parked by the woods overlooking Crabtree's farmhouse. Every light in the building was on. Police and private cars clogged the area. Although the house had activity, primary interest was in the barrel-shaped corrugated metal structure a hundred metres beyond the farmhouse. The doors were open and the interior was floodlit. Inside and out was a throng of people, some in police uniform, others casually dressed, yet others in the plastic coveralls of crime-scene technicians. DCS Sutton had moved fast.

Bennet turned his phone on, called him and said, 'I'm here.' He flashed his lights.

'I expected that. Meet me halfway,' Sutton said, and hung up.

After arresting Richard Turner, Bennet had called Sutton and been sent a patrol car to collect the councillor. The superintendent had ordered Bennet to remain with the prisoner so he could also go to the station and provide a statement. But when officers arrived at the stable, they found Turner alone.

One of the plastic suits started walking towards him. Bennet strode down the incline. They met exactly halfway between the farmhouse and the woods.

'I apologise for leaving Turner,' Bennet said. 'I'll go to the station after this, if you like. I just wanted to see the scene.'

'I can't let you down there,' Sutton said. Bennet nodded his understanding. 'Good call about this place. Can't promise it helps you much. You should have told me what you knew the moment you knew it.'

'I know. Maybe I was worried you wouldn't get a confession. Maybe I just wanted to hear it first. Maybe I was planning to hurt one of these people. I just don't know why I acted this way. And I'll take what's coming because of it. Crabtree helpful?'

'Oh yes. Eager to talk. We had to rush him to the station, he was that eager to start talking. And he showed us the burial site.'

'And you've arrested the others on the recording?'

'All but Lucas Turner. He wasn't at home and we don't know where he is. The others, the Keys as they call themselves, they were no problem. Awake and dressed and waiting for us. I think they were scared they'd get lynched by their own people. Because of that recording you played. That was quite a bizarre tactic, Mr Bennet. It could have been damaging to the case, except that so far everyone seems willing to accept their guilt. Time will tell. Why did you play it for the whole town?'

'I tried to think of a good answer for you on the way here. I couldn't find one. I can only put it down to a few days of having my head mixed up. With maybe a little bit of sticking it to Turner thrown in. You should have heard my original idea, before I knew about the audio recording. I thought about forcing Turner to call a village meeting. I'd get everyone in the town hall and have a sort of kangaroo court. Maybe build a wicker man to put the Keys in.'

Bennet grinned to show he was joking, but Sutton remained serious. 'This became very personal to you. I've never been there, so I can't judge. Your boss says you're a very good detective and I believe him. So, like you say, this has been a glitch. Go home. We'll worry about your statement tomorrow. Go back to your kid. I'll keep you updated.'

Bennet hadn't looked at Sutton throughout their conversation: his eyes were locked on the corrugated building. It wasn't where Lorraine had died, but it might have been her final resting place. Somehow, that made it seem more horrifying than the ranch where she'd been slaughtered. But it was about more than that.

'What have you found inside so far?'

'Mound of tarpaulin he said was used to cover the motorhome. And there's an area of churned soil we're rooting through. That's where the bodies lay. We've been finding all manner of items that had been in that motorhome.'

Now Bennet looked at the superintendent. 'I need to know as soon as you do. Please. It's my son's mother.'

Sutton gave him a careful stare. 'I know what's concerning you, detective. But we don't know anything for sure yet. We need to talk to all the others and we need to see what else we find at the crime scenes, and if anything changes once we can hammer away at Crabtree. At least that audio recording helps with the time frame. We know the film crew was at a local pub until just after 9pm on Sunday night, and the audio recording shows the bodies were found before 12.45 Monday morning. That gives us a time of death within just a few hours.'

Sutton had indeed fathomed Bennet's worry. With the arrests made and evidence found and questions answered, light had been shed where there had been darkness and it all felt like a great leap forward. The surface of the mystery had been laid bare and it was too easy to get hypnotised by it, and ignore the black abyss at the core.

If the story they had was true, then a killer was still out there.

60

Since they couldn't attend court on Friday because they'd been arrested late Thursday, Ronald Crabtree, Richard Turner and the rest of the Keys were due to appear at Southern Derbyshire Magistrates' Court on Monday, charged with a number of Public Justice Offences, primarily perverting the course of justice and obstructing a coroner. Lucas Turner was still missing and, along with Crabtree, he would face additional charges relating to the physical act of disposing of dead bodies and destroying a crime scene.

Until then, the seven charged got police bail. The still-unanswered question of who killed four film-makers and a little girl was a hot topic and opinion was split on whether or not the charged were also murderers. Upon their release, a gaggle of reporters, supporters and wannabe-vigilantes was waiting outside. Crabtree and all but one of the Keys had already made arrangements to stay with friends and family outside Lampton, but hopes of a quiet weekend were dashed as their vehicles were pursued away from the police station. The police did what they could to give the Keys a head start, but media folk had already obtained the addresses the Keys were headed to.

And the single Key who didn't choose to run and hide? Parish Councillor Richard Turner walked out of the police station like a man already acquitted, five steps ahead of his solicitor and a pair of bulky friends. If he expected thrown flowers and cheers, he got a shock. Within seconds, the heavies were forced to step closer and shepherd him to his car under a torrent of abuse. Someone launched an egg that splattered his suit.

Despite what he'd done – or because of it, hiding the bodies had been to save his village – he still had a number of well-wishers. Three large acolytes sat in a van parked across his driveway gates and held back the reporters who'd followed him home. Like his own SS-like group. But Turner couldn't ignore an audience. In the time it took to swap to a suit that didn't have an egg stain, the councillor appeared at his first-floor bedroom balcony, like the Pope, and addressed their questions.

'Are you a killer?'

Perhaps this worked sometimes, but Turner gave the answer everyone expected: no. 'I couldn't hurt a fly. Look into my history and you will see this is so. This is my first ever arrest, and the same goes for my son and for Mr Crabtree and the rest of us. We're model citizens. Our only fault was loving our home too much. That was why we did it. To avoid bringing the kind of attention it is now receiving.'

Bennet watched the whole thing on the news. What a twat, he thought. He wished he was there, with a slingshot. If this bastard had had his way, Lorraine and the others would still be buried for all time in a forgotten, shallow grave. Dozens, perhaps even hundreds of families and friends would still be in the dark about what happened to their missing loved ones.

'Do you understand how suspicious it was that you chose to hide the bodies in the very same place where a little girl's body was dumped?'

'Yes. I see your single-minded blindness, all of you. Take to the air, or load up Google Earth, and pick a better place. Yes, there are woods and rockeries and moors, but, as callous and hateful as it sounds, Lake Stanton is the perfect place to hide something out here. Whoever killed poor Sally Jenkins simply had the same idea as I did, that is all. I had nothing to do with killing little Sally, or the film-makers who came to document her story. Your focus should be on asking the police why they didn't think about searching that lake all those years ago.'

This was the crux of the matter. A simple case of probabilities. How likely was it that the murders of a young girl and of four people looking into that crime weren't connected? What were the odds that someone could dump corpses where one already lay and be oblivious to it? And when did anyone ever hear about so-and-so hiding bodies left by whatshisname? To most, Turner and his cohorts were a little puppy standing next to a pile of dog poo on a carpet.

But the Crown Prosecution Service seemed to think another dog might have sneaked into the house to dump a load and then fled. There were no plans as yet to charge Turner and his clan with murder, although Sutton's murder squad was still analysing the various crime scenes.

'Do you have any clue as to who killed five people?'

'I don't,' Turner bellowed from his perch. 'There's no proof yet that all five are the work of the same perpetrator. If anything, the method suggests otherwise. Killers of little girls don't then go on to murder four adults. And if it was so, there was no attempt to hide the bodies.'

'The film crew was shooting a documentary about the murder in 2010 – did it occur to you that perhaps someone didn't want secrets unearthed?'

'That would suggest a local killer, scared of exposure. I

implore you not to assume that these killers live in or around Lampton. Please. I know my people, and none of them would do such a thing. Whoever killed Sally was a transient. We are a tourist spot, after all. I would suggest the killers of the film crew are also visitors. There's no proof they were targeted because of this documentary. They could have upset someone in some other town or city. They could have been fleeing a danger. One of the deceased, John Crickmer, had a drugs past and the answer might well be found amongst dodgy acquaintances of his.'

That wouldn't go down well with Crickmer's people, Bennet knew.

'The police haven't officially ruled you and the others out of the killings. Do you expect additional charges for murder to be forthcoming?'

'That's all I have to say for the moment. Please remember that I am facing charges of perverting the course of justice. I didn't kill anyone. Now, please, you should leave my village alone. There's no need for you to be here, and no one will talk to you.'

'Where is your son hiding? Are you protecting him? Did he run because he's a killer? Why haven't you pleaded with him to give himself up?'

Turner had vanished into his bedroom, but this question prompted a return. Angry, he threw the curtains aside, stepped out, and slapped his hands on the railing.

'I chose not to do a silly TV news appeal for him to return because he will come when he's ready. He knows I want him back and saying it on TV will not help. He did not kill anyone, none of us did. I do not know where he is or how to contact him, and I told the police this. I love my son, and truth be told it would be better that he stayed away for a while. Because soon the police will have their proof that the killers they seek are still out there, and my son can return to avoid the kind of doubt and hatred I see on your faces. It's ironic that I have lost my son, and stand here now, facing these ridiculous charges, because of an obnoxious man's love of his own son. That is all. Now, you should leave my village because you won't get what you want from my people. Again, if you want answers, ask the police why they did such a weak job when Sally Jenkins went missing. Goodbye.'

And that was it: show over. Clearly, Turner was still angry about Bennet's interference. The bastard was too narcissistic to acknowledge that the 'obnoxious man' had helped grieving families find a little solace.

The balcony interview had been a couple of hours ago. Since then, Turner would have watched the seed he'd sown take root and blossom: Derbyshire police were coming under fire for their efforts long ago when Sally Jenkins went missing. Bennet had to admit the councillor had a point. A body of water like Lake Stanton, just a few miles from Lampton, should have been searched. But hindsight was a powerful tool. And as a major obstacle to the investigation, Turner had no right to condemn the police. If he'd planned to get the focus off himself a little, it had worked.

Turner had also probably learned how wrong he'd been about his people slamming doors in reporters' faces.

Plenty of Lampton locals had invited media people into their homes, and microphones had even been allowed into the shops and the Lion, where a mob had gathered to gossip. Again, opinion was split. Some respected Turner's unwavering care for their village, others hated what he'd done but understood his actions.

A handful refused to believe he was involved in any way but was willing to accept the blame to protect others, while some doubted someone of his power in the village could have no knowledge of the murders – either he was a killer or knew who was.

And a few people, thinking his power was gone and glad of it, took the opportunity to moan about insignificant things he'd done to them, like banning dogs from barking after 11pm. But for each of the latter, there was one who considered him omnipotent and wide-eyed, refused to say a word to reporters.

'Dad? Can I go again?'

Bennet put his phone away. He and Joe were at Rother Valley Country Park, just to get away from everything. Joe was on the playpark, laughing with the other kids, and Bennet envied his son's ability to compartmentalise his emotions. Here, by the lake, surrounded by green, Bennet had hoped to put the last few days out of his mind for a while. But it was no good.

It had helped Joe that he'd had some bright news emerge from the gloom. Lorraine's husband, Ian, had called that morning and suggested Bennet and Joe could attend her funeral. Joe liked the idea because he could meet his little half-sister, although he'd already said he didn't want to see his mother's body. For a child, he was quite adult in his diagnosis that seeing her dead, even touched up by the funeral home, would ruin the lively photos he had of her from her Facebook profile.

Bennet didn't like the idea of attending Lorraine's funeral, but was unsure why. He would go though. For Joe.

'Dad, can I go again?'

'As much as you want.'

While Joe ran off to play with the other kids, Bennet made another call.

'No murder charges yet,' Bennet said when Superintendent Sutton answered. 'You've got nothing yet?'

'We're still on the hunt. As yet, no. We could be looking at an unknown entity, you know?'

Bennet knew. He wasn't sure Turner and his gang were killers, but he wanted them to be. He needed them to be. He didn't want this whole thing unresolved for months. Or unsolved forever. 'Turner's on TV telling the world not to look in Lampton for the killer. He thinks anyone could have found that lake. And maybe that's right. But most people expect lakebeds to gradually slope down. Anywhere else, you'd have to push that motorhome right out into the middle to fully submerge it. Lake Stanton is different because it has that sharp ledge and a deep drop. Only locals would know that.'

'I know. We're looking into it. Everyone in Lampton will be spoken to, I don't care if they're eighty years old. And we'll trace everybody who lived in the area in 2010, even if they moved out of the country. But, bizarre as it sounds, the story we have could be the truth.'

'And you looked at their alibis? Like you said, we're looking at the murders of the film crew occurring between about ten fifteen and not long after midnight on Sunday.'

'Working on it. At that time, Turner and his son were at the Porsche showroom that Lucas runs. That's Turner's story and it's backed up by the employee in the petrol station across the road. He saw a workshop roller door open and heard work going on inside, and he saw movement.'

'He saw the faces of Turner and his son, and he's sure of the time? Turner's got this belief his people wouldn't ever lie to him, but what about *for* him?'

'No direct identification, no. It's not definitive and we'll break that alibi apart if it can be. I imagine if the station attendant was going to lie to save his councillor, he would have blatantly said it was him. So I don't think he lied and at face value the alibi looks good for the pair, at least until we find Lucas and hear what he has to say. The other Keys were at home and most have corroboration. Apart from Turner, these Keys are all pensioners or on the cusp, some infirm, and Turner's hardly a spring chicken himself. If they had something to do with the killings, it was with younger help. We're looking.

'Crabtree is the one with no clear alibi. He reckons he was with a prostitute, and didn't seem embarrassed at all to admit that. He gave us a phone number, which we traced to a pay-as-you-go device used predominantly in Derby centre. Nobody is answering it yet.'

'What about the Sally Jenkins murder? Have you checked alibis for everyone for March 2010?'

Sutton sighed. 'Bennet, you know how this works.' Bennet did: confirming alibis could take a long time. It didn't stop him being annoyed at the lack of progress.

'I'm sorry,' he said. 'I don't know myself recently.'

'Look, we do know a little. Crabtree and the others we're working on, but Turner's alibi is confirmed. On the night Sally Jenkins disappeared, he was in Baslow, at a restaurant function at Fischer's, about four or five miles away. Two dozen guests. Some were spoken to and confirmed he was there from around five in the evening until just past seven thirty. He left because his babysitter called him because his son was throwing up. And he went straight home. And the babysitter didn't leave until about half past eight. And since Sally Jenkins disappeared between about six pm and six forty-five, his alibi is good.'

'Who might have had motive?'

'What motive could someone have for killing a ten-year-old girl? If she wasn't taken by a paedophile, we're blank. Look, Liam, I know you want this solved. We all do. And your timing about motive leads me on to something I want to show you. A possible motive for the film crew's murders. We suspected they might have been killed because they were investigating the Jenkins killing. Now I think we have proof. We found a video.'

'Go on.'

'Well, I think you should see it. Lorraine is in it. It was shot on Sunday evening, before the crew went to the Red Lion. It could be the last pictures of her before her death. Do you want–'

'Send it.'

61

Sutton's team had found a memory stick at the burial site containing a number of video and audio files. Most of it pertained to the documentary, some of it just camera practice, and the audio files were narrative editing for voiceover. But one movie file had intrigued Sutton. The location was the kitchen of Crabtree's ranch, the time code Sunday the 19th of January, 8.18pm.

It began with an empty room, shot from one side with the kitchen door on the far left. The kitchen table, in the centre of the room, had a chair at each end and four or five sheets of overlapped A4 paper. The door opened to admit Francis Overeem, who passed the table and walked to the far wall, which was bare. He stood just inches from it, nose almost touching the plaster, like a punished child.

Next, Lorraine entered. She looked worried. Behind her came Betty Crute. No sign of John Crickmer, but he was probably behind the camera. All four were dressed as they had been at the Lion, suggesting they were soon to head across there.

Still facing the wall, Overeem said, 'Sit, please. Don't touch the documents.'

Documents? The fan of papers looked blank. Lorraine didn't sit and the worry on her face deepened. She looked round at Betty Crute, who stood in the doorway with her arms folded, as if blocking an escape exit. Lorraine returned her attention to Overeem and voiced a question on Bennet's mind: 'What the hell is going on?'

'You know what this is about. Am I wrong?'

'Of course you're wrong, you fool. How dare you accuse me of such a thing?'

Here, Bennet felt his heart thumping. This made no sense. What had Lorraine been accused of?

'I have proof,' Overeem said. He turned from the blank wall. 'Sit down and talk to me. I'll be happy to Alt F4 this joint.'

'No.' Strangely, Lorraine made a move as if she was straightening a necktie, even though she didn't wear one. 'I'm leaving. Don't contact me again.'

Here, Crute interjected. 'Hang fire. I don't think he'd leave this early. Not if he came all this way.'

Behind the camera, Crickmer said, 'Fair point. He needs to know how we know.'

Lorraine said, 'I wasn't going to leave. I was going to say I'm leaving unless you get right to the point. I reckon that's what would happen.'

Overeem waved for silence. 'Look, let's redo. Nobody interrupt. We'll keep the about-to-leave bit, so we can cover all eventualities. I'll follow the bastard out the door if he tries. Let's go again, John.'

Lorraine said, 'We could skip the entry bit. Why don't we pick up where we left off?'

'No, we'll redo the lot. Everyone out. You might as well just stay there, John.'

Crute vanished out the doorway. Lorraine gave a thumbs up and a smile and followed. Overeem got halfway to the door, then paused, then started walking towards the camera. 'Let me know how it looked from that angle.'

And he grabbed the camera off Crickmer. The screen went black.

What had Bennet just witnessed? A dress rehearsal for a confrontation between Overeem and another man, played here by Lorraine? But who? And what was he being accused of? The Sally Jenkins – at the time the video was shot – disappearance? Had Overeem, either during his post-production research or while filming around Lampton, discovered the identity of her killer? Was his evidence played here by blank sheets of paper?

It was a shame Overeem had cut the rehearsal when he did. Otherwise, he might have outlined his evidence, maybe even named his suspect.

The video was shot shortly before the crew visited the Red Lion: had they gone there to find this man? Had they somehow gotten a message to him, perhaps through someone at the pub, and set up a meeting for later?

Had Sally Jenkins' killer murdered four people and buried them where he knew a body could lie undiscovered for years, in order to keep his secret?

62

———

Sophie Turton answered the door without showing her face. The door clicked open a few inches and Bennet had to push it. He saw Sophie walking away up the stairs, not a word said. At first he wondered if she thought he was someone else, and he spoke her name. She heard, but continued walking. He followed.

He knew the bedroom she led him into was her dead son's. Space and astronomy was his thing and the window was covered with stickers of the planets. But all other indicators had gone. The room was empty except for an old blanket around the edges of the carpet and a craggy table stacked with paint tins, brushes and rollers. Sophie was in the process of turning the walls from green to cream.

She started to drag household cleaning gloves on. She was free of paint splatter except for a streak on one ear. Seeing his scrutiny of the room, she said, 'You think what I'm doing is wrong, don't you? This room should be a time capsule, that's what you think?'

'It should be whatever you want.'

'You think I'm trying to forget my son, don't you?'

'No.'

'I'm sorry if that sounded harsh. My brother... he flipped, seeing this. So I'm waiting for Ralph to shout at me when he gets home from work. That's right, I didn't tell him.'

It was just after 6pm. Bennet knew Ralph Turton stacked shelves at Asda from two till six, so his bus would probably drop him off in about half an hour. Bennet didn't want to be around when he returned, just in case an argument started. Not his business.

'We were contacted by your people,' Sophie said. 'You're no longer running the case. They wouldn't say why.'

She looked like she expected Bennet to fill in the blanks. 'Personal issue. I'll be taking over again next week hopefully.'

She snorted and grabbed a paintbrush and moved to a wall. 'Next week. There's confirmation nobody will be arrested today.' She dropped the brush onto the blanket protecting the carpet and turned to him. 'Sorry again. I keep snapping at everyone.'

'It's okay.'

'You could have stayed away. You could have thought, finally, I can get away from that weird couple and their silly dead son. But you didn't. You came here and you didn't have to. So, I'm sorry. But why did you come? I know it's not good news.'

Bennet removed something from his pocket. Sophie stripped off her gloves and virtually pounced upon it. When she smiled, he realised he hadn't ever seen this before. She clutched the bronze plaque to her chest. Bennet had engraved it with the words from the laminated dedication the Turtons had stapled to a bench in Buttery Park. 'How much do I owe you for this?'

That didn't even deserve an answer, and they both knew it. 'You can put it on the same bench. I got permission. Police clout.' A lie. He had paid Barnsley Metropolitan Borough Council £600.

A few minutes later, she walked him to the door, but called

him back as he headed down the path. He turned, but she said nothing, and he knew her words shouldn't be overheard. He moved closer.

'I shouldn't have asked you to do that thing. I'm glad you didn't. But I know you would have. So, I'm sorry and thank you. I'll wait for proper justice. One day, right?'

'One day,' Bennet said, and turned to leave. Sitting in his car, he noticed paint on his cheek from where Sophie had hugged him in the bedroom. He decided to leave it there for a while.

63

That evening, forty minutes before two bells went off and changed everything, Bennet loaded the file found on the flash drive and again watched the last ever video of Lorraine before she died. It was a purely selfless action though. Or so he told himself. He wanted to create a new video, sans Overeem, Crickmer and Crute. Lorraine alone. For Joe. Or so he told himself. He had free time because Joe and Patricia were upstairs and the pensioner was learning ten attack combos on a fighting game.

It involved watching the video numerous times to find relevant portions and to hone his cutting, cropping and transitioning skills with the video editing software he'd downloaded. And he'd found a beauty. In the video, when Overeem had sent everyone out of the ranch kitchen in order to reshoot, Lorraine had smiled and given a thumbs up. A perfect image and Joe would love it.

Unfortunately, he couldn't find a decent line of audio to sync it with. There was one that put a lump in his throat, because he wished she was still around to say it:

'Why don't we pick up where we left off?'

But there was one far more in line with history:

'I'm leaving. Don't contact me again.'

But none would fit with a thumbs up for a ten-year-old boy. He would have to try to cut and splice individual words to form a sentence, although he feared Lorraine would wind up sounding like a robot with its batteries running low.

So, he rewound, and watched again, and again, and–

That was when the first bell rang. It was in his head. He leaned back in his chair, sure he was wrong. But he knew he wasn't. Goosebumps rose on his arms.

As he stuck a hand into his pocket, bell number two sounded. This one was his ringtone. His phone started ringing as his fist closed around it.

It was Detective Superintendent Sutton. The man he'd been about to call.

'Sutton, perfect timing, I've got–'

'Wait, Liam, I just got some lovely news from Sally Jenkins' autopsy. Not cause of death, but an injury that says quite a lot.'

'You're going to like this more. I've got a real good clue as to who killed the film crew.'

Sutton's reaction to the name Bennet gave wasn't shock. 'I already know, Liam. I'm preparing a team to hit the house. You want in? Arrest and interview. I'll swing it for you, my treat, but we're on the road very soon. I'll tell you more en route. How quick can you be at the scene?'

With the line still open, Bennet grabbed his shoes, coat, keys, yelled upstairs to Patricia and Joe, and charged for the front door.

Stepping in the car to stepping back out: twenty-three minutes.

64

Bennet's car met the armed arrest team's van at the end of the street. The van led the way, Sutton's vehicle following, Bennet's car at the rear. But the gun-toting men in riot gear weren't needed. The truck of heavies guarding Ronald Turner's gates was still there, but only one guy remained. Seeing police, he shifted the vehicle and drove away, nice and casual. Bennet saw the man on his mobile, probably warning Turner.

Sutton, Bennet and another detective who'd ridden with the DCS rushed to the gate. Sutton used the intercom to call for Turner to open up. He barely gave the councillor time. At Sutton's wave, the van gave the gate a nudge and bust the lock. It parked inside, in front of Turner's car, but nobody got out. They weren't needed this evening.

Sutton's DC raced for the front door and rapped it hard. Police, open up. No reply.

Bennet and Sutton moved around the back, where Bennet saw a security light was on over the back door. Sutton tried the door, and it was unlocked. He flung it open and yelled for Turner to show himself. No reply. He vanished inside.

Bennet had seen this security light flick on once before and knew it meant someone had passed the sensor recently. He cupped his hands around his face to peer in the dark window of the surgery. No sign of Turner. And when he tried the door, it was locked. So his attention turned to the field.

Just in time to see the light in the stable office turn off. Bennet jogged through the dark.

The stable was unlocked. Bennet opened the door slowly, silently, and flicked on the light. Empty. He slammed the door behind him. It seemed like a cheap trick, but it worked. He heard a scrape from nearby. And below. There could be only one hiding place.

Bennet squatted before the trapdoor. The handle was a recessed wooden ring almost invisible against the floorboards. He yanked the door open. There, in the dark recess, sunken in junk and wires, knelt Turner, naked apart from tracksuit bottoms. He stared up like a terrified child.

Bennet said, 'You know, after his downfall, they found Saddam Hussain hiding in a hole.'

'Sunday, 2145: last known sighting of any of the film crew alive, when Francis Overeem checked out of the Panorama hotel. 0147 Monday morning: Keys meeting, at which a vote was passed to evict the film crew. 0245: reassembly of the Keys to discuss what to do with four dead found at Crabtree's ranch. Accounting for journey times for all parties, this offered a four-hour time frame: 2218 until 0215. In that period, four beating hearts at that ranch became five. Then four, three, two, and one. Then none. Agreed?'

'I would agree. How elegantly put.' Councillor Turner was slouched in the chair across the desk from Bennet and one of Sutton's DCs as if bored. His solicitor was in the station, but waiting in another room. Turner had chosen, at least for now, to be interviewed alone: he had nothing to hide. And he'd prepared: when escorted from the stables to his house to get dressed, he'd washed his face, brushed his teeth, and selected a grey suit.

Bennet leaned back in his chair, smiling. Interrogating suspects was usually something he left to trained constables and sergeants, but he missed the thrill of going face to face to strip the shield off a lie. Especially against this bastard. '0245: reassembly of the Keys to discuss what to do with four dead found at Crabtree's ranch. But we know all about that already, so we'll put it aside. Why'd you call that 0147 meeting? Why so late?'

'The film crew left the Lion. Everybody thought that was the last of them, that they'd finally left our village. Then we heard they were camped out at Mr Crabtree's ranch.'

'Their location was kept quiet, even from Mr Crabtree. How did you know?'

Turner paused to take a sip of water. 'I don't recall. I hear things.'

Bennet's phone was on the table. He clicked and scrolled and turned the device so Turner could see. On screen was a paused video. 'This video was taken inside Mr Crabtree's ranch at 2018 on Sunday. We think it shows a rehearsal for a confrontation with an unknown man.'

A habit of Bennet's was to outline his entire interview in chronological order, then shuffle the notes before facing his foe. The resulting jigsaw was clear in his own mind but would tip a suspect off balance. Turner's confused face broadcast the success of this tactic.

Bennet tapped the play button. Turner leaned forward to watch the short film, his expression blank throughout. Bennet had watched the video many times and could see without seeing: Overeem walking into the ranch kitchen, past the table with its fan of papers, to stand against the far wall; Lorraine following, but remaining on the door-side of the table; both then planning to retire, re-enter, repeat.

When it was over, Bennet asked: 'Have you seen this before?'

Turner leaned back and folded his arms. 'No, why would I have? Where did you get it?'

'As you saw, Overeem and the others arrived with the

unknown man. All entered the ranch together. Would you agree this means the film crew met their visitor somewhere else and travelled together?'

'If you say so.'

'How did you know they were renting the ranch?'

Turner gave a frustrated giggle, sans smile. 'I hear things. You clearly don't, since I've already explained this.'

'Who's the unknown man?'

'I hope I don't have to repeat this. I have no clue.'

Bennet used a finger on the video's scrub bar to rewind, and pause, and two fingers to zoom. Overeem's head filled the screen, frozen inches from the blank wall in the ranch kitchen.

'Ever seen this video before? Oh, wait, you said no already. Ever been to the Panorama hotel?'

'What? Yes, of course. Is that relevant?'

Bennet tapped the phone screen. 'Why do you think Overeem is standing here like this, just staring at nothing?'

Turner shook his head.

'Basic hotel rooms at the Panorama. Door in a central corridor, so it faces a window. Unlike this ranch kitchen, where the window is in a side wall. Overeem took a room at the Panorama. He'd dragged a tea table into the centre of the room, for two men to talk. Overeem rehearsed his confrontation with the unknown man at the ranch, but the live show, we'll call it, was to take place in that hotel room. That blank wall, come opening night, will be a window. Ever seen this video before?'

Turner snorted his frustration, but offered no words.

'Overeem checked into the Panorama on Sunday afternoon, bringing only a file folder and a camera bag. He was there for just minutes. Long enough to move the table, lay his documents out, and set up the camera. But here's the problem. Overeem left the hotel that afternoon and didn't return until 2145, and he was alone. He was back only to put away his documents and camera and check out. You've never seen this video before, right?'

Turner ignored the question in favour of one that hadn't been asked. 'You seem confused by his behaviour, Bennet, so let me clear that up. Overeem and his people had just left the Lion. Fast. They'd caused trouble in the pub and had decided, finally, to leave my village. He went back to the Panorama to clear out his things because they were running with their tails between their legs.'

'What if they weren't fleeing? What if Overeem went to the Panorama for his camera and documents for another reason?'

Turner shrugged. 'Why don't you just say it instead of–'

'The rehearsal video – here, look – is timestamped 2018. The film crew were planning a confrontation with the unknown man, but an hour later everything had changed. They left the Lion and, to use your word, fled to the safety of the ranch. But what if, in that hour, they changed the venue for their confrontation with the unknown man? And Overeem went to collect his camera and folder for that reason? You like Hennessy cognac, don't you?'

Turner gritted his teeth, clearly annoyed at Bennet's disjointed questioning. 'Again, just say it, detective.'

'You told me Sunday is your night at the Lion. I had that confirmed. Regular as clockwork, you pop in for a nip of your fine Hennessy. But you didn't go that Sunday, the 19th.'

'No. It's not written in stone. If you remember, I told you my son needed help with one of his cars. I was at his garage most of the evening. I was there at the time you say the film crew died. But obviously you're leading up to somehow trying to connect me to those murders. And I'd love to hear it.'

Bennet found another video on his phone and described it for Turner. CCTV from the Lion, Sunday evening. Francis Overeem at the bar, talking to the barmaid, Vicky London.

'Here, look: Overeem scans the lounge, then asks her a question. She tiptoes to also look at the patrons in the bar, shakes her head and looks at her watch. Doesn't that look like Overeem has just asked about a certain customer and he's not in? And the barmaid says, oh, he should have been in by now?'

Turner's reply to Bennet's narration was, 'I'm sure this silent video could be given a voiceover to mirror a famous movie scene, if we tried.'

'I think the film crew expected the unknown man to be at the pub that Sunday, because he usually is. Their plan was to take him to the Panorama hotel room for the confrontation. But the unknown man wasn't there.'

Next up for Turner's perusal was a printed sheet of paper. Bennet fingered a specific line. 'This is your phone data, and here, at 2104, you received a call. We know this was from Vicky London, the barmaid. We sat down with her and found her memory to be suddenly refreshed. She's admitted to police that Francis Overeem came to the bar and asked where you were. When he'd gone, she called you soon after and said a man was looking for you. You told her not to tell anyone she'd called you. I think that warning from Vicky is why you didn't go to the Lion for your weekly nip of Hennessy.'

Bennet fingered another line on the sheet. 'At 2113, you received another call, this time from an unknown number. I think that number belonged to Overeem. Let me ask again, have you seen that rehearsal video before today?'

'No. That's the last time I answer that question.'

'I have a couple more pieces of media for you.'

The first was a segment of the rehearsal video. It lasted three seconds. Overeem, with his face against a bare wall, said to Lorraine:

'I have proof. Sit down and talk to me. I'll be happy to Alt F4 this joint.'

'Alt F4 is a computer term, Mr Turner. In the context of this line, what do you think Mr Overeem mean by "Alt F4 this joint"?'

'I don't know. Leave? Leave this joint?'

'So you think Mr Overeem basically said, "I have proof. Sit down and talk to me. I'll be happy to leave this place". As in, give me what I want and I'll be out of your hair, right?'

Turner shrugged. 'At a guess. I've never heard this Alt F4 thing before.'

'Alt F4 is used on a computer to shut down the current window. It started as an online troll tool – so, a user in a forum might ask how to perform this or that action, and a joker will say it's Alt F4, which will kick the user out of the website. I'm sure to some it's a source of great mirth. But the term has evolved to become a buzzword meaning anything to do with stop, end, and, as you say, leave. Depends on the context. I'll bet you'd love to Alt F4 this police station right now. I want you to Alt F4 the acting all innocent. If I was beating answers out of you and my partner saw the chief constable coming, he'd tell me to Alt F4.'

'So, like you say, it's possible that Overeem's use of "Alt F4 this joint" was an offered deal: Talk to me and I'll be gone. But I don't think so. I think it was a threat. As in, talk to me, because if you don't, I'll have no problem shutting down this village of yours.'

Turner said nothing.

The final piece of media was an audio file. This wasn't from the rehearsal at the Crabtree ranch. It had been recorded, Bennet now knew, in a basement living room at the home of Sandra Gingham, where the Keys held their addendum gatherings. The recording was from the 0245 Monday meeting, at which Lampton's finest chose to hide a quadruple murder from the world.

Turner heard his own voice:

'*The film crew said it themselves. Their slang term, what was it? When they were done, they'd "Alt F4 this joint". Exit, in other words. So we pretend they did that. They exited.*'

'Mr Turner, you never saw the ranch rehearsal video. I think we established that. So when exactly did you hear the film crew say "Alt F4 this joint"?'

The councillor took a long time before answering. And his obvious disdain for the room around him and all its occupants was gone, replaced by worry. 'I can't remember. Maybe they said it to someone else and that person said it to me. Maybe I misspoke. I don't know.'

Bennet put his phone on the table. 'This is what I think happened. When the film crew couldn't find you at the Lion, Overeem called you and wanted to meet. Perhaps he asked, or perhaps he threatened. You agreed to meet. Perhaps you were curious, perhaps you were scared. But the meet would not happen at the Panorama. Perhaps it was too busy, too open, too centre of your world; perhaps you knew there might be a call for carnage. So Overeem got his camera and folder and checked out of the hotel, and he went to the only other place they could use for the live show. The ranch. That's how you knew where the film crew was staying.

'You were led into the kitchen, and it was there that Overeem threatened to destroy your life. Maybe he told you he planned to wait until morning to expose you. Maybe he gave you a deadline for admitting your crime to the world. Either way, you left that ranch angry and scared and knowing you needed a plan. A few hours later, you had that plan. You got a weapon, you went back to that ranch a few hours later, and you broke in. Four beating hearts in that ranch had become five.

'Francis Overeem, possibly working late, had fallen asleep at the kitchen table. John Crickmer was asleep on the living-room sofa. Betty Crute and Lorraine Cross were asleep in separate bedrooms. Four people, four separate rooms, all of them dead to the world. Perfect. With your weapon, you went from room to room. Five beating hearts became four, three, two, and one. And then you left. No beating hearts left. Your secret was safe.'

Turner said nothing. Bennet almost couldn't, so thick was the anger in his throat.

'Three of them never woke up. Maybe they never knew what hit them. One certainly did. Lorraine Cross. She woke and she fought back, but it did her no good.'

The only sound Turner made was the cracking of his fingers. His eyes were on the table.

'But now you had four bodies, and your village was doomed anyway. Unless you could hide the crime. But you couldn't clean the ranch and dispose of four bodies by yourself. So you call the Keys, and you convened for that 0147 meeting. Your plan was to arrange for people to visit that ranch under the pretence of evicting the crew. When the bodies were found, you called another meeting, at 0245, this time with the intent of getting help to hide the crime. Crabtree had to be part of it, of course, because it was his ranch and he had that big loader, perfect for digging holes.'

Still Turner didn't speak.

'But what of the accusation against you, councillor? What could this little film crew possibly have on you? This bunch of amateurs that was in town to tell the story of a ten-year-old tragedy? You were right after all.'

Turner looked up. 'Right about what?'

'About your people not lying to you. They all said they didn't kill little Sally Jenkins. You *knew* that to be true.'

66

After a break for Turner to consult with his solicitor, they went again. This time, the solicitor sat by his client's side in the interview room. Both men had worked on a prepared statement from Turner. The usual format was: suspect learns of damning new evidence, suspect retires to prepare a new statement, suspect's edited statement conveniently gives innocent explanation for new evidence.

Bennet was eager to see how Turner would try to explain away everything that pointed to him as a five-time killer, but the new statement tried no such magic trick. It was simply a more bloated and flashy repeat of the alibi Turner had offered ten years ago when the Sally Jenkins case was hot. At a function at the time Sally vanished, called home to sick son, stayed home all night. The alibi was good, undisputed. But prepared-statement-aware detectives always held a little back for the next round.

Bennet said, 'At first glance, there was no external sign of how Sally Jenkins died. No damage. Until the post-mortem. Sometimes, you see, a blow hard enough to smash bone doesn't even lacerate the skin or flesh. There's a springiness to the skin. Sally Jenkins had no damage to the flesh and skin on the top of her head. No visible clue anything was out of the ordinary. But underneath, her skull was broken.'

He showed Turner a photo, but the councillor didn't want to look. The bone showed two clear breaks connected by a fracture in a semicircle.

'The pathologist was quite certain about what broke the bone and pushed fragments deep into her brain. Look at the shape. Isn't it clear? It was a horseshoe. She was killed by a massive kick to the head from a horse. And you owned the only horses in the village back in March 2010.'

Turner looked horrified, but it wasn't the look of a man who'd been caught. He stood up. His hands were shaking. He was ordered back into his seat, but instead he snatched Bennet's phone from the table. The DC next to Bennet stood up and got two words into an objection, but Bennet grabbed his arm. Bennet wasn't outraged, simply curious. He doubted the councillor was about to call in a rescue team or instruct a disciple to burn evidence.

Turner dialled a number and paced in the small area between the table and the back wall as it rang. He was furious. Bennet was nervous with anticipation. He knew this phone call, whoever it was to, was about to change everything.

'Lucas? It's me. I'm with the police,' Turner virtually screamed into the phone. Both detectives raised an eyebrow – so, Turner had known how to contact his son after all: at the end of a phone nobody knew about. The councillor then gave the address of the police station. 'You've got some explaining to do. Get your arse down here, *right now*.'

67

Bennet and Sutton agreed that they were going to see fireworks if Turner and his son were together, so they arranged for both men to sit in the same interview room. And this time Sutton wanted in, even though he hadn't attended the interview of a suspect since he was a detective sergeant. The wait was agonising, probably more so for Turner, who was left alone with a uniformed officer, instructed not to say a word. The detectives wanted Turner to stew in his own thoughts.

When Lucas turned up, in a car nobody recognised, uniforms raced across the car park to intercept him. The young man wore trousers and a shirt, neatly ironed, and his face was smooth. Wherever he'd been since fleeing his home and his village, it clearly hadn't been a box in a cardboard city. Lucas walked towards the officers as if to meet old friends. The officers surrounded him, but nobody made contact other than to snap on handcuffs. Lucas looked terrified, but the cause of it wasn't his new location. Outside the door of the interview room, he stopped and took deep breaths. His own father scared him more than the police.

Bennet opened the door and ushered Lucas inside. Lucas

was brought into the interview room where his dad sat. He came in like a man to the gibbet, and his father leaped to his feet upon seeing him.

'You lied to me, Lucas,' Turner yelled. 'To me, of all people. And you're burned with me now. Sit down. Sit down and tell them what you did. *Now.*'

Mesmerised, the detectives standing nearby watched the young man sit across from his father, but his eyes were anywhere but on the older man. Yet it was to his father he spoke, as if both men were alone in the room.

'You would be out all evening at your function. The babysitter would be stuck in front of the TV again. I crept out of the back door, across the yard, and scaled the wall. I was at the playpark soon afterwards, watching the entrances for Sally...'

And the reason for this secrecy? Lucas's father had always been in the house when Sally rode Reeve, making it impossible to have a sly go with B'fly, the giant Clydesdale she was determined to master. But now there was a chance! The day before the party, he and Sally had hatched a plan. Sally would leave the party one hour earlier, so they could have some secret time together. With his father away and the babysitter locked into her TV drama, Sally would get her ride, and Lucas would get his kiss.

'Deal done,' Lucas said. 'I guess her fate was sealed in that moment.'

Across from him, Turner watched with anger on his face. When his son paused, the councillor said, 'So that was the first lie. You told me she came to ours to borrow your bike. Continue.'

Lucas needed no time to consider. So, together he and Sally sneaked out of the park and along the streets. They knew who had cameras, who liked to watch out the windows, and puddles of darkness and cars helped them find hiding spots as they made their way to Turner's home. They hopped the wall and approached the stables. Sally was virtually jumping for joy as B'fly was brought out. Using a stool, she tried to climb aboard.

'I smacked him. He moved as she was climbing up. He knew she'd fall, and she did. So I smacked him for it. But she was on her knees in the mud, behind him. My smack made him kick. I didn't see the impact, but I saw her fly through the air. There was no blood, but she wasn't moving.'

Richard Turner leaned forward, shaking his head. 'And that's when you strangled her to death.'

It wasn't stated as a question, or even a fact. It was a line loaded with sarcasm. Another lie exposed. Bennet wanted to sit, but feared a single movement might break the spell entrancing the two Turners. Still, the young man could not look up at his father.

'No. But I thought you'd believe that. No blood. I didn't even see an injury.'

'But there was one. Her skull was smashed.'

The files were still on the table. Turner slapped the sheet of paper aside, seeking the one he wanted. Neither detective moved a muscle as paperwork skimmed off the table and onto the floor, in case it broke whatever spell father and son were under. Turner snatched up the sheet he wanted – the photo of the break in Sally Jenkins' skull – and stopped little short of ramming it into his son's nose.

Lucas leaned back so his eyes could focus. Even when Turner dropped the photo and it hit the table and glided to the floor, those eyes followed it. It was face down, but still the young man stared as he said, 'I knew you'd be angry. Angry because I went behind your back to let Sally ride B'fly. So, yes, I lied. I'm sorry.'

Bennet was shocked. To cover the fact that he'd disobeyed his father's wishes not to let Sally near the Clydesdale called

B'fly, ten-year-old Lucas had instead claimed he'd killed her. And Turner seemed more upset that his son was a liar than a killer. How messed up was that? If only Turner had also warned his son never to pretend to kill little girls.

'Continue,' Turner ordered his son.

Ten-year-old Lucas Turner dragged Sally's body into the stable, put B'fly away, and sneaked back into the house, into his bed, and there he yelled for the babysitter. He was ill, in pain, and needed his father. She got on the phone, and within minutes Richard Turner was driving home from his bash. Lucas was waiting in his room, crying. Turner sent the babysitter home. Alone now with his father, Lucas's story poured out: Sally had come to borrow a bike, but she tried to open the stables to see B'fly. He said no. She insisted. They fell out. They fought. He was stronger. She couldn't unsnap his hands from around her neck. Neither could he. Turner left his son in the bedroom and went out to see the body for himself.

And here, a twist that shocked both detectives. Lucas looked up at his father, and in his voice was such rage the councillor jerked back in his chair.

'And then she got up, now suddenly alive, and ran away from home, right?'

The councillor found it hard to speak at first. Their roles seemed to have reversed, with Lucas now the accuser and his father weak and nervous. 'What else could I do, son? You were ten. You wouldn't have understood.'

Lucas stabbed a finger at the hypnotised detectives. 'So tell them. Tell them what you told me.'

Turner looked at the policemen, one at a time, then back to his son. He folded his arms and visibly relaxed. An hour earlier, Bennet would have assumed the councillor had suddenly renewed a belief that he could lie or parry and escape the anvil hanging over his head. But everything was different now. This, he knew, was the calm that filtered through those unwilling to fight any longer.

'I told you she was alive,' Turner said. With his skills as a vet, he'd brought her round. She had only been choked unconscious and, revived, Sally had run away. Lucas feared she would tell her mother and he'd get in trouble, but Turner had told him not to worry. Sally hadn't run home. She'd told Turner she was leaving the village, running away forever. 'And off she ran.'

'I believed you,' Lucas said. 'We all did. But I didn't believe you for long. Nobody saw her, nobody heard from her. When I was older, I knew. She wasn't living a new life somewhere. She'd been dead all along. And you fed that theory of her running away to the whole world. You lied to everyone, and you have the nerve to sit there and scold me for a lie? So tell it. I know what happened, because it's obvious now. But I want to hear something truthful from your face.'

Turner nodded and began telling it. Sally had been quite dead when he found her and he'd dragged her behind the stables until he could think what to do. That night, after Lucas had fallen asleep, Turner loaded Sally's body into the boot of his car and left her there until daylight. In the morning, as the village was becoming increasingly panicked about the little girl's disappearance, he drove out of Lampton to dump the body. He knew about Lake Stanton, a place he and friends had swam in as kids. He also knew a body could lay at its deep bottom for years. A decade later, the location had proved its worth and once more received the dead.

From a charity shop in Castleton, a few miles north of Lampton, he bought an old steamer trunk. By Lake Stanton, he loaded Sally's body into the trunk and inserted rocks in the spaces around her to cut down on the amount of air that would be trapped, so it would sink. He dragged the trunk to the water, slid it in, and kicked it over the submerged edge. Once the rippling lake had calmed, he turned his back. The easy part was done. Now it was time for the real test.

In his car, Turner lifted an item he'd bought from the charity shop along with the steamer trunk. It was a black dress for Sally's mother. He'd planned to get his car serviced as a reason for leaving the village that morning, but had worried that such a selfish action would invite scorn, perhaps even suspicion. The purchase of the dress, so Anika could present well before the media, would make an honourable cover story instead. Might win him some brownie points with the watching world. Might even impress Anika enough to allow him to slide that dress off her body one night.

When his story was told, Lucas was a wreck, hunched over so far his chin was on his chest and he looked ready to tumble off the chair. But Turner was sitting up, alert, and he straightened his tie. He looked at Bennet and gave a smile. 'Make that two things I was right about. Didn't I promise you Sally had no *murderer*?'

68

———

When it was over, Lucas Turner was taken away to be arrested and processed for his part in disposing of the bodies of the film crew. Charges for his actions ten years ago would follow. His father was rearrested for his own part in the Sally Jenkins tragedy and returned to his cell. Although the conversation between him and his son had seemed genuine, no good detective would accept it at face value. Later, a pair of interrogators would reinterview both men and try to chip away at their story. It wasn't impossible that the councillor and his son had invented the whole thing, knowing they'd fare better if a ten-year-old kid rather than an adult was charged with disposing of a corpse. Lucas's anger at his father could have been part of the charade. Turner was certainly the sort to let his son take the blame, and Lucas was awestruck enough by his dad to go along with it.

Bennet, though, believed what he had heard. Without a further role to play, and doubtful any new revelations were on the cards, he had no reason to stay. But he got permission for a final chat with Turner. He didn't have any questions; he just wanted the last word, although he was unsure what it would be. Turner unwittingly helped him with that.

Bennet flipped the hatch on Turner's cell door and was pleased to see the man tearful on his bunk. Bennet had learned to suppress the hate he felt towards this man, just feet away, who'd hammered a spike into Joe's heart. And his own.

The councillor looked at him. 'You heard the last thing my son said to me. He was grateful. I saved him. That's what this was all about, Bennet. And that pleases me. I'll take that to prison and it will keep me warm.'

Bennet understood why Turner had contradicted himself so often, on the one hand arguing that a Loper had abducted Sally, while also continuing to claim she'd ran away: the latter was a lie he had to perpetuate for his son. Even long after the fallacy disintegrated as child became adult.

Bennet gave no response, but Turner clearly wanted one. 'You and me, Bennet, are the same. We overstepped lines in pursuit of the same thing. Like you, I was just a father trying to do right by his son.'

'You should have bought him a Lego set,' Bennet said, and shut the hatch.

69

———

Bennet sipped his water and looked up from his phone, watching Joe running with the other kids in the pub beer garden. The boy was having a lot of fun, but Bennet wanted to get going soon.

He returned to his phone and the email Detective Superintendent Sutton had sent him. In the three days since Richard Turner and his son had been arrested concerning the death and unlawful disposal of Sally Jenkins, Sutton's team had acquired more information and evidence. A search of the councillor's surgery had uncovered a missing tool: a graft passer. It was a hook-like tool used for feeding a graft through a joint. The missing implement hadn't been found, but the pathologist who'd performed the film crew's post-mortems believed such an item could have caused their neck wounds. Turner couldn't say where he'd disposed of the weapon, but he had come clean and admitted murder. Exactly as Bennet had outlined it to his face: room to room slowly, starting with the males. Each victim incapacitated by a blow to the head and murdered by throat slice.

And Lorraine, woken by a noise as Turner approached her

bed, three already down, had fought her attacker, screaming for help that fell on dead ears.

The police had learned more about Lucas Turner too. Before Sally vanished, he had been known around the village as more than just the tearaway Bennet had diagnosed. *Weird* was the term some employed. He'd been caught on more than one occasion exposing himself to older women. He shoplifted obsessively. And there was a rumour that he'd killed four or five cats. All of these things had been spoken about in hushed whispers because he was Councillor Turner's son.

Most telling: since the arrests, Anika Jenkins had changed her opinion on the relationship between her daughter and Turner's son. Now unmenaced by fear of speaking out, she'd said Sally and Lucas had never truly been friends. Sally had been creeped out by his behaviour towards her, tolerating it only because she had to in order to ride his dad's horses. Sally had certainly died by horse-kick, but had the rest of Lucas's story happened the way he told it? He was sticking fast to his version, so maybe Sally had willingly gone with him that night, and maybe she hadn't.

Bennet looked up to see Joe running with little Tessa on his back. It brought a tear to his eye, much as it had at Lorraine's funeral two hours earlier when the children had met each other for the first time. They had sat together at the gathering and stood side by side at the committal. Watching them watch their mother's coffin being lowered into the ground, Bennet had had to sit down on the grass, his legs jelly. He had arrested the man who'd killed her, sat in the back of a police car with him, and interviewed the man for two hours, all of it while within reaching distance. And he had held his composure. But if Richard Turner had been in that graveyard right then, Bennet would have throttled the bastard until he was as cold as those who called it home.

'Another drink?'

Bennet looked up to see Ian, Tessa's father, standing by him. Bennet stood. 'Actually, no, I think it's time we got going.'

'If you're sure. Help yourself to some of the food if you want.'

Bennet thanked him and called for Joe, who came running with his new best friend.

'So, I'll text you about Saturday,' Ian said. Earlier, the fathers had arranged a bowling outing at the weekend. Joe and Tessa versus the adults. A sleepover was on the cards for the future, as well as various days out. It could be the start of something long-term.

The kids were eager, but the plans had been made on this emotional day and Bennet wondered if it would all fall through as time passed. He hoped not. Joe needed the company of good people. His last conversation with Richard Turner had set him thinking.

There was every chance that a loose screw in the councillor's head contributed to his son's obvious social and mental problems – that was the media angle. But how much had a home *sans* a mother during his adolescence pulled him off track? It was hard not to worry about the future of Joe's journey along that path towards adulthood.

EPILOGUE

The next afternoon, Bennet met with Liz at a pub in Sheffield. She had returned from Spain the previous night, with no resolution to her ongoing case. He tried to shake her hand, but she leaned in to kiss his cheek. A week ago that would have given him a buzz, but not today, with his head still in a maelstrom. Not for a while, maybe.

Her first question, even before the kiss, was about his job. He still had one, for now. There was a back-to-work meeting in two days that he was required to attend before he'd be struck off compassionate leave, but he was also going to face questions and possible reprimand about his actions in Lampton. He wasn't thinking that far ahead, but there was a stillness in his gut that spoke volumes. He told her he wasn't sure he wanted to go back to work.

'I think you should. Throwing yourself into work will be the best way of getting past this.'

'That's not what I mean. I've changed. Remember Pond Street?'

'What about it?'

Pond Street was the unofficial operation name of a double

murder they'd both worked back in December. While chasing a lead in Wales, she'd suggested they should work in that country without informing the local police. He'd agreed.

'You're talking about breaking protocol?' she said as they walked to the bar. 'Heck, I was the one who suggested it. That makes me worse.'

'I also led a suspect to a crime scene to force a confession, instead of recording the interview in a station. And he got killed.'

'I know. That haunts me too. But it wasn't your fault. You're worried about your morals, is that it? What you did the system would frown upon, but it was the only way. We wouldn't have solved that case otherwise.'

Maybe, maybe not. But there had been other transgressions over the last few days. He'd broken into Ronald Crabtree's house and threatened the man; he'd played a mammoth piece of evidence for the public; worst of all, though, the CaraHome... Lorraine's body... or maybe it was that he'd planned to hurt Don The Man, chief suspect in the Buttery Park stabbing. He could think of a dozen activities that he could be sacked for, that would irritate his moral fibre.

She waved the barman over. After they were served and heading back to their table, she said, 'But you got the job done. At least it was all about what was right. And if your boss thought you'd really overstepped the line, he wouldn't be welcoming you back to work in a couple of days.'

'He's been my friend for years. There's bias. He would have suspended anyone else.'

They sat and sipped in silence for a moment. 'You're a good man, Liam, and you know it. Your boss knows it. And if you go before a misconduct panel, they'll know it and it will count for a lot. Look, what are you telling me? That you want to quit because you don't think you're right for the job? After all these years?'

'It's not after all these years. I've changed. Recently.'

'This is the first time that a case was personal. Your son's mother. Completely understandable. Maybe the next time a family member is hurt, you'll do the same. But you can't worry about such a thing all the time. The police service needs people like you. And I know you won't want to bow out of the Buttery case right now. You can't just abandon that unfinished. It'll eat you up. That's something your moral compass definitely can't handle, especially if the killer gets away with it.'

He wasn't sure. 'Anyway, even if they keep me, there's no guarantee I'll be returned as SIO of that investigation. The boss is leading it at the minute and it's not impacting his workload. Besides, I've been thinking about spending more time with my son. He doesn't see me enough. I rush out of the house at all hours.'

'Well that would be a better reason. But you've coped so far. And he loves being around Patricia.' Liz grabbed a menu and leaned back in her chair. She hadn't mentioned wanting to eat, but if they did, that would make this a dinner date. Again, a week ago he would have loved that... 'Don't think about work right now. And I should take my own advice. We're here to relax. I've been stuck with work for the last week and I don't want to talk *la hada*.'

'What's *la hada*?'

'Spanish thing. I think gang members use it to describe the police. I got called it over there. I ask you, does any other profession have such a vast amount of negative nicknames? Don't all these criminals realise vigilantes would lynch every single one if we didn't exist?'

Bennet grunted. 'Like peelers. I got called that one recently.

In the last few days I've heard everything from Lopers and Alt F4 and peelers and now *la hada…*'

'What on earth is Alt F4? Is it… what's wrong?'

She'd seen his face change. He felt it: the blood draining from his cheeks. He stood up and kissed her cheek.

Sanderstead Avenue was a commercial drag in Wombwell and there was a small car park behind the Co-op. Bennet parked on double yellows and strolled past shops, towards a Triumph bike showroom and a Weldricks pharmacy. Between them was a thin alleyway that delivered him into a backyard with an iron spiral staircase leading to a peeling green door above the pharmacy. He saw that the door – probably to a first-floor flat – was open. A Rhianna song floated out.

Halfway up the staircase, he smelled burning and knew why the back door was open. He knocked on the door, but quietly. And said hello, but not too loudly. If he was later questioned about why he'd entered the house unbidden, well, he'd knocked and called out and gotten no answer, and the open back door was a red flag.

He stepped inside and crossed a small kitchen, sparse and grimy. The washing machine, flashing a warning light, seemed to be the cause of the burning smell. A door ahead was also open. No knock this time.

The living room was small and made tinier by a four-seater sofa under the window overlooking the commercial drag. The only other seat was an armchair facing the TV, its back to him. Poking over the backrest was a blonde pixie cut with a hint of blue. He could see a hand with long green nails holding a mobile phone.

Bennet stepped up to the chair and the girl's legs came into view. She wore a short skirt, no shoes, and he saw a life-sized skeletal foot tattooed over her own instep.

The girl was also wearing headphones, which would aid Bennet's lawful entry excuse. He leaned closer so he could read her phone. A text message from The Man said:

3 FOR £20 & GARLIK BREAD YOU WANT THREE?

As the girl typed her reply to The Man at the speed of light with two thumbs, Bennet extracted his warrant card and lowered it slowly in front of the girl's face. Peripheral vision should have alerted her long before the card slid in front of the phone, but such was her obsession with what she was typing, the wallet eclipsed the top of the device before she noticed. And when she did, she jumped as if plugged into the mains.

The teenager got to her feet and backed off, right into the sofa, which tripped her into its embrace. Bennet sat on the armchair and held out his hand.

'Why'd you just walk in here?' the girl said.

'Let me have the phone, Erica. The one you told us you lost. The one that, somehow, all your friends and family didn't have the number for.'

Erica clutched the phone with both hands, as if Bennet might just rip it from her with telekinesis. 'How did you know?'

He couldn't help a grin. Liz's use of police slang in the restaurant had sparked a connection between two people. Helium Girl, who had called the Buttery Park stabbing incident room from a phone box: *I don't have anything for you peelers. I was wrong. So I won't be coming in. But I know it was a black man from Bradford what did it.'*

And this young lady, Erica Smith, girlfriend of the prime suspect in the murder of sixteen-year-old Mick Turton. When defending her partner's alibi for the night of the stabbing, she had said to Bennet: '*So, what, you peelers saying I'm lying as well?*'

But he explained none of this to Erica. He just continued to hold out his hand. 'I don't know where Don is. I haven't seen him for ages.'

Bennet said nothing. His hand waited. Eventually, Erica tossed him the phone. She then stood, but he suggested she should sit. She did.

Bennet cycled through text messages, rolling back the days. Such was the text energy of youngsters these days, it took a while. Hundreds of texts. Erica just sat there, watching.

Soon, he found the all-important date. Thursday January 2nd. He flicked by inert morning texts from Erica to a friend, and then the afternoon flicked by with only a single contact with her mother, and then the evening of the stabbing came onstage with an explosion of messages.

At 1959, eleven minutes after he'd slid a blade into a boy's flesh, Don The Man wrote:

Hey babe.

Her return message:

Whos this?

The Man. New phone. Tossd mine cos cops can work out where it was. You gonna have to toss yours. Cant tell police what phone numbers we have. Trace.

What talking bout? Why cops want phone?

I stab someone babe. Kid in park tried it on stab him.

Bennet's heart almost stopped. The proof he needed.

He dead? You dick.

Dunno. I'm coming round to yours, need you to say I was there all night. You watch summat on tv?

You dick. Gotta stop doing that. Just watching Australian bushfires. Carla reckons they could burn all earths oxygen away.

Then thats what we watchd together. Be there in twenty. You gotta tell me some things the people on tv said so it looks like I watchd it.

You owe me for this.

Love you babe.

Not enough. Owe me.

Tagged onto that final message of Erica's was a picture. It was an engagement ring.

Bennet scrolled through a horde of nonsense texts between the loved-up teenagers that had nothing to do with the stabbing, until he reached Thursday the 16th. Here, Erica besieged The Man with messages. Where was he? Was he with that bitch again? She was going to mess them both up if he didn't answer. No reply from Don.

Until the following Saturday. At 11.34 in the morning, he finally got back to her with a denial to all accusations that he was with another girl. The following argument took place over ninety-eight texts within under an hour. At 12.27 Erica wrote:

I'll tell the fucking cops you stabbed that kid.

I'll fuckin stab you. You threatn me? Yeah, I was with a girl last night. Shaggd her silly and we cussd you down. Better shag than you.

It all made sense now. Erica had called the police on that Thursday because she was angry with Don The Man. Woman Scorned had intended to ruin his life because he'd been with another girl. So, with a voice disguised by helium, she had called the police to say she would meet and give them the killer. This had been her plan right up until her next call to the police, on the Saturday, at which she'd claimed a black man killed Mick Turton. Now, Bennet saw the reason for her change of heart.

Early on Saturday, Don The Man had sent a text:

Sorry babe I love you.

what me and the bitch you mean?

No just you I lied about other girl your only one for me can I come round?

Why should I let you?

The final text from Don The Man that day had been a picture. Another engagement ring. Erica had told him he was forgiven and to come round. End of argument. End of her plan to sell him down the river. It didn't matter: this was beautiful evidence.

Bennet stood up. 'No more games. This is serious. Don is going to prison. You need to think about whether you want to go there too. No phones allowed there, Erica.'

'I don't.' She wiped a tear away.

'Then I need you on my side. Don is done, but you're not yet. You can still come out of this a free woman. But you have to help me. Invite me into your home. Offer me the text messages on your phone. Don't fight us and things won't get worse for you.'

'You won't find him, you know? He knows people. He's been reading spy stuff about counter-intelligence. He's a ghost. So what are you going to do?'

Bennet had to suppress a laugh. He sat on the sofa, facing the doorway. 'He's a ghost who's planning to share three pizzas and garlic bread with his girlfriend. So I'm going to do what all coppers these days do, according to my son's friend. Sit on my fat arse and wait for him to come to me.'

THE END

ACKNOWLEDGEMENTS

As you've probably heard before, no one writes a novel alone. Behind the scenes are editors and publicists and publishers, all of whom do their bit to convince an author that the dross she's so proud of needs work before it can be handed to readers. The convincers in most need of thanks for this book are, as always, Betsy Reavley, Ian Skewis, and Tara Lyons.

All the good stuff is down to them; each confusing or misplaced snippet, and every unfunny joke, is an instance where I put my foot down and insisted I knew what I was doing. However, if you come across certain aspects of police procedure, history or geography that furrow the brow, know that I took few liberties for the sake of drama.

Cold Blood is a loose follow-up to my first novel, Dead Cold. If you haven't read it but would like to know about the previous adventure of Liam Bennet and Liz Miller, it's available from Amazon right now. For those of you who already have a big reading list and no time to add my book, I suggest getting friends to download a copy so they can fill you in. If a hundred or so friends read a chapter each, you could know everything by day's end. #Justsaying.

And a final piece of business for those who also read the thanks page in my second book, Don't Believe Her: *...The Librarian says, 'They're beeehiiiind you!'*

A NOTE FROM THE PUBLISHER

Thank you for reading this book. If you enjoyed it please do consider leaving a review on Amazon to help others find it too.

We hate typos. All of our books have been rigorously edited and proofread, but sometimes mistakes do slip through. If you have spotted a typo, please do let us know and we can get it amended within hours.

info@bloodhoundbooks.com

www.ingramcontent.com/pod-product-compliance
Lightning Source LLC
Chambersburg PA
CBHW050801190726
48285CB00005B/1742